To R
Look up!
(Luke 21:25-28)

REVELATION, THE NOVEL

DARE TO EXPERIENCE THE BOOK OF REVELATION!

Will Carson

WILLIAM C CARSON

This book is a work of fiction. Names, characters, places, and incidents are products of the author's imagination. Any resemblance to actual events or locales or persons, living or dead, is entirely coincidental.

WILLIAM C CARSON

All Scripture references are from the King James Version of the Holy Bible.

Copyright © 2014 William C Carson

All rights reserved. This includes the right to reproduce any portion of this book in any form.
ISBN: 1500269247
ISBN 13: 9781500269241

Acknowledgements

Many thanks go to my wife Jeanne, my sister Emily Carnes, and my writing coach Larry Leech who read and re-read my manuscript for flow of thought, conversations, grammar, spelling, and doing reality checks.

Many thanks to Vasily, a Russian Christian, who helped me locate the Russian postage stamp at the beginning of "March of the Four Horsemen." The image of the stamp is used by permission.

ONE

The Arrival

The Roman battering ram shattered the door of the Apostle John's home early on the Lord's Day. A squadron of fully armed and armored Roman soldiers swarmed though the opening toward him, brandishing short swords. The house rattled with the sounds of hobnailed boots and clanking armor. The fifty people along with John scrambled out of the soldier's path, pressing themselves against the walls. John knew their thoughts: they could be killed or taken to prison.

The Roman captain came face to face with John and stared at him. He looked at the people huddled against the walls and motioned to another soldier. The captain took a scroll from the soldier and read from it: "The Emperor Domitian charges you with asserting there is another Lord to be worshipped other than His Majesty, the Emperor. Therefore, you are charged with sedition against the Roman Empire. Since you are not a Roman citizen either by birth or by purchase, you are hereby condemned to work in the copper mines of Patmos until time the Emperor himself shall judge your case."

The captain nodded to another soldier ready with hand irons. The soldier showed his gnarly teeth while he clamped them onto the hands of the ninety-plus-year-old apostle. John cried out in pain when they pinched his wrist.

"Loosen those a bit. They really hurt."

The soldier said, "That's how we treat criminals. I'm glad it hurts."

One of the bolder Christians spoke to the captain. "Did you bring enough men to capture this ninety-year-old man?"

A snicker worked its way through the house but stopped when the captain pointed his sword at the heckler.

The soldier who clapped irons on John's hands shoved him out of his house and forced him into a mobile prison cage. The soldiers attached it to a team of horses.

The citizens of Ephesus lined the roadway. They recognized John as the Romans took him to their headquarters. John saw them boo the Romans but keep their distance. He was glad people risked arrest for his sake. Bolder citizens threw garbage at the soldiers. One person threw a spear through the spokes of the prison cart and disappeared into the crowd. The spear broke the wheel and John fell against the bars when the cage hit the ground. People cheered at the Romans' misfortune. The soldiers had to protect themselves from the crowd while fixing the broken wheel. They had to endure ridicule from the people for requiring twenty men to capture the Apostle John.

An hour after the arrest, John arrived at the Roman headquarters. He spent a hot September night in a prison cell that reeked of human waste and sweat.

The next day, the Romans chained John and other criminals below deck of a prison ship bound for Patmos. He knew the Lord would not abandon him, but did not relish going to prison. John thought of Peter and Paul who had spent time in prison for their faith. Both of his friends had given their lives for their faith in Jesus.

About nine o'clock in the morning, the boat departed for Patmos.

The boat trip lasted a few hours. The ship handled the rough sea well. The boat stank like fish and salt water and John became seasick. After only an hour on the ship, he threw up.

After the boat docked, the Romans unchained John and the other prisoners and took them off the boat onto the island. Work masters fitted the new prisoners with leg irons that allowed them some freedom of movement.

Early in the afternoon, Roman guards took them to the copper mines. Fully armored guards surrounded the prisoners. Their helmets covered most of their faces. Most guards had short swords and spears. They shouted at the captives often and pushed them to the ground when they didn't obey commands fast enough. Pushing and shoving seemed to be what they did best. John's work master gave him a pick and shoved him into his assigned cave.

The mine supervisor looked at John and pointed. "Get over there. Pick at this vein of copper." Several other old men slumped over the vein, struggling to swing their heavy picks. He joined them.

John whispered to a fellow worker, "Why are they mining copper?"

"Because where you find copper, as a rule you find silver."

At the end of the day, John was exhausted. The Romans herded a small number of prisoners into the dining hall and fed them bad food. John looked at the food. He considered fasting, but decided to eat anyway. The prisoners could not talk with each other while at the dining hall. Each prisoner went to the latrine before going to their sleeping quarters.

The guards took John to the barracks. When he entered, he almost vomited because of the odors: sweat, urine, and fetid odors from the beds. Even the bricks in the walls stank. A glimmer of twilight showed through the barred windows. In the dim light, he could see several Mediterranean cockroaches flying around.

Thirty men shared the same barracks. Fifteen men slept on each side of the aisle. The guards took them one by one and chained their feet to the end of the bed nearest the center aisle. This insured the safety of the guards and allowed a little movement by the prisoners.

The last guard to leave stopped at the door. "Keep it quiet in here tonight. You have another hard day ahead of you tomorrow." He left, slamming the weathered oak door shut. The prisoners heard the sound of the door being barred.

John lay quiet to recover from the day's activities. He wondered if he could survive the hard labor. His mind went back to his home in Ephesus and prayed for the Christians there.

After a few minutes, one of John's fellow prisoners blurted, "Hey, who's the new guy?"

John said, "My name is John. I'm from Ephesus."

"I'm Demos. My name real name is Demosthenes, but people tend to spit when they say my real name. I'm from Ephesus, too. What did you do to get promoted to hell?"

"I am a disciple of Jesus Christ who dared to name someone other than the Emperor 'Lord.' I have churches in seven cities of the Empire: Ephesus, Pergamum, Smyrna, Thyatira, Philadelphia, Laodicea, and Sardis. The Emperor himself took notice of my actions."

"You certainly get around, don't you?"

Another prisoner chimed in. "I've heard about Jesus. Wasn't he called 'Christus' or something like that?"

Demos said, "That's Nikos who did not introduce himself."

Nikos said, "Getting back to my question, was he the person we heard about named 'Christus'?"

John rolled over to talk to Nikos and let out a cry of pain.

John said, "It is hard to turn over. My whole body aches. I haven't done such hard labor in years. My wrists and sides are throbbing."

Nikos said, "I remember how I ached my first week or two here. The pain will go away."

John recovered from the pain. "You're talking about Jesus, the Christ."

A third prisoner introduced himself. "My name is Jared, by the way. What does Christ mean?"

John said, "In Jewish terms, the Messiah, the Savior."

Demos said, "I've heard about him. People claim he rose from the dead. And crazy things like doing miracles. How did you hear about him?"

John grimaced and rolled over again to face Demos. "He chose me as one of His twelve disciples."

The prisoners within earshot said, "Oooooh."

John said, "I saw him get crucified."

At the mention of the word 'crucified', the barracks fell silent. Most of the prisoners knew it could be their way of death.

After a couple of minutes, another prisoner said, "We all know about crucifixion. And my name is Petros".

John said, "Thank you for introducing yourself, Petros. I saw Him after He rose from the dead. I was there when He performed miracles."

Petros said, "Well, I don't believe in such stuff. I don't believe in much anymore. I especially don't believe in the Emperor. He's as human as the rest of us. As a matter of fact, if I could get to the Emperor right now—"

A guard opened the peephole in the main door and said, "Yes? What might you do if you could get to the Emperor right now?"

Petros said, "Uh, I'd tell him what a great guy he is. We'd drink some wine and talk about women."

A couple of prisoners chuckled. The guard shut the peephole and walked off.

Petros waited a bit before breaking the silence. "But only if there is a guard around." Several prisoners laughed but John shook his head.

Another prisoner said, "Hey, John, don't let Petros bug you. He's here for having sex with the governor's wife."

Petros said, "Hey, she didn't tell me who she was married to."

"But you knew she was married", said Melek. "Oh, and my name is Melek."

Petros said, "So did she." He chuckled at his reply.

Demos said, "Enough."

Nikos said, "I got sent here for stealing a little money to buy food for my family. I didn't know it was the home of a Roman captain nor did I know that he was the Emperor's nephew. If I had known, I might have stolen from somebody else. I'll be much more choosey next time I steal from someone."

Another prisoner said, "If there is a next time. My name is Dragon."

John asked, "Dragon? Is that your real name?"

Dragon answered, "No, my real name is Alexander. I thought my friends called me Dragon because of my fierce behavior, but later I found out it was because of my breath."

Nearby prisoners laughed hard at his comment.

John turned over again to talk to Dragon. "How did you get here?"

"I refused to worship Caesar at a public ceremony in Cyprus. I think he's ugly. He's as human as the rest of us. I got put in jail there and later sent here." With sarcasm, he added, "I must be important."

John lay on his back to massage his wrists.

Demos said, "Well, I accidently knocked over a statue of the Emperor in the town square."

John asked, "How can you *accidently* do something like that?"

John saw Demos listening for the guard. When he heard no footsteps he said, "I got tired of looking at the Emperor's ugly face and decided the township could use a little beautification. I meant to chip off his face, but I leaned on the statue too hard."

7

Nikos said, "Yeah, and if he had someone watching his back, he wouldn't have done it in front of a Roman soldier."

The other five prisoners roared with laughter.

Even in the dim light, John saw Demos' face turn red.

Demos said, "Oh shut up."

John rolled his eyes.

John asked, "Demos, have any of us ever done anything violent?"

Demos responded, "Only Melek."

Melek grinned, "You got that right. I set fire to the Roman headquarters in Damascus, Antioch, Perga, and Attalia before I got caught. The Emperor decided to try me. I've been waiting here five years. Maybe the Emperor has forgotten about me."

Demos added, "We all await our time before the Emperor. None of us wants to stay here, but none of us wants to go to Rome, either."

Snoring sounds interrupted the conversation. John turned his head and saw Petros sound asleep.

Demos asked, "You said this man Jesus did miracles. What kind of miracles? Was he a magician or a sorcerer?"

John turned his head toward Demos. "No, He was none of those things. He was the Son of God."

Demos said, "Really? How did God have a son?"

Dragon interrupted. "Hey, it is getting late. I'm tired, and I bet John is, too. He will still be here tomorrow if he lives through the work. Now let us go to sleep."

The six prisoners around John murmured approval and went to sleep.

For the first time, John realized God might have a purpose for him being on Patmos. With that thought, he relaxed and went to sleep.

Two

Getting to know John

John's second day of work made him look forward to the evening time of rest. Once a week, after the meal and the latrine, the guards made them stand under a tub of water and poured it over them.

Chained to his bed, John used his blanket to wipe the mud from his eyes. He let his aching muscles relax. When the last guard left for the evening, the barracks quieted.

John had been praying all day. He wanted the others to initiate the conversation, so he pretended to go to sleep.

Demos broke the silence. "Wake up, John."

John opened his eyes and turned his head toward Demos.

Demos asked, "What was this Jesus like? Did He really rise from the dead?"

Showing interest, Melek, Petros, Jared, Nikos, and Dragon propped themselves on their elbows.

"Jesus was interesting to be around. He frequently did something unexpected. One time he fed a crowd of several thousand on a few loaves of bread and some small fish He borrowed from a little boy. He often spoke of what He called the 'Kingdom of Heaven'."

Melek said, "Did He do miracles for real?"

"Yes, He did. I *saw* Him work many of them. He healed many sick people with a touch from His hands. One time He made mud from spit and put it on a blind man's eyes. When the man washed it off, he could see. Sometimes He only spoke and the disease disappeared. He even healed a Roman centurion's servant."

Nikos said, "Why did He help a Roman centurion?"

John said, "Because the centurion asked Him to."

Silence rippled through the barracks.

John explained. "The centurion perceived He had authority over diseases by watching Him. Jesus gave me the same authority and I've done many miracles in the Name of Jesus."

Melek said, "For real?"

John said, "Yes, for real. Many people who came to my churches couldn't see, hear, or walk. God healed them through my prayers. Many times friends brought sick people to church so I could pray for them. Many people in my church prayed for sick people and saw miracles."

Melek said, "Well, I can't wait to get sick so you can pray for me."

The little group of men laughed.

Demos switched topics. "Is there really a hell?"

John said, "Jesus said there is a place called hell. He told a story about a rich man suffering there."

Nikos said, "I bet it wasn't a pleasant story."

Petros said, "You haven't said anything about Jesus rising from the dead yet. Tell us the story about the rich man in hell later."

John turned his head to face Petros, Jarad, and Dragon only to find out Dragon and Jared snoring. He shook his head. "This is not the first time people have gone to sleep in church. Petros, shake them."

Petros roused Jarad and Dragon from their sleep. He said, "This is important. You can sleep after you hear this." Jarad and Dragon turned toward John after being roused.

John thought for a minute. "Okay. Jesus told us ahead of time about the crucifixion, but we didn't want to hear it. He even told us He would be in the grave for three days and three nights, but we didn't want to hear it. We didn't believe it could happen. When the Romans crucified Him, our last hope vanished. We thought we might never see Him again."

Petros broke in and asked, "Was Jesus truly dead?"

John made the effort to roll over and face Petros. "The Romans used much cruelty when putting Him to death. Blood, bruises, cuts, and gashes covered His body. You could not recognize Him by His face. He was quite dead.

"They buried Jesus in a tomb a rich friend donated. Since He made public statements about rising from the dead, the religious leaders asked the Romans to make sure He didn't. They put a seal on that tomb and set guards around it. We were so scared, we hid behind locked doors. We tried to think of ways to get out of Jerusalem without getting killed."

Melek said, "I think if I were you, I would have visited those soldiers in the middle of the night with my trusty dagger."

John ignored Melek's remark and continued. "Three days later, one of the ladies we knew visited us. She claimed she had seen Him alive. We didn't believe her even then. Without warning, He appeared in the midst of us. *In person. We could touch Him. He spoke with us.* We saw Him for about forty days. Many people in Jerusalem saw Him. One time, five hundred people gathered around Him while He walked the streets. All of Jerusalem was in an uproar."

Melek chimed in and said, "I like uproars."

Demos nodded and agreed. "Yes, you do."

John heard Nikos let out a yelp, and heard several slapping sounds. John said, "What is going on? I can't see what is happening."

Nikos said, "One of those roaches landed on my face. I hate them. Sorry for interrupting you."

John continued. "Then, while talking to us, He rose into Heaven."

Nikos asked, "You mean He flew?"

"No, God Himself took Him in a cloud. God is Jesus' Father."

Petros said, "So, there are two gods?"

"No. Jesus is the very essence of God."

Demos lay on his back and thought for a minute. The he asked, "So what's in it for you?"

John replied, "Maybe you should say, 'What's in it for us, too?'"

Demos said, "Please continue."

John turned to face Demos. "Jesus told us He would prepare a place for us in Heaven. God wants all of us in Heaven with Him, but sinners can't go there."

Petros said, "That's bad news for all of us."

John continued. "Jesus told us to preach the Gospel. It is *good news*".

John could see Demos had a question. He looked at Demos and asked, "What is on your mind?"

Demos said, "Um, get to the essentials, please. If sinners can't go to Heaven, how do we avoid hell?"

"Confess in public Jesus is the Lord of your life and believe in your heart God raised Jesus from the dead and you will be saved."

Demos said, "Is there anything else we need to do? I know I've sinned an awful lot. Will God forgive me? What else do I have to do to get into your Heaven?"

John said, "Jesus gave His life to pay for the sins of the world. If you repent from your sins, accept Him as your Lord, and believe in your heart God raised Him from the dead, you will be saved. You will go to Heaven and not to Hell when you die."

Demos said, "What a good deal. But how do I know God raised this man Jesus from the dead? Did you see Him in person afterwards? Could you touch Him?"

Petros looked at Demos and said, "Bonehead. John already told you he did."

Demos' face turned red with embarrassment. He said to Petros, "Oh yeah, I knew that. I did. Yes, I did."

Petros said to Demos, "John didn't only hear about this Jesus. He spent three and a half years with Him. I think he is telling the truth."

Petros thought for a minute and said, "I believe Jesus is alive. I'm calling Him my Lord."

John looked at Demos. "What about you?"

Demos thought for a moment. "Well, that's good enough for me. Since you knew Him, I'll say you know what you're talking about. Okay. I'll believe in this Jesus, too. I believe God raised Him from the dead like John said. I will call Him 'Lord', too. Caesar will have to fend for himself and get along without me. I'll do my best to live for Jesus the rest of my life. Even if I get out of here."

Demos smiled after stating his belief in Jesus. His face showed signs of relief. He said, "You know, it feels like a whole load of rocks lifted off of me. I've don't know when I've felt better. Even here on Patmos, I feel good."

Melek asked John, "Will it cause an uproar if I believe, too?"

John said, "You will cause an uproar with the devil if you do, and there will be cheering in Heaven."

Melek said, "I think I'll cause an uproar again. I believe in Jesus, too."

By this time, over half of the men in the barracks showed interest.

John looked at them. "Did you understand, too? Who else here will believe in Jesus?"

Half of John's fellow prisoners in the barracks raised their hands, including Jarad and Dragon.

John said, "Good. I will share more tomorrow. But let us go to sleep now. Remember, the day after tomorrow is our day of rest."

John looked at Melek and Demos in the dim light. For the first time, John noticed a peaceful look on their faces. John smiled and went to sleep.

Three

The Lord's Day

During the next several months, John's hard work earned the respect of his fellow prisoners. He kept his cool, settled fights, and kept a clean mouth. Each night he told the other prisoners stories about Jesus.

John tolerated the quality of food offered at the dining hall. It wasn't good, but he got used to it. The routine continued: rise and eat, work a lot, rest a little, work a lot, eat at the end of the day, then back to the barracks.

John asked the work master if they could clean their barracks. That is, scrub the floors and walls a little. They obtained permission to do so. The improvement, although small, seemed to lift the spirits of the men. John's first summer at Patmos approached and the cold nights turned into hot ones.

In spite of his age, John became accustomed to the work at the mines of Patmos. His character and peace made an impression on the other prisoners.

***

Ten months elapsed after John's arrival to Patmos. He rose early on the Lord's Day to spend time in prayer before the others woke. He stood with his hands and eyes lifted. His leg irons hung on his ankles and remained attached to the floor.

In the middle of worship, John found himself caught in a vision. He wasn't aware of it at first. From behind, a voice like a loud trumpet startled him. The voice said, "I am Alpha and Omega, the first and the last: and, What thou seest, write in a book, and send it unto the seven churches which are in Asia; unto Ephesus, and unto Smyrna, and unto Pergamos, and unto Thyatira, and unto Sardis, and unto Philadelphia, and unto Laodicea."

Those cities sounded familiar to John because he had founded churches in them. He turned around. He saw Jesus standing in front of a large menorah. But Jesus looked different this time. His hair was white and his eyes shone like fire. His feet looked like polished brass, and His voice boomed like thunder.

He held seven stars in His right hand. A two-edged sword came out of His mouth. His face shone bright like the sun. John felt dizzy and started seeing white. He slumped over and fell to the floor.

John thought he dreamed of Jesus when he felt someone trying to rouse him. He came to and felt the cold floor of the barracks. He looked and saw Jesus stooped over with His right hand on his shoulder. Jesus took his hands and helped him to his feet. John's strength returned to him.

John found a desk next to him with a parchment, ink well and a quill on it. He wondered where it came from and why it was there. He remembered the voice telling him to write.

John looked into Jesus' face and could see the excitement in His eyes.

"Fear not; I am the first and the last: I am he that liveth, and was dead; and, behold, I am alive for evermore, Amen; and have the keys of hell and of death."

Jesus commanded John with a strong voice, "Write the things which thou hast seen, and the things which are, and the things which shall be hereafter; The mystery of the seven stars which thou sawest in my right hand, and the seven golden candlesticks. The seven stars are the angels of the seven churches: and the seven candlesticks which thou sawest are the seven churches."

John sat on his bed, picked up the quill and dipped it into the ink. He unrolled a parchment and recorded Jesus' words and waited for Jesus to preach. He didn't have to wait long.

"Unto the angel of the church of Ephesus write; These things saith he that holdeth the seven stars in his right hand, who walketh in the midst of the seven golden candlesticks; I know thy works, and thy labour, and thy patience, and how thou canst not bear them which are evil: and thou hast tried them which say they are apostles, and are not, and hast found them liars: And hast borne, and hast patience, and for my name's sake hast laboured, and hast not fainted. Nevertheless I have somewhat against thee, because thou hast left thy first love. Remember therefore from whence thou art fallen, and repent, and do the first works; or else I will come unto thee quickly, and will remove thy candlestick out of his place, except thou repent. But this thou hast, that thou hatest the deeds of the Nicolaitans, which I also hate. He that hath an ear, let him hear what the Spirit saith unto the churches; To him that overcometh will I give to eat of the tree of life, which is in the midst of the paradise of God."

John had not seen Jesus preach with such fervor. When Jesus preached, He paced and waved His arms around. John sensed the urgency in His voice.

Jesus reached behind and extinguished one of the flames in the menorah with a flick of His finger. He hit the menorah so hard that it wobbled. The flame next to it almost went out, but recovered. John knew what to preach if he ever made it back to Ephesus.

John knew part of the blame belonged to him. Since he did not want the Church at Ephesus to die, he had to tell them about returning to their first love with Jesus. He wrote His message on the parchment.

Jesus started preaching again. "And unto the angel of the church in Smyrna write; These things saith the first and the last, which was dead, and is alive; I know thy works, and tribulation, and poverty, (but thou art rich) and I know the blasphemy of them which say they are Jews, and are not, but are the synagogue of Satan. Fear none of those things which thou shalt suffer: behold, the devil shall cast some of you into prison, that ye may be tried; and ye shall have tribulation ten days: be thou faithful unto death, and I will give thee a crown of life. He that hath an ear, let him hear what the Spirit saith unto the churches; He that overcometh shall not be hurt of the second death."

John knew about the persecution in Smyrna. He was proud the saints there did not collapse under pressure and remained faithful to Jesus.

He dipped his quill into the inkwell and wrote. He glanced at the prisoners beside him and saw them sleeping. They appeared to be in a dense fog.

Jesus resumed preaching. "And to the angel of the church in Pergamos write; These things saith he which hath the sharp sword with two edges; I know thy works, and where thou dwellest, even where Satan's seat is: and thou holdest fast my name, and hast not denied my faith, even in those days wherein Antipas was my faithful martyr, who was slain among you, where Satan dwelleth. But I have a few things against thee, because thou hast there them that hold the doctrine of Balaam, who taught Balac to cast a stumbling block before the children of Israel, to eat things sacrificed unto idols, and to commit fornication."

The old apostle motioned to Jesus to slow down. When he caught up, he nodded and Jesus resumed.

"So hast thou also them that hold the doctrine of the Nicolaitans, which thing I hate. Repent; or else I will come unto thee quickly, and will fight against them with the sword of my mouth. He that hath an ear, let him hear what the Spirit saith unto the churches; To him that overcometh will I give to eat of the hidden manna, and will give him a white stone, and in the stone a new name written, which no man knoweth saving he that receiveth it."

Jesus extinguished a second flame from the menorah with a quick flick of His finger. The menorah didn't wobble this time. John suffered cramps in his hands from the rapid pace of writing.

John knew he should visit the church in Pergamos, too. He didn't know Balaam and the Nicolaitans had influence there.

Without a pause, Jesus resumed preaching. "And unto the angel of the church in Thyatira write; These things saith the Son of God, who hath his eyes like unto a flame of fire, and his feet are like fine brass; I know thy works, and charity, and service, and faith, and thy patience, and thy works; and the last to be more than the first. Notwithstanding I have a few things against thee, because thou sufferest that woman Jezebel, which calleth herself a prophetess, to teach and to seduce my servants to commit fornication, and to eat things sacrificed unto idols. And I gave her space to repent of her fornication; and she repented not. Behold, I will cast her into a bed, and them that commit adultery with her into great tribulation, except they repent of their deeds. And I will kill her children with death; and all the churches shall know that

I am he which searcheth the reins and hearts: and I will give unto every one of you according to your works."

John's face turned red from embarrassment. He taught the people of Thyatira to abstain from lustful behavior. They knew better. He knew if he ever visited Thyatira, they'll get more than a short, sweet sermon.

Jesus continued His preaching. "But unto you I say, and unto the rest in Thyatira, as many as have not this doctrine, and which have not known the depths of Satan, as they speak; I will put upon you none other burden. But that which ye have already hold fast till I come. And he that overcometh, and keepeth my works unto the end, to him will I give power over the nations: And he shall rule them with a rod of iron; as the vessels of a potter shall they be broken to slivers: even as I received of my Father. And I will give him the morning star. He that hath an ear, let him hear what the Spirit saith unto the churches. "

Jesus extinguished third flame on the menorah.

He was glad a few didn't fall into sin. John completed writing the message to the church at Thyatira. He took another glance at his fellow prisoners. They were almost invisible.

Jesus continued. "And unto the angel of the church in Sardis write; These things saith he that hath the seven Spirits of God, and the seven stars; I know thy works, that thou hast a name that thou livest, and art dead. Be watchful, and strengthen the things which remain, that are ready to die: for I have not found thy works perfect before God. Remember therefore how thou hast received and heard, and hold fast, and repent. If therefore thou shalt not watch, I will come on thee as a thief, and thou shalt not know what hour I will come upon thee. Thou hast a few names even in Sardis which have not defiled their garments; and they shall walk with me in white: for they are worthy. He that overcometh, the same shall be clothed in white raiment; and I will not blot out his name out of the book of life, but I will confess his name before my Father, and before his angels. He that hath an ear, let him hear what the Spirit saith unto the churches."

Jesus snuffed out another flame. Three flames still burned.

John shuddered at the terrible message. He decided to double his prayers for the church at Sardis. They deserved a special visit from him when he left Patmos. Or if he left Patmos. He wondered how his writings might make it out of Patmos if he didn't. John didn't have much time to wonder. Jesus resumed His preaching.

"And to the angel of the church in Philadelphia write; These things saith he that is holy, he that is true, he that hath the key of David, he that openeth, and no man shutteth; and shutteth, and no man openeth; I know thy works: behold, I have set before thee an open door, and no man can shut it: for thou hast a little strength, and hast kept my word, and hast not denied my name."

This message made John smile.

"Behold, I will make them of the synagogue of Satan, which say they are Jews, and are not, but do lie; behold, I will make them to come and worship before thy feet, and to know that I have loved thee. Because thou hast kept the word of my patience, I also will keep thee from the hour of temptation, which shall come upon all the world, to try them that dwell upon the earth. Behold, I come quickly: hold that fast which thou hast, that no man take thy crown. Him that overcometh will I make a pillar in the temple of my God, and he shall go no more out: and I will write upon him the name of my God, and the name of the city of my God, which is new Jerusalem, which cometh down out of heaven from my God: and I will write upon him my new name. He that hath an ear, let him hear what the Spirit saith unto the churches."

Jesus looked at the menorah but didn't extinguish a flame. Three flames remained.

John smiled because Jesus said only good things about the Church at Philadelphia.

"And unto the angel of the church of the Laodiceans write; These things saith the Amen, the faithful and true witness, the beginning of the creation of God; I know thy works, that thou art neither cold nor hot: I would thou wert cold or hot. So then because thou art lukewarm, and neither cold nor hot, I will spew thee out of my mouth. Because thou sayest, I am rich, and increased with goods, and have need of nothing; and knowest not that thou art wretched, and miserable, and poor, and blind, and naked: I counsel thee to buy of me gold tried in the fire, that thou mayest be rich; and white raiment, that thou mayest be clothed, and that the shame of thy nakedness do not appear; and anoint thine eyes with eye salve, that thou mayest see. As many as I love, I rebuke and chasten: be zealous therefore, and repent. Behold, I stand at the door, and knock: if any man hear my voice, and open the door, I will come in to him, and will sup with him, and he with me. To him that overcometh will I grant to sit with me in my throne, even as I also overcame, and am set down with my Father in his throne. He that hath an ear, let him hear what the Spirit saith unto the churches."

Jesus extinguished another flame. The two remaining flames represented the churches at Smyrna and Philadelphia.

While writing these words, John became sad to know of the state of the Church in Laodicea. He knew he must visit them again.

John expected this message from Jesus to be the end of his vision. He was wrong.

Four

Shock and Awe

Jesus stopped preaching and John dried the ink on his parchment. He heard the same trumpet-like voice again. It said, "Come up hither, and I will show thee things which must be hereafter." John looked up and saw an open door in the sky through the roof of his barracks. Bright rays of light came out of it.

John didn't have time to admire the beauty of the door. He found himself propelled with high speed through it and found himself on the floor of God's Throne Room. His parchment, quill and ink fell on the floor next to him. John noticed a beautiful table and chair standing next to him. He picked up his writing equipment and parchments and put them on the table. He slapped himself to find out if he was awake. He was awake. His body and clothing were clean. The clothes smelled fresh. John's leg irons were gone.

God's Throne Room was spacious and had no ceiling. A bright green rainbow surrounded the throne, which was about one hundred yards away. God had the appearance of polished jasper or sardonyx. Lightning and thunder came from the throne.

Each of the seven lampstands that surrounded the Throne was topped by a large ball of fire. The roaring energy coming from the

Throne sounded like a huge waterfall. John's mouth and eyes grew wide with astonishment, taking in the wonderful sights. The intensity of colors in Heaven impressed John.

John saw twenty-four beautiful thrones surrounding God's Throne and the Altar and wondered why they were there.

The transparent floor of crystal in front of the throne looked like a sea of glass.

Four living creatures stood in a circle around the Throne, each one ninety degrees from the other. A creature with a man's face stood in front, a calf creature on the left, an eagle creature behind the throne, and a lion creature on the right. They had six wings and eyes all over them. John remembered similar creatures from the prophecies of Daniel.

When a trumpet sounded, they bowed and worshipped God on the Throne. John joined in. The worship of God thrilled John. Love and admiration for God welled up inside of him.

Twenty-four Elders entered the Throne Room. When they approached, John realized these thrones belonged to them.

Every now and then a loud trumpet sounded and the four living creatures, the Twenty-four elders, and everyone he could see bowed down and worshipped the Lord. The elders threw their crowns toward the Throne and said, "Thou art worthy, O Lord, to receive glory and honor and power: for thou hast created all things, and for thy pleasure they are and were created." John worshipped God with everybody else but remained by his desk.

A sundial stood near John. He touched it and wondered why it was there. He also wondered how it worked since light came from every direction.

God's throne sat on a large dais. Many angels flew in the air surrounding the Throne shouting "Holy, Holy, Holy is the Lord God Almighty". Seven powerful angels guarded the throne.

John sat on his chair, picked up his quill, dipped it in ink, and wrote what he had seen. He wanted to remember how wonderful he felt at this time. When he completed his writing, he checked his inkwell level. The inkwell remained full. "Interesting", he thought.

John could hardly wait to see what would happen next.

Five

The Book in God's Hand

John saw a scroll in God's hand. It had writing on the inside and outside. He thought, "Hmm. It must be a legal document of some kind."

A strong angel flew into the vast space of the Throne Room and shouted, "Who is worthy to open the book, and to break the seals thereof?" Angels searched all of Heaven and Earth for somebody worthy enough to open the seals, but didn't find anyone. John was sad at this news and started to cry. He wanted to know the contents of the scroll. For a moment he thought, "I've been called here, and now nobody is worthy enough to open these seals."

One of the Twenty-four elders approached John. He was handsome, well-dressed, had a stylish beard, and looked distinguished. John noticed he seemed old, but his facial skin seemed quite young. The mix of old and new puzzled John.

He greeted John and said, "That scroll is the title deed to the Earth. God removed His church from the Earth yesterday and His Church is here now. God is giving the final call for repentance to those left upon the Earth through terrible signs and wonders."

The Elder continued. "Weep not: behold, the Lion of the tribe of Judah, the Root of David, hath prevailed to open the book, and to break the seven seals thereof." The Elder pointed in the direction of God's Throne.

John watched Jesus approach the Throne. He wore a sheepskin having seven eyes and seven horns draped over His shoulders. He took the scroll from the Hand of God.

When Jesus took the scroll, the Four Creatures and the Twenty-four Elders worshipped God. They played worshipful music on their harps and opened bottles full of aromas. The fragrances filled the air.

The bottles also released voices. John heard sorrowful and joyful voices. He realized they were the prayers of the saints. The voices captivated John's attention to the point he almost forgot to write about them.

John stood, inhaled the fragrances, and watched the prayers rise to God. He realized the importance of our prayers to God from even the least of the saints.

The elders continued playing their harps. John stopped writing for a minute as he listened to the beautiful music. The music blended perfectly and suited the occasion. John reminded himself to keep writing.

John noticed thousands of people assembled in the Throne Room. They sang a new song: "Thou art worthy to take the book, and to open the seals thereof: for thou wast slain, and hast redeemed us to God by thy blood out of every kindred, and tongue, and people, and nation;

And hast made us unto our God kings and priests: and we shall reign on the earth."

Millions of angels shouted, "Worthy is the Lamb that was slain to receive power, and riches, and wisdom, and strength, and honor, and glory, and blessing."

John could see every creature. He heard them saying, "Blessing, and honor, and glory, and power, be unto him that sitteth upon the throne, and unto the Lamb forever and ever." Then the Four Creatures said "AMEN". The Twenty-four Elders fell on their knees and worshipped God. After a brief period of worship, they stood again.

John tapped the Elder's shoulder and asked, "Who are those people on the Earth if God removed His Church?"

The Elder replied, "This is prophetic. All of creation glorifies God. The sea creatures, the land animals and people, and the citizens of Heaven all glorify God. What you have seen will be fully realized when Christ rules on the Earth."

He let those words sink into John.

The Elder continued. "This is a big event. This is what you have been called here to see. God brought you here to witness the breaking of the seals and to witness the final judgments of God. Your writings will give the saints comfort until Jesus returns to the Earth. Keep your quill ready."

Six

The First Four Seals

The First Seal

The thundering sound of all creation worshipping God subsided. People in the Throne Room became quiet and directed their attention toward Jesus. John could hear a pin drop. When John saw Jesus reach for the first seal on the scroll, he waited on the edge of his seat to see what might happen.

Jesus broke the first seal. A low rumble of thunder filled the Throne Room. The floor shook. John heard the creature with a man's face say, "Come and see." Seeing this eerie creature talk disturbed him, but the Elder, who stood next to him, acted like everything was normal. John thought, "I will have to get used to this."

At the sound of the creature's voice, two angels brought in a beautiful table covered by a red velvet cloth. Another angel placed a sword and a crown on it.

The clomping of a horse's hooves broke the silence. Through a door near the Throne, John saw a white horse walk into the Throne Room with a rider. Everybody's attention focused on them. A helmet concealed most of the rider's face. He wore strange clothing and carried a bow but no arrow. An angel picked up the crown from the table and gave it to him. The rider placed the crown upon his own head.

A voice coming from somewhere said, "Go and conquer." A wicked smile appeared on the rider's face. It made John's blood run cold. He watched as the rider guided his horse off to the side to witness the breaking of the next few seals. The rider stopped, turned around and waited.

The Second Seal

John saw Jesus reach for the second seal on the edge of the scroll. When He broke the seal, the "calf" creature intoned, "Come and See."

A red horse came into the Throne Room with a rider. He received power to cause wars and to cause the death of many people. An angel picked up the great sword on the table and gave it to the second rider. Skill went into the creation of this horrible sword. Skulls on the handle added fear to the engraved message on the blade, "Peace is now banned on the Earth and Death reigns." The rider's raspy voice echoed in the Throne Room while he read the message on the sword. Then he swung his sword around a few times and grinned. He rode off and joined the first rider.

John remembered the command of his Lord. He recorded the frightening event. He knew terrible things will happen when this rider is turned loose.

The Third Seal

Jesus broke the third seal. John looked in the direction of the Four Living Creatures. The "lion" creature roared, "Come and see."

A black horse came with a rider. A foul odor like rotten food accompanied them. The rider held a pair of balance scales in his left hand that jangled as he moved. A somber voice came from the midst of the Four Living Creatures and said, "A measure of wheat for a day's wages, and three measures of barley for a day's wages; and see thou hurt not the oil and the wine." A feeling of horror came on John. This voice told of hunger and want.

The sinister figure directed his horse to join the first two riders and stopped to watch the next seal broken.

The Fourth Seal

Jesus the Lamb broke the fourth seal. John watched as the "eagle" creature said "Come and see."

A gaunt, pale-green horse entered. His rider looked like a living skeleton, and his name was Death. A man followed behind the horse named Hell. He brought the foul odor of sulfur and brimstone with him.

A voice somewhere among the Four Living Creatures said, "You have the power to kill a fourth of mankind with the sword, famine, hunger and wild beasts." He and his companion joined the other three riders who were waiting nearby.

At that time John noticed all four of them had the same face.

When the fourth rider arrived, he nodded at the others. They galloped out of the Throne Room, and descended to the Earth.

Seven

March of the Four Horsemen

"Vasily's Stamp and Coffee Shop" in Brooklyn displayed a large picture of a Russian stamp in the front window. Early in the morning, many office workers dropped in for a hot cup of coffee, a bagel, and time to read a newspaper. Vasily tuned the coffee shop's TV to the news.

The lead news anchor started his story. "Good morning. I'm Mirek Trinka with Channel 6 News. The world is still in a state of panic as the result of the Great Disappearance earlier this month. There has been no reasonable accounting for the number of people who disappeared.

"Public services such as bus lines, subways, and air travel have returned to normal. The thousands of vehicles that collided as a result of the Disappearance have been cleared off the roads. Hiring is at an all-time high as businesses seek workers to replace those who are gone. Fire and emergency services have also returned to normal.

"Not all has improved in the last month. This disruption has triggered fighting among the nations. A total of forty-two new conflicts have started since the Disappearance and there seems to be no end to the killing. New conflicts erupt every day. No conflicts have touched our shores yet. Please keep your fingers crossed. Now, Tina Levy, our National News anchor."

The camera moved from Mirek Trinka to Tina Levy.

"Food supply chains have broken down and groceries have disappeared off store shelves. Local grocery stores look more like mob scenes than anything else. Food is getting scarce and prices are taking a sharp upturn.

"This craziness has even affected animals. Many fierce animals have escaped from zoos all over the country and have attacked people in the streets. Similar reports have come from Europe, Asia, and South America. Our Medical anchor, Dr. Kees Vorhees, has another story of national importance."

The camera switched to Dr. Vorhees, a retired Dutch doctor.

"Massive populations died of AIDS in Africa this month, but seems unrelated to the current crisis. According to the CDC in Atlanta, it is a factor of the disease reaching maturity in large numbers of people at the same time. The CDC also confirms that the number of AIDS victims is increasing in the US and Europe as well. They also claim the population of the Earth has declined by about two billion in the past month. And now, our Local News Anchor, Dean Braxton."

The display behind Dean showed an open Bible.

"The sale of Bibles at bookstores is at an all-time high and so are their prices. As a result, many Bibles have vanished from motel and hotel rooms. Many countryside preachers urge people to turn from their sins. People have been spotted in public places displaying posters about the world coming to an end. With the current events in mind, you might want to take them seriously. And now, our International News Anchor, Jan Metz."

The camera switched to Jan and a photo of Charti Nist appeared behind her.

"Charti Nist, a UN peace negotiator, is making the rounds with various heads of state to coordinate emergency forces. He is arranging meetings with various warring parties using his high-ranking UN position. His main goal is to cool the hot spots in the Middle East oil fields, North Africa, and then to other theaters of conflict. He already has resolved eighteen conflicts. And now, Nate Perkins with our regional weather."

The camera switched to Nate, who stood beside a weather map.

"We are experiencing the usual September heat in the Greater New York City area. Highs today will be in the upper 80s to the low 90s…"

The parade of news anchors continued babbling.

***

From Heaven, the Apostle John watched people on the Earth. He noticed they treated the Great Disappearance as an unusual disaster but not as a sign from God. John expected much soul-searching repentance in the people left on the Earth, but he found only a little.

He sat at his desk and waited on the next seal to be broken.

Eight

The Fifth Seal – The Martyrs Revealed

Back in the Throne Room of Heaven, Jesus broke the Fifth Seal of the scroll. Something like a curtain moved under the Altar of God, revealing millions of people.

John looked at the Elder and asked, "Who are the people under the altar?"

"They are martyrs who have been killed over the centuries. Listen to them and write."

Their shouting sounded like thunder. "How long, O Lord, holy and true, dost thou not judge and avenge our blood on them that dwell on the earth?"

Jesus listened to them. He ordered a pure white robe given to each of them. He spoke to them saying, "You should rest for a little while longer until your fellow servants also and their brethren, that should be killed as you were, should be fulfilled." That message satisfied them for the moment. John knew what those words meant more Christians will be martyred.

John asked the Elder, "Why are these *terrible* things happening?"

"There is a two-fold purpose. The first is like the time the children of Israel approached the Promised Land. God sent hornets ahead of them to soften up the resistance. By the time Jesus arrives on the Earth, they will ready for Him. The second purpose is to get people's attention so they will repent and be saved."

John didn't write that down, but did make a mental note of it.

The Elder said, "Get your quill ready. Jesus is about to break the next seal."

Nine

The Sixth Seal – A Shock Wave from Heaven

Jesus broke open the Sixth Seal and John saw a shock wave launch from Heaven toward the Earth. He didn't know how he could see these sights so far from Heaven, and the Elder didn't bother to explain.

The shock wave hit the Earth so hard it caused a planet-wide earthquake that lasted for thirty minutes. It hit at 6:45 p.m., New York time and occurred three months after the Great Disappearance.

Most major landmarks collapsed: The Golden Gate Bridge, the Empire State Building, Sydney's opera house. The Leaning Tower of Pisa finally fell. The Eiffel Tower fell. Most Manhattan skyscrapers collapsed. London's Big Ben tower crumbled. Highway interchanges no longer existed. There wasn't a single city on the planet left untouched. Falling buildings killed millions of people. The earthquake destroyed countless landmarks.

All islands shifted in latitude and longitude. Mt. Everest, K2, and Kilimanjaro moved. GPS units failed to work worldwide because all coordinates had changed.

Dust from collapsed buildings filled the air and the sky darkened. The Sun appeared to be a black, smoky ball and the Moon appeared to be blood-red.

People trapped by the earthquake in the dark had to wait for daylight before they could be rescued.

Showers of meteors hit the surface of the earth and injured thousands.

When the dust settled, God pushed the sky back like a scroll and revealed Himself to the world. This filled people with terror and they sought out caves or whatever cover they could find to get out of God's sight.

But not everyone thought it was something to be afraid of.

Ten

The Reaction of Uncivilized Indians

The Elder said, "Here is something I think you will enjoy seeing." He directed John's attention to a certain location on Earth. He pointed to certain South American Indians in Venezuela. John watched them and listened in on their conversation.

After the earthquake, these Indians picked themselves off the ground. They managed to dodge the falling coconuts and trees. When they saw the image of God in the night sky, they bowed to the ground and worshipped Him.

The chief pointed to the image of God. "This is God, Whom we lost many ages ago. Our legends say we knew God and walked with Him, but somehow we lost Him. Our rituals include searching for God. Now we have found Him. Let us ask Him to visit us in person."

The Indians gathered together and their chief led them in prayer. "Great Spirit, accept our sacrifice. Please come and walk among us. We want to get to know You."

After praying to God, they sacrificed a chicken in His sight.

The chief's assistant said, "I hope He will be pleased by our actions. I wish to know Him."

"It will be a fulfillment of our tribe's legends if we found God."

The entire village gathered in a clearing so all could see God without obstruction and waited with great expectations.

John spoke with the Elder. "This is so amazing. I hope someone visits them soon with the Gospel."

Eleven

The Yellowstone Hikers

The Elder pointed to the Earth and said, "Watch these people." John looked down and saw two hikers.

Holly and her boyfriend Scott took a winter vacation in Yellowstone. They wanted to get away from the panic in the cities caused by the Great Disappearance. They parked their minivan at the campground and started hiking. Five minutes later the earthquake hit. The thirty-minute quake threw them to the ground. Many trees fell, random boulders rumbled past, and thousands of tiny meteorites rained on them. With the earth still experiencing aftershocks, they picked themselves off the ground.

After getting over the immediate shock of the massive earthquake, Holly said, "We got away from the panic in the city. Now we've experienced panic in the wilderness."

Scott said, "I'm still shaking. I've never been in an earthquake before. My head is still spinning. How long did the quake last?"

Holly looked at her watch. "Half an hour. Look at the sun. It is barely visible through the dust clouds, and the Moon is a dull red. It is 5:15 p.m., and the sun is about to set."

"I thought the quake might never end. Those fallen trees protected me from the meteors. I heard them hit all around me. Did you get hit?"

"I got zapped by a little one on my ankle, but nothing bad." She rubbed her ankle to soothe it.

Scott said, "What is that red dot on your forehead?"

Holly said, "You have a red dot on your forehead, too. Where is it coming from?"

Holly saw a pencil-thin beam of light coming from the sky to his forehead. She turned her head and saw the image of God in the sky.

Her eyes grew big and she pointed at it and said, "Look at that."

Scott turned his head and saw the image of God.

Holly shouted, "There's a cave over there. Let's hide there."

Scott said, "Follow me."

They scrambled into the cave going in deep enough to escape the frightening image in the sky.

Inside the cave Holly said, "What an earthquake. I've been through several tremors and a couple of major quakes. You come to expect them in Southern California. But we're in Yellowstone. And thirty minutes? Was this the major quake everybody was talking about happening here? And what is that *thing* in the sky?"

Scott went to the mouth of the cave, stuck his head out and saw the image of God. He pointed in the general direction of God in the sky. "Do you mean that? What do you think? What does it look like to you?"

Holly replied, "Well, don't you think that thing up there is God?"

Scott didn't answer her.

They turned on the flashlights they carried on their belt loops and walked deeper into the cave.

Scott said, "Let's explore this cave and see if we can find a place to stay for a while."

Holly put on a ball cap so anything that wiggled or crawled wouldn't get into her hair. The air inside the cave felt cool and moist. Holly touched the cold walls of the cave and felt the moisture. Her boyfriend searched the ceiling for bats and looked ahead for puddles and obstacles.

Holly shrieked when her hand went through a spider web on the wall. She wiped her hands on her jeans to remove the sticky web and brushed herself off in case a spider jumped on her. Then they continued their exploration.

Holly asked, "Do you think a bear might live here? I don't smell any bear odors."

"No, I don't either. Probably not."

Holly discovered a small brook in the cave. The source of it came out of the wall near the end of the tunnel. She saw Scott catch a stream of water in his canteen and sample it.

"It is drinkable. This cave is made of limestone. You can taste it in the water. There is no sulfur taste in this water like at my parent's home in Florida. At least we have a never-ending supply of good water."

Holly felt something jump on her neck. She let out a high-pitched shriek and brushed it off quickly. She jumped forward a couple of feet and turned her flashlight around to see what it was. A frightened lizard lay on its back. The light caused the lizard to scurry off. Scott laughed at Holly's misfortune. Holly glared back in return for his laughter. Scott apologized.

When they turned a corner a little deeper into the cave, they discovered a rather spacious room with a dry floor. The cave dead-ended there, so they checked out the features of the room and found dry rock formations to sit on. They put their flashlights on the floor so the ceiling could reflect light to the entire area.

Holly said, "We can camp here since it is protected and dry. Our zip-up tent will keep out bugs while we sleep. The kerosene lamp in our minivan will give us all the light we need. And we have a solar charger for our flashlights."

Holly saw Scott's face and knew he still thought about the image of God in the sky.

Scott asked, "Are you *sure* you saw it?"

"Yeah, I saw it. I hoped you hadn't seen it. I've had a few beers."

"Well, I've had a couple, but now I wish had had drunk more."

"Okay, if it is God, what'll we do?"

"I tell you what I'm going to do. I'm going to stay inside this cave until whatever it is outside goes away. "

"And if it doesn't go away?"

"Then I'll be here a long time. I'm scared of it. It stared right at me."

After a couple of minutes, Scott asked, "Do you have a radio? It's probable an earthquake lasting a half hour did damage in nearby cities."

Holly pulled her mp3 player from her pocket, "I only have this. There's a radio in my backpack that runs on emergency power, a crank, or solar cells, but it is still outside."

She put on her ear buds and tuned the radio on her mp3 player. After listening for a while she said, "They're saying this earthquake is not a local event. It happened worldwide. Cities all over the world have been reduced to dust and rubble. Thousands are dead from the earthquake in Salt Lake City alone."

She paused while listening to hear the next item of news. "And everyone in the world is seeing that thing in the sky. Scientists don't know what it is yet."

Scott scoffed. "Oh, really? Well, we do. How can they not know?" He made a grim smile.

Holly put a finger to her lips and thought before speaking. "I had a friend before the Great Disappearance who said stuff like this was in the Book of Revelation. Massive earthquakes, things falling from the sky, seas boiling, water turning to blood and similar stuff. At least, I think that is what she said."

She noticed her words made Scott think.

"I wish they'd made a movie out of it. I hate to read. My question is this: Why is God staring at us at a time like this? Did you see how the sky moved and God became visible?"

"I have a few ideas. It started with the Great Disappearance three months ago, all of those wars starting in the last few weeks, food prices skyrocketing, massive epidemics, volcanoes erupting everywhere, and now this earthquake. Maybe God is giving us His final warning."

Holly noticed Scott appeared less than comforted.

"It is food for thought, isn't it? God's final warning?" Holly could see the impact of her words on her boyfriend. He stayed quiet for about ten minutes.

Holly broke the silence that had settled over the cave. "Speaking about food, I left our food and supplies outside in my backpack."

"Well, go out and get it."

Holly whined, "With God looking at us?"

"You left your backpack outside. It has our food and supplies in it. I've got my backpack. It has the tent inside and our sleeping bags on top. It helped cushion my fall and it is still on my back."

"Well, my backpack fell off during the quake. I didn't leave it out there on purpose."

Scott offered a solution. "Okay. I have a coin. The loser goes out and gets the backpack."

He took out his coin and flipped it into the air. "Heads or tails?"

Holly called out, "Heads."

He smacked the coin against his wrist and showed it to Holly. "Tails."

She cringed. "Two out of three?" She paused.

"What if I wait about an hour? It might go away by then."

"I'm hungry now."

"Okay. Here I go. I'm hungry, too."

She eased out of the cave. When she stepped from the cave, the red dot appeared on her forehead. The image of God looked directly at her. She shuddered at the sight. Since it was dark, she turned on her flashlight, and retrieved her backpack. She decided to pick up some extra supplies from their vehicle: food, the gas grill, radios, solar generators for their batteries, and a first-aid kit.

Before re-entering the cave, Holly stopped and measured the image of God in the sky. She held out her arm and spread her fingers. The width of the image measured one full hand span, and its height was one and a half spans. She noticed God's features, but only in shades of grey and white.

She brought the food to the interior of the cave and cooked it. While eating, Holly said, "There is a big crack in the road. Our minivan won't be able to go any further. Too many trees have fallen across the road, so we can't go back the way we came either. Not for a while."

Scott said, "After we eat, I will set up our solar battery recharger and organize our supplies. We'll have to make plans for survival. There are plenty of deer in these parts. I have my hunting bow and plenty of arrows in the minivan."

Two hours later they both ventured out of the cave to retrieve other supplies.

On the way back, Holly pointed, "The image of God is still in the sky. It looks different than it did a couple of hours ago and has an eerie glow."

The pair stayed in the cave all night making survival plans.

***

Vasily, the stamp and coffee shop owner in Brooklyn, repaired his restaurant. His building was a local bank in the 1950s, designed to withstand small bombs, earthquakes and floods. Yes, he kept his "dough" in the safe. He had the lock cut off, so he couldn't lock himself in it. The front window had shattered so he mounted a hand painted sign on the front door to let people know his shop was open for business. His generator powered the lights and coffee urns. His gas lines were still intact, so he had gas for cooking. He turned the heat on full blast because the missing window let the cold December air in.

Vasily went to his supply closet to find his sweater. While there, he inventoried his supply of coffee, flour, and other supplies needed to run his shop. Fortunately, he had plenty of supplies.

Many rescue workers took advantage of the coffee and breakfast foods. The non-existent window served to take the aromas of his shop into the neighborhood. Across the river in Manhattan, rescue workers had their work cut out for them. Vasily's patrons watched news on Channel 6. Mirek Trinka, a favorite TV personality, walked the streets with his camera crew. He wore an overcoat to keep warm and a face mask to keep dust out of his lungs.

"I'm Mirek Trinka, on the streets for Channel 6 News. New York City is in ruins. The thirty-minute, 7.4 earthquake that started at 6:45 p.m. yesterday evening destroyed most of Manhattan and the surrounding boroughs. Most major buildings have either collapsed or suffered severe damage. Rubble is hindering rescue and emergency services. Fires started by gas leaks are everywhere."

Mirek held his mike and pointed to firemen extinguishing fires.

"Clouds of smoke from the fires and rubble have darkened the daytime sun. Everyone will wear face masks or breathing apparatus until the dust settles."

An ambulance siren drowned out his reporting when it passed by.

"Loss of life is estimated in the thousands. Rescue workers in the area are looking for trapped victims and bodies. Thousands of homeless people wander the streets seeking shelter. It is an icy day in New York City with temperatures in the low 30s. Looting is rampant, and many routes of access have been blocked, thereby limiting police and the National Guard. The mayor's office ordered first aid stations set up at Battery Park and every two blocks on Broadway and the Avenue of the Americas, with several at Times Square. A flashing green light will mark them. I've been told if anyone wants to volunteer, please report to your closest police precinct building and they will direct you where to go. Now back to our studio in Mount Vernon."

"I'm Dean Braxton, City News Desk. Many residents of New York City don't have power or water, and may not have it for weeks. Channel 6 is using emergency generators for our radio and TV transmitters."

Behind Dean, a screen showed ConEd employees repairing generators and re-connecting power lines.

"Essential government workers must come to work today. President Callaghan is assessing the damage to the United States and has ordered FEMA to get into high gear. FEMA will send emergency supplies like water and medicines to the hardest hit areas. And now to Ronnie Einstein, our Science News reporter."

Ronnie was in his early 30's and had brown hair, glasses, and a lab coat. "Most of the communications network is down. Land lines are down throughout the Greater New York City area, and cell phone usage is spotty because of the number of collapsed towers. Internet service is also limited.

"From satellite communications, we know this massive earthquake happened around the world. The major cities on all continents have been reduced to rubble and have suffered many casualties. An earthquake this long and planet-wide is unprecedented.

"Also, the frightening image in the sky is being seen around the world. Our scientists don't have an explanation for it yet."

A photo of the image of God in the sky appeared behind the reporter.

Vasily shook his head. "This is terrible. It's like 9/11 over again, but much worse."

Several patrons nodded.

Vasily said, "I wish I were someplace else, but where?"

Twelve

A Change of Scenery

The Elder took John to a window in the Throne Room. He pointed to a couple who arrived in Heaven a few minutes ago. Ed and Ava, a couple in their eighties, became born-again a few days after the Rapture. They went to church before, but it wasn't much more than a social club. They understood they missed the Rapture, and prayed together to receive Christ as their Savior. A couple of Sundays later Ed had a heart attack while driving to church. They both died when their car ran off the road and hit a tree.

The Elder said, "Do you want to meet them?"

"Of course."

"Let's go."

They left the Throne Room and walked to the Reception Area. John and the Elder embraced the couple and welcomed them to Heaven. They could see that the glories of Heaven overwhelmed Ed and Ava. Their eyes beheld new and wondrous sights, sounds, and smells.

John discovered when he met people in Heaven, he 'knew' their names. John expected Ed to recognize him.

Ed said, "You're the Apostle John, aren't you?"

John smiled. "Yes I am. And this is your lovely wife Ava, isn't it?"

John saw other saints in Heaven rush to meet the newcomers. An endless crowd hugged and welcomed them. Beautiful music filled the air. Friends and relatives they had not seen in years greeted them. The new arrivals and long-time residents of Heaven praised the Lord.

A boy approached Ed and Ava and hugged them. They recognized their son, Ronnie, who died two weeks after being born. He said, "I've looked forward to the day when I could meet my parents. I'm so glad you are here."

Ed held back tears and said, "Ronnie, I'm so glad to see you. It broke our hearts when you died. We are so glad the Lord brought you here."

Ronnie said, "I've been playing with my cousin Chris and his two sisters who came in the Rapture. They're lots of fun." He saw Ed and Ava overcome with emotion at this reunion, but the tears of sorrow soon gave way to rejoicing.

An old man approached them. John knew it was Abraham. He greeted John, and turned his attention to Ed and Ava. He hugged them and welcomed them to their eternal home.

Abraham said, "I'm going to take you on a tour of Heaven." He motioned to the Elder and John and said, "Both of you come with me, too." Abraham looked at Ronnie and said, "You can go back to play with your cousins now."

Ronnie hugged his parents and said, "I'll see you later. I know where you live." He waved as he left.

Although John had experienced the awe and sights of the Throne Room, he had not yet ventured into the City of Heaven until now. He watched Ed and Ava's reactions.

While they walked with Abraham along one of Heaven's streets, Ava remarked, "The flowers smell so good here."

Abraham replied, "You will see many new kinds of flowers here."

John noticed that Abraham's pace was slow and deliberate. He was not in a hurry.

Ed heard singing and music in the air. He said, "The music here is wonderful. I could live with this. I need to find a guitar." As they walked by, Ed saw people with musical instruments playing praises to God. John heard Ed singing along with the people when he walked past them.

John noticed the bright sunlight, and the clear blue sky. In the distance he could see snow-covered mountains. He felt a gentle breeze on his face. It was neither hot nor cold, but comfortable.

The Apostle John studied Abraham's appearance. Abraham's skin looked young while his overall appearance suggested great age. He looked like the Biblical patriarch he was.

John noticed Ed and Ava no longer looked their age, but appeared to be much younger.

Abraham led them through the City to an extravagant and expensive-looking house.

It looked like a mansion suitable for a Hollywood actor. The lawn looked perfect, and flowers filled the air with their fragrances. Ed and Ava wondered why Abraham brought them here.

Ed asked, "Who does this home belong to?"

"This is the home the Master designed for you. It has all the features you like. Does it please you?"

John saw the surprised look on Ed's face.

Ed replied, "Why, yes. Are you sure this is our house? It looks like it belongs to someone important. It probably cost a lot of money."

"Yes, it does belong to somebody important. God considers both of you important. The Lord spared no expense to make this home for you. It will be your home for all eternity. Do you like it, Ava?"

John could not miss the shocked expression on Ava's face as Abraham talked with her. She said, "Why yes, of course I do. The flower bed in the front of the house has my favorite flowers: hydrangeas. Look at all these other flowers. I've never seen many of them before. Oh, they smell so good."

"Yes, the Lord knows you love flowers."

John heard a rustling in the hedge leading to Ed and Ava's home. The noise startled Ed, and for an instant he jumped. Out of the hedge, a grey cat howled and landed into Ed's arms.

Ed's mouth hung open. He said, "Pepper. I didn't expect to see you here."

The cat replied, "Well, you asked the Lord to bring me here, and He did. Is your grandson Chris here?"

Ed replied, "Yes, he is here. You will see him later."

It took Ed a few moments to realize he was talking to a cat. "Do you mind if I carry you around for a bit?"

Pepper said, "Not at all. I like the way you hold me. I've missed you."

Holding tears back, Ed said, "I haven't seen you for twenty years. I've missed you, too."

Pepper purred as Ed stroked him.

The Apostle John saw a red-bearded, chubby man approach. He knew in an instant it was King David.

David said, "Abraham, may I show these new citizens of Heaven around? I'll take John and the Elder off your hands, too."

Abraham nodded.

John saw a sparkle of recognition in Ed's eyes.

Ed asked, "Where are your royal clothes?"

David said, "It's not like you think here, Ed. We are all servants." He took him by the arm. "Let me show you around the city."

Abraham walked off and said to them, "See you around."

David asked the new arrivals, "Could you use a glass of water?"

Ed and Ava said in unison, "Yes, please."

A beautiful river of crystal-clear water flowed from the Throne Room and through the City. Costly, transparent goblets sat on stone pedestals along the way. King David picked up four cups. He dipped the cups into the river and gave each of them a cup of water.

Ed and Ava said together, "Mmmmmm. The water is delicious."

Ed asked, "What is this cup made of? It's heavy."

"Gold."

"Gold?"

"What else? It is useful metal here. We make cups and streets out of it. Let's go."

"But it is transparent."

"It is refined gold."

John, the Elder, Ed, and Ava walked with King David. As they walked, they passed a gold tray with delicious fruit on it. Ed started to reach for a piece of fruit, but took his hand back. David said, "It is okay to eat the fruit. It is here for you anytime you want."

Both Ed and Ava picked a piece of fruit and ate it.

David said, "Let's move on. There is a lot to show you."

The small group of people followed David.

Ed noticed something and looked behind David. He had a puzzled look on his face, but kept quiet. David said, "I know what you are looking for, but you won't find them. There are no shadows here in Heaven. Let's keep moving."

King David showed other houses to them. One time, he took a short-cut across a flower bed. Ed and Ava watched their steps to avoid smashing the flowers, but the flowers moved out of their way. When Ed and Ava passed by, they noticed the flowers turned toward them.

Ava said to Ed, "It looks like those flowers can see us."

John thought the same thing.

King David said, "Yes, they can see you. I imagine it is unnerving at first, but you will get used to it. By the way, do you two know of the Apostle Paul? I know John does."

Both Ed and Ava said, "Yes."

David pointed and said, "Well, there he is."

The small group with David saw Paul with several people sitting around him. He was sitting in a park with seats arranged in a small circle. Paul's seat was in the center. They were discussing the Holy Scriptures. Bible scholars and preachers from many time periods surrounded him. They included Sir Isaac Newton, John Hus, Elisha Hoffman, William J. Seymour, and Timothy, a student of the Apostle Paul.

The Apostle Paul recognized them and said, "Hi there, David. Hello, Ed and Ava. And a special 'Hello' to my good brother John. I heard about your arrival here for a short visit. I am pleased you are here."

John greeted his old friend. "You have fared well since I saw you last. I am glad."

"Yes, I have fared well. I see you and the Elder are taking a tour of Heaven with Ed and Ava. It is good to see them here with the rest of their family."

Ed said, "Yes, Praise the Lord Jesus, we're glad to be here. And I'm glad the rest of my family is here, too."

Ava chimed in, too. "Everything is so beautiful here. The people here are so nice."

The Apostle Paul said, "I'm glad."

King David said to Ed, Ava, John, and the Elder, "Come along now. There is someone else I think you'd like to meet."

As they walked off Paul waved to them and said, "See you later."

King David led them into a park along one of the streets of Heaven. John noticed that Ava recognized a lady sitting on a bench. Ava asked, "Are you Fanny Crosby, the famous hymn writer?"

The lady said, "Yes, but I don't know about famous. You are Ava, aren't you? I know King David and the Elder. One of the other men is your husband, Ed."

She turned her attention to the Elder. She asked, "Who is your other guest?"

The Elder replied, "He is the Apostle John. You really knew who he was, didn't you?"

"Yes. But something tells me he is not yet a permanent citizen here, but he will be."

"You're right. His ministry isn't over."

It made John glad to hear the good news. John saw Fanny Crosby turn her attention back to Ed and Ava.

"I'm so glad you two are here."

Ava said, "I loved your hymns and I wish I had my hymnbook. I will miss the hymns you wrote."

Fanny said, "You have it backwards. The hymns came from here. They are still here."

Ava said, "I am glad then. Let us talk more about them later."

Fanny looked at both of them and said, "You have something to look forward to. You will be meeting Jesus soon. You must go now. I'll see you later."

Ava said, "Aren't you going to say 'good-bye'?"

Fanny said, "Why should I? We never say 'good-bye' here." She smiled and waved when they left with King David.

John could have spent the rest of Eternity touring Heaven with them. But the Elder told John, "We need to get back to the Throne Room."

John said to Ed and Ava, "I have to go now. I'll see you two later."

Both he and the Elder walked back to the Throne Room. The Apostle took one last look at Ed and Ava. They were lost in love and continued walking with King David.

Nobody was in a hurry in Heaven. Nobody there had any worries.

Thirteen

The 144,000 Evangelists

John returned to the Throne Room and saw four angels leave the Throne Room. They flew toward the Earth and stopped when they reached the atmosphere. One angel remained stationary and the other three took off in different directions.

When they moved into position, the four angels grabbed what looked like transparent sheets in the air. They pulled the sheets taut. All the wind on the planet stopped.

Another angel flew in from the circle of the Earth with the Sun behind him. He had the Seal of God in his hands. He shouted, "Hurt not the earth, neither the sea, nor the trees, till we have sealed the servants of our God in their foreheads."

***

Vasily's business thrived during the cleanup of New York City. Many construction workers from Brooklyn who cleared the rubble made his store their favorite breakfast stop.

Jackie, a bobcat operator said, "Can you turn on the news? Someone changed the channel to the Home Shopping Network. I'm about to go crazy."

Vasily said, "That channel drives me crazy, too. Someone must have found the remote control. I'll change it back to Channel 6 now. I'll hide the remote so it won't happen again."

Mirek Trinka had good news to report. "The Great Disappearance happened four months ago, and the massive earthquake a month ago. The cleanup in New York City continues. Traffic is permitted in Manhattan and most of the boroughs as well. Distribution centers for water have been combined with clinics for minor injuries or sicknesses."

Jackie said, "They won't mention the image in the sky, will they?"

Vasily nodded. "I wish they'd tell us what it is. It still scares me."

"I think it is God looking at us."

"It could be. Let us hope He still cares for us."

Vasily swept the floor of his shop and waited for the next wave of customers.

Mirek Trinka on Channel 6 News completed his story. "Today, electricity and water are being restored to the residents of Staten Island and Yonkers. And now, our meteorologist, Nate Perkins, who has a most unusual weather story."

A weather map of the world showed on a display beside Nick.

"This is the rarest of all weather events. At this moment in time, there isn't a breeze blowing anywhere on the planet. All winds have stopped."

Nick pressed a button and said, "This map shows the normal wind patterns of the planet."

He pressed a second button and said, "And this is what the wind patterns look like now."

The map showed no winds.

"Meteorologists have no explanation for this strange phenomenon. Scientists contend the recent planet-jarring earthquake is a probable contributor since the mountains and the islands are all in different places. The earth's axis shifted 180 feet during the last earthquake. To give you a comparison for severity, the Japanese earthquake a few years ago shifted the earth's axis six inches.

"Satellite transmissions from buoys off the coast of Greenland show the North Atlantic Current has experienced changes in direction and temperature."

A picture of one of the buoys appeared on a monitor behind Nate.

"It will doubtless take a few years before weather patterns make sense. The earthquake caused much ice to break off the polar caps, somewhat reducing the size of the polar caps. This fresh-water influx may cause a shift in the salinity of the ocean, which could change weather patterns."

Vasily said, "I think I will step outside and see if there are any breezes here. There's always a breeze in front of my store, even if it is a gentle one."

He went out the front door of his shop, wet his finger and held it up. "What do you know? No breeze."

***

Rabbi Elijah Morgan from Jerusalem sent a message to Jewish communities all over the world. He asked them to meet with him at Petra to seek their Messiah. Not all Jewish communities accepted his invitation, but in a few days, a city of tents formed there. Several million Jews gathered there.

At the appointed time, Rabbi Morgan asked for everybody's attention. "We must pray and seek the Lord's face. I know in my heart that the people who vanished in the Great Disappearance were Christians who knew God. We need to overcome our pride and get acquainted with our Messiah. God will meet us here, I know."

The Jews agreed and spent hours in prayer. God heard their prayers.

When darkness fell, the glory of God descended on their meeting place. It looked like a huge, sparkling cloud of light. It settled fifty feet above the ground. A fog left the glory cloud and descended on them. The assembled Jews stared at the glory cloud with their mouths and eyes wide open. It mingled with them all night long and God communed with them. They listened while God spoke to them.

They worshipped and said, "Yes, Lord. We accept Yeshua as our Messiah. Please forgive our times of ignorance and rebellion. Show us what You want us to do."

John saw the angel with the Seal of God fly in. The angel sealed twelve thousand people from each Jewish tribe. The mark on their foreheads was invisible to them, but not to John or beings in the spirit world. The angels and demons could see the Seal of God on their foreheads.

God commissioned the 144,000 Jewish Christians to cover the Earth with the Gospel of Jesus Christ. They knew their job: preaching the Gospel to everyone left.

After the angel sealed them, they danced, and God anointed them with joy. They danced wearing their prayer shawls and yarmulkes. A spirit of worship fell on them again.

***

John watched them from the Throne Room. God gave each one of them a vision. One of the sealed Jews had a vision of himself preaching near Sugarloaf Mountain in Rio de Janeiro. Another had a vision preaching in an Indian village in the jungle of the South America. An Israeli Jew received the desire to travel to Tokyo and preach there. A Russian Jew desired to return to Red Square in Moscow and conduct a meeting. Another Jew saw himself preaching by the Space Needle, one of the few surviving landmarks. One brave soul received a call to preach near a mosque in Tehran. God directed each sealed Jew where to go. They continued their celebration for the rest of the night.

The next day, these Jews acted on the vision God gave them. They left the shelter and safety of Petra. Most of them headed for the airport and traveled to every country on the planet. God provided for them in miraculous ways. Many of the evangelists went to large cities and others went to remote areas. The 144,000 preached in every county. Remote Indian tribes and aborigines received visits from these Jewish evangelists.

The few that stayed in Israel conducted impromptu meetings in city streets. They preached Jesus as the Messiah. Awesome signs and wonders accompanied their message. People received Christ in large numbers. Miracles of healings occurred when these evangelists prayed. The angel with the Seal of God marked the new believers, too. Often the new believers would also have meetings of their own in which people received Jesus as their Messiah.

***

One of the evangelists found the Indians in the Venezuelan jungle. An interpreter came with him. The evangelist entered the village and met with the natives.

The evangelist pointed to the image of God in the sky. "The God in Heaven, whom you all see in the sky, sent me here. God sent His son, Jesus, to die for your sins so you can go where He lives for eternity. Also, He wants to live in you now. He will give you eternal life if you forsake your sins and believe in His Son, Jesus, whom He raised from the dead after being an offering for all of your sins.

"Indeed, God sent me here because of your prayers. God remembered your sacrifice and your desire to know Him. His Holy Spirit will live in each of you who accept Him as your Savior."

Everyone in the village received Jesus as their savior at that meeting.

The leader of the Indians said, "Thank you for coming. We are pleased God heard us and we welcome your message. All of us here believe in this Jesus you tell us about."

The leader's assistant said, "We are glad we finally found God. We have searched for Him for generations."

John saw the angel with the Seal of God mark their foreheads, too. The whole village celebrated because God came to them. They at long last found God, or perhaps God found them. Laughter found its way into their culture.

***

One month passed since the 144,000 evangelists left their camp in Petra. This didn't go un-noticed by the media. Vasily in Brooklyn would find out shortly. As the morning rush ended, he cleaned up his coffee shop. He sat to enjoy a cup of coffee and watched the news before the lunch rush.

The mid-morning news anchor had an unusual story.

"I'm Tina Levy with Special Edition News. The surge of Christian evangelism by this large team of Israeli preachers has been going on for four weeks. The planet is covered with them and they are getting their message out. They are experiencing a large number of converts."

A video of one of their meetings appeared behind Tina.

"These preachers don't stay in one place long. Most meetings are impromptu. They leave behind hundreds, sometimes thousands of converts. I suppose times being what they are, we could use a little good news."

Vasily shook his head at the thought of Jewish evangelists preaching about Jesus.

Tina Levy interrupted his train of thought. "And now our International Desk anchor, Jan Metz."

"In International news, Charti Nist of the UN has obtained an unprecedented meeting of Jews and Arabs to discuss the Peace of Jerusalem. This conference will take place next week. It is unprecedented because rumors state the Arabs may consider giving control of the Temple Mount in Jerusalem back to the Jews and may stop hostilities. The possibility of recognizing the State of Israel is also on the table.

"Nist, a UN negotiator originally from Turkey, is also planning to meet with important heads of state afterwards. He will be discussing what national leaders what must do to promote world peace. Nist's

UN negotiating experience has been sharpened because of the large number of conflicts he has resolved in a few months."

Vasily thought, "This man has his work cut out for him. It will take a miracle to have the Middle Eastern Jews and Arabs to agree to anything."

Fourteen

A Peacemaker Arrives On the Scene

The massive earthquake occurred three months ago. Even then, most of the people at Times Square consisted of cleanup and repair crews. It was the middle of March, and noon, the temperature was sixty-five degrees.

Luigi Campion owned Times Square Communications, LLC, and sold time on the Jumbotron at Times Square. His subscriber list consisted of major news outlets and advertisers. Today, Channel 6 News had the noon hour. The big story of the day was Charti Nist's Arab-Israeli conference.

Jan Metz, the International News anchor announced her story. "In a striking accomplishment, Charti Nist of the UN has obtained signatures of Arab and Israeli parties to create the Seven Year Pact of Peace. All parties agreed to the terms suggested by Nist."

A video behind Jan showed Nist talking. Then it showed Arabs and Israelis signing the agreement.

Nist said, "The Israelis have been given full control of the Temple mount, provided they do not disturb existing Muslim buildings. The WAQF relinquished administrative control of the Temple Mount this morning. Half of Jerusalem will be under UN administrative control for seven years, and UN forces will enforce peace in the city.

"Israel will keep its current borders. Both Israelis and Arabs will be given free access to all sectors of Jerusalem. The UN will also enforce the current borders of Israel until a permanent solution can be agreed upon.

"UN Troops are replacing both Israeli and Arab armies at the borders as I speak."

A video behind Jan showed UN Troops moving in and the Israeli and Arab armies moving out.

Jan Metz continued her story. "Tomorrow, the Jews will commence construction of their Third Temple. The plans have been in existence for years, waiting for the right time. Arab reaction is cool, but not hostile.

"In a surprise announcement, Prime Minister Horowitz of Israel revealed the original Ark of the Covenant will be taken out of hiding and placed in the Third Temple. The Ark has been in the country since the mid-1980s and has been guarded by certified Levites.

"Animal sacrifices will start soon after completion of the Temple despite protests by animal rights activists."

A photo of the Ark of the Covenant displayed on the monitor behind Jan. "And now our National News anchor, Lawrence Powell, with a related story."

The camera switched to Lawrence Powell.

"Nist will land in Washington in a few hours. He will meet with President Callaghan to discuss solutions for world peace."

A video of Nist appeared behind Lawrence. Nist said, "I am asking the world and the UN for more power and cooperation. Things need to get done in a timely manner if we want to survive these crises, and it will take authority and action to get it done. All countries will have to give up some of their sovereignty for the prospect of world peace and safety."

Cheers broke out among the workers and shoppers at Times Square at the news of peace.

***

The next day, patrons filled Vasily's coffee shop, eager to hear more good news about the meeting between the president and Nist. Vasily cleaned the TV screen and made extra bagels for the anticipated crowd.

Jackie, a regular at the coffee shop, arrived early for the broadcast. Jackie was an electrician who also operated a backhoe. Before the special news broadcast he said, "That Nist must be really smart to get Jews and Arabs to agree on all the items he asked for. How did he do that?"

Vasily said, "You got me. I can't even get my neighbor to agree to keep his dog out of my yard."

Channel 6 news opened with the anticipated news. "Good morning. I'm Lawrence Powell. Nist met with the President Callaghan earlier today and gave him UN mandates to follow in order to speed world peace. Nist made it clear these mandates are not optional, but mandatory."

A video of Nist speaking appeared behind Lawrence. "The mandates I have given your president are for the good of the world. They must be followed. Severe penalties will be assessed including military action by the UN if these mandates are not obeyed. The people of this country will be required to turn in their guns and all other weapons to promote world peace. People should turn in their weapons at their nearest police station. A cash reward will be given for each weapon turned in.

"No nation is exempt from these UN requirements. Nist will be making his rounds to key people not able to get to Washington. His reputation of tough negotiator seems to be well earned."

A video of Nist giving a speech played on a monitor behind Lawrence.

During the broadcast, Jackie said, "Hey, look. There is a mark on Nist's forehead."

Vasily turned to look, but the mark was gone. "I don't see anything."

"I saw it there a few seconds ago. I know I saw something. Can't you rewind it? Don't you have a DVR on that TV?"

Vasily said, "No, I don't. Sorry."

Lawrence Powell continued his story. "During a stop in New York, Nist announced his plans to build his international 'World Peace Organization' headquarters north of New York City. Nist requisitioned two hundred bureaucrats and consultants from the UN to join his organization. Also joining with him is his former secretary at the UN, Stile Vastens. Channel 6 will give you more updates when available. And now to our Weather news…"

Vasily turned to Jackie and said, "Imagine that. World Peace headquarters about thirty miles away from here. And, let's hope he is as nice in person as he appears on TV."

Fifteen

An Important Discovery

The day after Nist moved into his building, he met with his staff in a series of meetings. By five o' clock, the office was empty except for Nist, an intern, and Stile Vastens, his secretary.

The intern connected computer and phone lines under Nist's desk and Stile worked in the next room. Office equipment, file cabinets, computers, and telephones littered the floor while Nist arranged his office.

Charti Nist received a call on his personal cell phone. He had a short conversation. When he ended the call, he smiled.

Nist said, "The UN has given me what they call 'Unlimited Power' to resolve issues. I can command military and have far-reaching executive powers. This is a life-long goal, and it has come to me at last."

The intern under the desk said, "Lucky break."

"Lucky, nothing. This has taken careful planning. What is your name, son?"

"Jesse Castaldo."

Nist reached under the desk and shook the intern's hand. The intern stood and looked at Nist. Jesse wore black glasses and looked like the stereotype computer geek. He had a set of electrical tools on a leather belt, and held electronic testing equipment in his left hand, which he laid on Nist's desk.

"I normally wouldn't say this to someone at your level, but this is good news."

Jesse said, "You said something about a goal?"

"Oh, yes. Years ago I paid a think tank to create these plans. I have done everything they suggested."

"Plans?"

"Yes. The think tank I hired told me to work in the background until a severe crisis came along. Or, perhaps, a crisis of your own making. Then offer solutions for peace. The Great Disappearance provided that crisis. I couldn't pass it up. It was too good of an opportunity. Millions of people disappear and the whole world is in a panic. What a great disaster."

Nist noticed the surprise on Jesse's face. He asked, "What is surprising about what I said?"

"'Great' isn't a word I'd use to describe the turmoil that followed the Great Disappearance."

"Oh, but it *is* great. Others tried to create a crisis with things like that fake global warming garbage, but it didn't move people since there is no real science to it. Global warming doesn't get people where they live. So, I didn't go along with it. My plan is similar to one Hitler used."

Jesse replied, "Did you say Hitler?"

A smirk creased Nist's face. "Yes. Remember after the Great Disappearance lots of so-called 'conflicts' broke out? I started them. I sent out teams to provoke those conflicts. Later I came in and solved them. Oh, the massive death because of the AIDS epidemic wasn't my idea or my doing, but it did help me at the perfect time. Not everything that happened was my doing, but I have taken advantage of it. Don't you think my last step was a great success?"

"You mean the Arab-Israeli solution?"

Nist smiled. "What else? A lot of behind the scenes bribery took place on both sides, but it worked. The think tank told me exactly what I needed to propose to get an agreement."

"So, you really don't care about the peace in Israel?"

"No, I don't. But it will lessen world panic because oil prices will stabilize. That will make me real popular with most people. I'm thinking I might move my headquarters to Jerusalem. And these accomplishments will get me what I want."

"What's that?"

"Cooperation. I'm getting known as the man who has all the solutions to all of our problems."

"Do you?"

"Of course, I do. The Middle East solution is just the beginning. There will be lots of crises I will have to create in order to solve them."

"Create?"

"Of course they have to be created. Do you think these things just happen? No. You've got to make them happen. I caused these wars. Then I stepped in and fixed them. A lot of worthless people will die as a result, but so what? It gets me instant popularity. These wars also drive up food prices by jamming normal food distribution channels. It is the next best thing to a famine because it creates the worldwide panic, and that will create the needed financial crisis. But, I am getting ahead of myself."

"What's your next step?"

"Well, the next thing the think tank told me to do is to get rid of the religious crowd. I hate Christians and Jews in particular. There is something about them I hate. I can't hate them enough. They seem to be the biggest sector of resistance to my way of thinking. Hitler and Stalin tried to kill them, too. The religious people champion the individual over the State. They always talk about God, and I hate even the mention of God. They'd have problems with the things I'll be doing, anyway. Their loyalty crosses the importance of the State, and I don't like that."

Almost shouting, Nist said, "The *State* has the highest importance. To be more precise, I have the highest importance."

After regaining his composure, Nist said, "But I shall succeed. That is why the next thing on my agenda is to get rid of those idiot preachers running around the globe."

He could see the disagreement on Jesse's face.

Jesse asked, "Then what?"

Nist put his hands together in the shape of a cup. "I almost have it in my hands now. It is hard to believe. My ultimate goal is to rule the entire world. My powers are being upgraded all the time. I have only a few more goals to attain to make it complete."

He tapped his forehead and said, "I'm getting ahead of myself. The think tank told me how to control the world's finances. So, the next thing on my agenda is seizing control over every financial transaction. I will be able to bring rebellious nations to their knees in moments without firing a shot. They also told me I needed to create some kind of loyalty test or badge. I haven't been able to come up with it yet. But I'll figure that out in time.

"Also, after collecting all the weapons, I'll be able to control the whole world with my own police force."

The look of shock on Jesse's face amused Nist.

Jesse asked, "But didn't you ask people to turn in their guns and weapons to make the world a safer place? I have noticed large numbers of people turning them in. Won't that make the world a safer place?"

Nist smiled. "It will be a safer place for *me*. You ought to know better. It is only a trick to disarm the public. People are much easier to control if they don't have any weapons."

He could see Jesse losing his composure. His mouth hung open, and his hand shook.

Jesse came to a conclusion and said, "So, you caused these wars and mass killings we've seen in the last few months to gain control of the world? It appears you don't care for the people on this planet."

"As a matter of fact, I don't. I don't. The planet could use a little depopulation. I learned that in the UN. All I care about is me. I know what is best for everybody. To sacrifice a few or even many doesn't mean a thing to me except I attain my goals."

Jesse asked, "Why did you jack up food prices so high?"

"I already told you. It is a natural and planned result. It will bring the financial crisis to the individual level. This will give me the leverage to offer my financial solution. All citizens will put pressure on their governments to ease their stress. Then I will step in and offer my solution."

The expression on Nist's face changed from exuberance to anger. "Do you have a problem with me?"

Jesse fumbled and said, "Uh, no."

"Well, I think you do. And I have a problem with you now. You know my plan. And you don't approve. I have to kill you now."

He took out a gun from his inside coat pocket.

Jesse said, "You can't be serious, can you?"

Nist removed the clip from his gun and counted the bullets. Then he snapped it back in and cocked the gun.

Jesse begged, "Please don't do this. I won't say anything. Nobody ever believes me."

He ran for the door, but Nist fired two shots into his back. Jesse collapsed on the floor, choked on his own blood and died.

Nist said to the intern's dead body, "And you were such a good intern."

Sixteen

New Age Meditation

Charti Nist took an elevator from his office to his secure, underground bunker for the night. He had no safety concerns because armed teams of hand-picked UN soldiers patrolled the whole compound.

After locking the door, he took off his coat and tie, and changed into some comfortable clothes. He glanced at the pictures of Hitler, Stalin, Castro, Karl Marx, and Friedrich Engles on his walls. His library, below the pictures, contained their books.

He put meditation music on his sound system, and ate a small dinner of stir-fry vegetables and wine.

After dinner, he entered his meditation room. He lit a few sticks of incense, turned on the burner to his hookah and loaded the water with powerful drugs. He put cushions on the floor, positioned himself in the Lotus position, took several pulls on the hookah pipe, and melted into a trance.

Ten minutes later in a drug-induced stupor, his eyes rolled up, and he smiled. He inhaled at regular intervals from his drug-laden hookah, blew out smoke above his head and lapsed in and out of consciousness.

***

Smoke formed a dragon above his head about the size of a baby alligator. It writhed in figure eights above him in silence with its red, glowing eyes fixed on Nist. Occasional red scales reflected light. Nist inhaled deeply. The dragon demon entered him through his nostrils because it sensed his extreme hatred for God and extended its influence through his mind. Something different about Nist made the demon summon Satan himself.

The Devil appeared beside Nist and walked around him several times. He had not felt such arrogance and wickedness in a single person in sixty years or more. With Nist's position in the world, he knew he could accomplish much with him. Nist was willing to do his bidding.

Satan summoned a powerful demon of mass murder. He had a distorted human body, a head full of red scales, and claws designed for shredding human flesh.

Satan said, "Don't you sense the *wickedness* in Nist? I think you will find him a suitable environment in which you may exercise your powers. You may enter."

The demon nodded and entered Nist.

Satan invited demons that once lived in Hitler, Stalin, and Mussolini to enter Nist. These entities of ego, pride, hatred, and greed entered Nist. The drugs opened areas of his soul to the demons.

The Devil had not entered a human for a number of years. He had been looking for the right person and decided to possess him. He waited for Nist to inhale. When he did, Satan slithered in.

After looking around his new home, Satan said to the demons, "Invade every corner of his mind. Make decisions to kill and enslave as many people as possible. Justify any means at his disposal to erase the mention of God and overrule his thoughts at every opportunity. With this man, we can kill everyone on the planet."

The Devil singled out a specific demon and said, "You go out and direct the choice of his spiritual advisor. Interfere with anyone else who might be eligible. Our man in Iraq will be perfect. You know who I am talking about."

The demon nodded and left Nist's body seeking a particular advisor.

The dragon's power grew and it puffed out large volumes of smoke. The other demons petted the dragon as their powers grew. For a few seconds, Nist's eyes glowed red. Then he smiled.

Seventeen

The Anti-religious campaign starts

Charti Nist felt new powers inside of him when he woke up the next morning. He couldn't wait to get to work. He called Stile Vastens, his secretary, to his office and gave her details of a press release he wanted her to write.

Nist said, "Write a story about these preachers running around the planet. Make them look like unstable people who threaten world security by their teachings. Write that they make threats of violence to government officials, advocate bombing of federal buildings, instigate rebellion against moves for world peace, and spread dangerous rumors of judgment from God.

"Say they preach about sin, which is an outmoded concept. Make sure you say that these are the most *intolerant of intolerants* that exist on this planet. It is an emotional word and should do the trick."

Nist added, "Also, set up an 800 number for reporting these fanatics. Ask people to call our 800 line if they spot one of these preachers and offer a cash reward of $10,000 for information that leads to a capture."

Stile said, "Okay, Charti. I promise you, it will be good."

"I know it will be. You always did good work for me at the UN."

Nist received a call from Stile two hours later.

"Your story is ready and the 800 number is set up. I've e-mailed you my story."

"Okay. I will read it now."

After reading it, Nist called her and said, "This is good, Stile. You've earned yourself a nice bonus."

"Thanks. I can use it."

"This is your next task. Call all major news networks and tell them to broadcast my story tonight. Record the responses of each. I want to know who is loyal to me. Offer them $100,000 in cash if they cooperate. The cash will be delivered here in half an hour. Get a good courier service to deliver the money. Remember, the delivery is conditional on the story being broadcast tonight."

Nist paused while Stile took some notes. Then he said, "Next week, I will give you a list of banking executives to call. We will discuss creating a world banking system to make local and international transactions safe. Set up the meeting next month in Hawaii. I'm sure that will get most of them there."

"Will we be merging banks or buying them?"

"The conference subject matter will say 'merging', but I will be buying them. Jack Delson, our Financial Advisor, is writing the subject matter of the conference. Do you know him?"

"Yes, Charti."

"Good. Set up a meeting with me and Jack for Monday morning."

***

Stile worked her list for the press release. The first executive on her list was Stephen Theily with the National News Network in Atlanta, Georgia.

She dialed and waited for the call to be answered.

Theily answered his call. "Hello?"

"Stephen Theily, I'm Stile Vastens from World Peace Organization headquarters. Charti Nist has a favor to ask of you. I need your cooperation in airing Nist's agenda item for world peace. This story needs to be broadcast tonight. Can you do it?"

"Do we have an exclusive?"

"No."

"What can we do to get an exclusive?"

"You don't have that kind of money to get an exclusive on this story."

"What is the story about?"

"It's about getting rid of those subversives who call themselves preachers and run around the planet interfering with Nist's peace efforts."

Theily asked, "How are they a threat?"

Stile perceived the curiosity in Theily's voice.

"They have been bombing World Peace Organization buildings worldwide, murdering UN officials, advocating assassination of high-ranking government officials, and advocating the violent overthrow of stable governments. This is contrary to the needs of world peace."

Stile paused to let her words have an effect on Theily. "Also, there is $100,000 cash reward for you if the story is broadcast tonight." She listened for any hesitancy in his voice.

He responded, "I see."

Stile knew she had cornered the executive. Nist was a powerful man, and dangerous to oppose.

She noticed the hesitation and made her closing statement. "Is that a yes?"

Theily waited a few seconds and said, "Of course."

Stile smiled and made a check by his name on her list. "I'll record your response and the date the story is broadcast. I'm e-mailing the story to you and your editorial office now. Have a great day. The cash will arrive after the story is broadcast."

She ended her first phone call.

***

Theily wasn't happy. He sat in his chair stunned at what he had done. He pressed his intercom buzzer and requested Sam Chase, the night news editor, to report to his office. A few minutes later, he entered his office.

The executive greeted his editor. "Sam, I'd like to discuss the World Peace Organization story they sent us. Do you have it?"

"No, I haven't seen it yet."

"Check your e-mail, write the story, and then we'll discuss it."

"What's so special about it?"

"You will see. Now get to work."

Sam stood and left the office.

***

After thirty-five minutes, the editor returned to Theily's office. He had a grim look on his face.

"Why the long face, Sam?"

"I think you know. The story the World Peace Organization sent in claims the preachers loose on the planet demand the death of government officials, and should be killed. I refuse to broadcast this story."

"Can you verify what Charti Nist is saying about them?"

"Steve, there's not a word of truth in it and this broadcast will sign their death warrants."

"Run it anyway."

"Are you kidding? There's enough trouble in the world without creating more. What's he got against them anyway? I admit lots of problems require force to solve, but this isn't one of them. I'm not excited about those preachers either, but this is not a good idea. You won't let anybody else get away with something like this."

"Nist promised a nice bonus if we broadcast it."

"How much is he offering for our souls?"

"It will mean $10,000 for you if the story runs tonight. It will be in cash *and* unreported."

"How much are *you* getting for my soul?"

Theily did not answer. "Just do it. I'll give the cash to you after tonight's broadcast before you go home. Remember, it will be in cash."

Theily saw the disgust on Sam's face.

Sam left Theily's office without saying anything and slammed the door shut.

Theily waited a few seconds and said, "The deed has been done." He didn't like what he did, but he didn't want to get on Nist's bad side.

***

Sam Chase looked at his story and wrote his version for the International news anchor, Sandy Cramer.

He saw Sandy approach. She asked, "What's the news tonight?" She looked over his shoulder at his computer screen. Her look went from 'What's new?' to 'anger'.

"What? You gotta be kidding. We can verify almost anything else, but this story is pure B.S. What is your source?"

"I got it from the exec, and he got it from World Peace Organization."

"I don't care if he got it from the Pope. I'm going to the Exec. We can't broadcast this."

***

Sandy Cramer stormed through the hall to Theily's office. She knocked on his door but Theily did not respond. She tried to open the door, but it was locked. She shouted, "Hey, let me in. I need to have a word with you. I know you're in there. I've got to speak with you about the news story you released for tonight."

She heard nothing. She uttered a sigh of disgust and shouted, "I'll be back. You haven't heard the last of this." Then she stomped away.

***

Theily watched Sandy Cramer storm off on his security camera. Then he picked up the phone and dialed a number. "Replace Sandy Cramer with Terry Berger for tonight's news." Then he hung up.

During the six o'clock news, he watched the World Peace Organization story from his office. The new International News anchor, Terry Berger gave the story.

"It is official. The war against the subversives has begun. The self-appointed preachers who have spanned the globe are causing massive disturbances. They advocate among other things violence against government officials, resisting peace initiatives, and encouraging disloyalty in their respective countries. We have reports of these subversives bombing government buildings and child welfare centers. These *intolerant of intolerants* threaten listeners with hell unless their ideas are accepted. If you see one of them, call the 800 number on your screen. There is a $10,000 reward for information leading to a capture."

After the broadcast, Theily received hundreds of angry e-mails from his employees. They expressed shock at the story. They knew they could not get away with broadcasting such lies and wondered why he allowed it.

After the news broadcast, a courier arrived outside of Theily's office and knocked on the door. He saw the courier on the security camera and pressed a buzzer that unlocked the door. The courier entered and said, "I have a package you need to sign for." He signed for the package and the courier left. Inside the package was the $100,000 in cash along with an unsigned note. It said, "Your cooperation is appreciated."

***

The next day, the wire services reported eighty-seven evangelists killed. Sam, the night news editor, read the stories and left work early with the $10,000 in cash. He went to his apartment and got drunk. The alcohol could not cover his guilt, so he loaded his handgun and shot himself.

***

In the Throne Room of Heaven, John shook his head. He spoke to the Elder and said, "This man is doing everything the first four horsemen set out to do. He is conquering, killing, causing food shortages, and now he is warring against God's saints. This is what I saw when Christ broke the Fifth Seal."

The Elder nodded and said, "And worse things will come."

Eighteen

Preachers in Season

In the shadow of the Space Needle, evangelist Yosef Rosen prepared himself for a meeting. He prayed for hours in preparation. He had his Bible, yarmulke, prayer shawl, and his assistant, David. The weather was perfect: a clear March sky, and a warm, gentle breeze. Hundreds of people enjoyed the rides, the food, and the shops. His assistant put a small, square platform about a foot and a half tall in the middle of the plaza. Yosef climbed on top of it and shouted, "Hey, hey, hey, let me have your attention."

He didn't have to wait long before a crowd gathered.

He shouted, "I'm glad you made it here today."

A lady covered with body piercings and tattoos shouted, "I wish you *hadn't* made it here today."

Yosef laughed and waved to the heckler. "We have the proof that Jesus is the Messiah, or the Christ." His assistant, David, passed out flyers with information about Jesus.

"Look at point number one on your flyer. The prophet Daniel specified the exact number of days between the order for

Jerusalem's restoration and the day Jesus rode into Jerusalem. Read Daniel 9:22-27. A British astronomer, Sir Robert Anderson verified this prophesy.

"Point number two, the prophet Micah predicted His birthplace: Bethlehem. Read Micah 5:2.

"Point number three, the prophet Isaiah predicted the manner of His death. Read Isaiah, chapter 53.

"Point number four, Jesus predicted His time in the belly of the earth: three days and three nights. He likened Himself to Jonah, who spent three days and nights in the belly of a big fish."

The heckler shouted, "Sounds like a whale of a story to me." Several in the crowd laughed at her comment.

Yosef continued. "Point number five, He was born of the tribe of Judah, the House of David, and in the city of Bethlehem, like the Scriptures predicted. Look up the Scripture references on your flyer when you get home.

"Point number six, God, His Father, raised Him from the dead. We have historical proof of the Resurrection of Jesus. See the web links on your flyer.

"Many other Bible prophesies have come true. The most recent one came from the prophet Zechariah. He prophesied the division of Jerusalem by the nations in Zechariah 14:2. It happened a few weeks ago.

"The Great Disappearance, which happened six months ago, is in 1st Thessalonians 4:13-18. This "Great Disappearance" is in your Bibles, and is known as the "Rapture of the Church". We didn't pay attention to God's messengers, nor did we pay attention to His written word. That is why we are still here.

"Salvation is only in His Name. To demonstrate Jesus' power, we ask you to bring the sick and diseased here. We will pray for them in the Name of the Messiah, Jesus, and they will be healed. More proof will come from your changed lives."

Sick and disabled people came to the front of the crowd. Yosef prayed and miracles happened. Amazement filled people who had never seen miracles and crowded near the preacher.

After the prayer for the sick, Yosef continued his message. "You will be tried, even to the point of death. But don't worry. Six and a half years from now Jesus will return to this planet. The Great Disappearance happened six months ago. We are six months into the seven year-period of intense trouble described in your Bibles. Who will give their lives to Jesus now?"

Many of the people in the crowd raised their hands.

"Pray with me now. 'I now receive Jesus as my Lord and Savior and believe in my heart God raised Him from the dead. I am forsaking my sins. Please forgive me. Thank you, Heavenly Father, for saving me. In Jesus' Name, Amen.'"

After prayer, Yosef saw the heckler move closer. He motioned for her to approach.

She said, "I'm sorry I ridiculed you. I had no idea this was real. I want to get saved."

Yosef asked, "What is your name?"

"Tara."

Yosef led Tara to Jesus using the Sinner's Prayer. He laid hands on her and the power of the Holy Spirit came on her and she passed out. Many people came closer to look.

Yosef said, "Don't worry about her. The Spirit of God is doing His work. She will recover in a minute or two and be a different person."

The crowd cheered and broke into applause.

***

John and the Elder watched these events from the Throne Room.

John said, "His preaching was awesome. He has an excellent knowledge of the Holy Scriptures."

The Elder pointed and said, "Look what the Angel of God is doing."

John watched as the Angel of God put the Seal of God on the foreheads of people who accepted Jesus as the Lord and Savior.

***

Yosef encouraged the new converts. "But be faithful to the Lord. Keep your behavior above reproach; love one another as Jesus loves you. Depend on the Lord to guide you. Read your Bible every day. If you don't have one, get one soon. Read the Book of Revelation and be warned about what is coming."

He saw Space Needle security guards approaching and knew he had to leave.

"I have to go now. God's has much work for me to do in a short period of time. Blessings to you all."

His assistant picked up his little platform and they walked to the curb to hail a cab. The security patrol stopped their approach.

The crowd cheered as he and his co-worker made their exit.

While Yosef looked for a cab, a reporter with a camera crew in tow approached. The Holy Spirit prompted him to give an interview.

The reporter said, "I'm Karen Chatham with Action News here in Seattle. Can I get a word with you before you leave?"

"Sure. Make it quick because I don't have a lot of time."

"This is a question everybody is asking. Why are you doing this? Don't you think your message is a little narrow-minded and insensitive to people of other religions?"

Before he could answer, a paper airplane made from one of the flyers sailed between the reporter and Yosef. They both ducked, not knowing what else might be hurled at them. A heckler shouted, "That's what I think of your preaching." His remarks were picked up by the microphone.

Yosef recovered. "I'll answer your questions in the order you asked them. First of all, I'm doing this because God has commissioned me to do so. A lot of people need to hear this. There is not a lot of time left to make a decision for Christ. To answer your second question, this is God's message from God's Word. God made a narrow walkway to Heaven. It's as wide as the cross. And yes, it is right to be on a narrow path if it is the right one."

A loud explosion rocked the crowd at the Space Needle. Everybody hit the ground and covered their heads. After a minute of silence, people looked around. Someone discovered the remains of a cherry bomb that exploded in a trash can.

Yosef, David, and the reporter picked themselves off the ground and stood. A cab approached and David hailed it. The driver pulled up to the curb where they stood. David took the platform and flyers and entered the opposite side of the cab.

Yosef said, "Bye for now. I've got to go."

He opened the cab door when the reporter said, "One more question, please. What do you think of the World Peace Organization's report on your activities?"

Yosef thought as the cab driver honked his horn and yelled, "Hey, come on. I haven't got all day." He knew the reporter's motive for asking and got in the cab.

***

Soldiers authorized by World Peace Organization hunted evangelists and patrolled city streets in Jeeps.

A lieutenant commanding four soldiers received a call on his radio to meet with a tipster who lived on the outskirts of Taos, New Mexico. His GPS led him to an abandoned gas station converted into a cheap residence. Cactus plants grew in the yard and the car parked in front was old and rusty. The soldiers got out of their Jeep and knocked on the door. A sloppy, half-drunk man came to the door.

The lieutenant asked, "Are you the tipster for one of those subversives?"

"Yup. I sure am. Got the reward money? If you're gonna make out a check, make sure you spell my name right. It is Jack Renshaw. R-E-N-S-H-A-W."

The lieutenant said, "We deal in cash, so don't worry about a check. But you don't get the money until we get the man you reported."

"I know esh-zactly where he is preaching. I came from there a half hour ago."

"Well, hop into our Jeep and tell us how to get there. Breathe in the other direction. I don't want your breath bleaching out my uniform. You better be right or you'll go to jail."

Jack replied, "Okay".

The soldiers helped the drunk to sit upright in the back seat of the Jeep. The driver followed Jack's directions.

Moishe Kranmann preached the Gospel in a plaza located in the tourist area of Taos, New Mexico. Close to one thousand people listened to him. The Jeep stopped and the soldiers told Jack to stay put. He could hardly sit up by himself anyway. The soldiers scrambled out of the Jeep and prepared their weapons. The lieutenant gave the order to shoot. They shot the evangelist in the head. Ladies screamed and most of the crowd fell to the ground. Some covered their heads while others ran away. The soldiers shot a few people near Moishe to instill terror.

Using a bullhorn, the lieutenant read a message to the crowd: "World peace has been strengthened by killing this subversive. Let it be a lesson to all of you."

The soldiers handed cash to the snitch while the stunned crowd watched. They radioed to headquarters to announce their success.

The soldiers got back in their Jeep and drove off. They left the dead bodies on the ground to show their contempt.

***

Moishe's body lay in the center of the plaza. Blood covered his tallit. His Bible remained in his hands. Several other bodies added to the pool of blood.

A person closest to the dead evangelist still shook from the gunfire. He said, "What did these people do to deserve getting shot? Moishe was a man of God and we could have been one of these dead people. We should give them an honorable burial."

The man said, "Yes, we should. I am glad he preached enough of his message so I could get saved."

A woman said, "Praise God, my sins have been forgiven. I am so happy right now. I wish I had paid attention to my preacher before the Great Disappearance. Now I'm living for God no matter what."

People nearby nodded.

***

Jack, the informer, counted his money as the Jeep sped back to his home. He saw a liquor store and asked to be dropped off there. He said, "Don't worry about me. I can find my way home."

The soldiers helped him to his feet. Jack said, "Give me a shove in the general direction of the front door and I'll make it the rest of the way." They complied and drove off.

After leaving the store, Jack walked home. He stumbled on the edge of the road and a passing car killed him.

***

Looking through a window of the Throne Room, the Apostle John saw Moishe Kranmann arrive along with the others caught in the gunfire.

The Elder said, "Let us leave the Throne Room and welcome them." The pair walked out to meet them. John saw Abraham approaching and knew what he planned to do.

John watched Jesus approach the martyrs. Cheers broke out as He walked in their midst. Angels brought in a lavish table with fruits, pastries and heavy gold cups filled with pure water.

John and the Elder returned to the Throne Room and saw a huge crowd of people – more than they could count. Each wore a white robe and held palm branches in their hands. They shouted, "Salvation to our God which sitteth upon the throne, and unto the Lamb."

At the conclusion of their song, the angels, Elders and the Four Creatures bowed and worshipped God. "Amen: Blessing, and glory, and wisdom, and thanksgiving, and honor, and power, and might, be unto our God forever and ever. Amen."

John returned to his writing desk and wrote their song.

John felt the Elder tap his shoulder. He pointed to another group of people and asked the Apostle, "Who are these people dressed in fine white clothing? Where did they come from?"

He didn't know for sure. He pretended he knew the answer and said, "You know."

The Elder smiled, "These are they which came out of great tribulation, and have washed their robes, and made them white in the blood of the Lamb."

"Is this all of them?"

"No, not yet. There will be many more. Therefore are they before the throne of God, and serve him day and night in his temple: and he that sitteth on the throne shall dwell among them. They shall hunger no more, neither thirst any more; neither shall the sun light on them, nor any heat. For the Lamb which is in the midst of the throne shall feed them, and shall lead them unto living fountains of waters: and God shall wipe away all tears from their eyes."

John recorded his words.

The Elder motioned for John to get up from his table. He said, "It is time to watch the breaking of the Seventh Seal."

Nineteen

The Seventh Seal

John and the Elder saw Jesus sit on His throne. He took the scroll, broke the seventh and last seal, and unrolled the document. Standing next to John, the Elder whispered, "It is the title deed to the Earth."

John noticed all people in Heaven stopped their conversations. They looked in the direction of the Throne Room. He *felt* the silence. It lasted thirty minutes, and seemed like an eternity.

The silence was broken by an angel who brought in a table covered with a bright red cloth. Seven beautiful silver trumpets lay on it. The seven angels who surrounded the Throne left their posts and assembled in front of the table. Each of them received a trumpet.

Another angel came to the altar and God gave him a large amount of incense. He put the incense on the altar, and ignited it with Holy Fire. As the smoke rose, beautiful voices went with it. John heard people praying. Crying. Rejoicing. Worshipping. All at the same time.

The angel took fire from the altar with his hand, filled his censer with it, and then threw it onto the earth. John's watched the fire fall from Heaven to the Earth.

***

Vasily's business slowed after 2:00 p.m. The evening rush started in another hour or two. He had another five hours to go before closing time, so he listened to his TV while mopping the floor and cleaning tables. He poured dirty water from the mop bucket into a drain behind his kitchen. Seconds after he put the mop into its corner, another earthquake began.

Pots and pans fell off the shelves, salt and pepper shakers spilled their contents onto the floor, and the front window cracked. Vasily kept an eye out for falling objects and braced himself for the duration, however long it took.

While being tossed around, Vasily heard deep laughs, groans, and what sounded like church choirs singing praises. A number of screams could be heard from the immediate neighborhood. The quake lasted three minutes and his shop suffered minor damage.

***

The earthquake knocked baseball players off their feet at Wrigley Field in Chicago. When the rumbling stopped, the managers bolted onto the field. The Cubs' manager wanted a replay because his player missed a routine fly ball, and the Met's manager wanted a replay because his player fell rounding third base and should have scored.

While the managers fussed with the umpires, a weather radar display replaced the game stats on the giant matrix board.

The announcer said, "We interrupt this game to announce a dangerous lightning storm, which is approaching. Fans must leave the stadium immediately. The game has been postponed. Please take immediate cover." The warning message remained on the screen while players left the field and fans fled the stadium.

Dark clouds swept over Chicago and other cities of the world. A crack of lightning hit a building across the street from Wrigley Field and thunder shook the century-old stadium. Panic filled the fans while they fled and headed for cover. A bolt of lightning struck and killed eighteen people leaving the stadium, adding to the panic.

***

In Brooklyn, people stranded at Vasily's shop after the earthquake decided to wait out the electrical storm that followed. Traffic jammed the streets because many lights went out. Powerful lightning bolts lit the sky and thunder rattled the front window.

Vasily tuned the TV set to Channel 6 News. "Let us find out what is happening." Lawrence Powell, the Local News anchor gave his report.

"Today's three minute earthquake comes eight months after the record-breaking, half-hour earthquake in December. An apartment building in Harlem collapsed killing eight. Local hospitals also report several minor injuries."

A photo of the collapsed building appeared on the monitor behind Lawrence.

Vasily said, "I know somebody in those apartments. I hope they weren't one of the victims."

Lawrence continued his story. "The New York City area escaped major casualties with only eight lives lost. Power is out in many areas of the city and traffic signals are not working. ConEd, New York's electric company, has workers out restoring power. First Aid stations will go up soon in Manhattan and the surrounding boroughs by order of the Mayor's office. Look for the flashing green lights. And now, Jan Metz with Channel 6 International news."

"The whole planet felt today's quake. Most cities of the world suffered only minor damages. No aftershocks have been detected, but Nist, the world leader, has been taken to an emergency bunker for his protection. He will be kept there for a short period of time. Today's earthquake interrupted purchases of major financial networks by the World Peace Organization. And now, our Science Desk reporter, Ronnie Einstein."

"Weather scientists at the Global Hydrology and Climate Center theorize the changes in the jet stream have caused an electrical imbalance resulting in this world-wide electrical storm. They estimate it will last twenty-four hours. Data collected will be used to forecast storms like this in the future. Please stay indoors if you can."

***

The Apostle John saw a few prayers in the form of voices and smoke reach Heaven, but not many. He told the Elder, "I thought this would cause more people would turn to God."

The Elder replied, "This is only the start. Worse things will follow."

Twenty

The First Trumpet – Hail, Fireballs and Blood

John saw the first angel raise his trumpet and blow. John covered his ears. On Earth, people looked to the sky when they heard the trumpet. One month had elapsed since the three minute earthquake.

At 5:10 p.m., New York time, high winds blew dark clouds all over the world. Hailstones the size of grapefruit fell. The hail killed thousands. People caught outside hid under bridges. Semi-trucks. Trees. Dumpsters.

Rain added to the mix. Many people leaving businesses and shops ran to their cars to avoid getting wet. In the parking lot of the Mall of America in Minneapolis / St Paul, a lady caught in the open rushed her baby to the car. She used one of her purchases to shield herself and her baby from the hail. When she opened the door, she noticed blood covering her baby. Great drops of blood fell on her arms, clothes, and hair, and blood covered her packages. She couldn't stop screaming while she scrambled to get her baby in the car and head for home.

Hailstones killed or injured people on the beaches of Hawaii. The rain turned into blood and many bloody and battered swimmers fled for their hotels or cars for shelter.

Wipers smeared blood when drivers tried to clear their windshields. The stench of blood permeated the air and pools of blood filled the streets and yards. Many cars collided on the slippery roads.

Fireballs raining from the clouds and did more damage than the hail. Thousands of homes caught on fire. Millions of acres of rainforest caught on fire. Fear paralyzed people who saw fireballs and hailstones rain from the sky and destroy their possessions.

***

Rachel and her friend Diane chatted over coffee when the hailstorm hit her Tallahassee, Florida home. The hail sounded like gun shots when it pelted the roof. They panicked and they ducked under the kitchen table for shelter. Through the Plexiglas storm door, they saw huge hail stones hitting the ground. Later they noticed the fireballs raining from the sky. They screamed for thirty minutes.

Rachel almost pulled her hair out by the roots. She screamed, "What in the world is going on? Hail and fireballs? Are we under attack? I hope my house doesn't catch on fire. What are we going to do?"

Diane trembled and said, "Who is attacking us? Can you see my house? Is it on fire?"

Rachel poked her head out from under the kitchen table and looked.

Diane said, "It is the house behind yours."

"I know where your house is. No, it isn't. Not yet."

Both ladies shouted at each other to be heard over the sound of hailstones striking the roof and sides of the house.

A hailstone crashed through the roof of Rachel's ranch-style house and hit the floor in front of them. Both screamed. Glass fragments flew everywhere when the hail shattered the windows.

Rachel saw Diane regain her composure. "That was close. I think I peed in my pants."

Diane patted her chest over her heart. "I think I did, too. I've never had a close call like that."

Rachel noticed an odor and sniffed. "Do you smell blood?"

Diane sniffed. "Yes, I smell blood. But it isn't mine. I wonder where my cat is. She is probably hiding in the deepest crevice of my house."

Rachel peered out from under the table again to look out the door. "Is the rain red, or is it blood?" She saw fireballs falling from the sky. "It *is* raining blood and fireballs in the middle of a severe hailstorm. This is nuts."

"Maybe God is mad at us. It's the thing in the sky, you know."

The sound of the hailstones hitting the roof seemed to slacken. The ladies breathed a sigh of relief.

"Why should God be mad at us? We haven't been that bad, have we?"

"Need I remind you about our affairs when our husbands are on business trips?

"Well, so what? There are worse things we could be doing. We're both bored out of our skulls staying home. In the last few months, we've had two major earthquakes, and now hail, fireballs and blood. What disaster will be next? I'm scared to death. My husband is off doing business somewhere and he is away most of the time. With this storm, I don't even know if either of us will live through it, so I'm going to live my life to the fullest."

"Well, that *thing* in the sky there might not be pleased with us. I know I'm just as guilty. I've been sleeping with my son-in-law while my daughter works, for the same reason. I'm bored to death and my husband is gone most of the time on business trips."

"You could have picked a wealthier guy."

"I don't care about money at this point. I need companionship. Has the hail stopped?"

Rachel noticed fires burning in her back yard. "I think my hose is outside the door. I don't smell any smoke yet, so at least this house is not on fire. I think your house is okay for the moment. Do you see it?"

Diane poked her head far enough out to look through the door. She breathed a sigh of relief when she saw her house intact. "It is okay."

"How many more disasters like this one will we have to endure?"

"Don't even *say* that. I'm scared to death and trying to deal with this disaster."

Rachel agreed. "Me, too. One of those forbidden preachers held a meeting not too far away from here last week. I wanted to go to one of those meetings, but I couldn't make myself go. I didn't feel right after sleeping with my neighbor's husband the night before."

"I'm afraid to go there because I don't want to get shot. If I get shot, who will take care of my kids? Anyway, I don't know why those preachers are such a target. Aren't there more important things to do these days than shooting at preachers?"

"Yeah, like getting out of this disaster alive."

"You got that right."

Rachel turned to look out the Plexiglas door. She heard fireballs rolling off her roof and saw them burning in her yard. She clenched her teeth and shook with fear. She saw the same look of fear on Diane's face.

Rachel sniffed and said, "I smell smoke. My house is on fire. Smoke is coming from the living room."

"We gotta get out of here."

"Where to? The hail will kill us if we go outside."

"Either that or get burned. What should we do?"

A hailstone hit the gas meter outside of the house. The escaping gas made a loud, hissing sound.

Rachel said, "Do you smell gas?"

Before Diane responded, a fireball hit the gas meter detonating the house, killing them both.

x x x

When the storm stopped, people who still had electricity tuned to the news programs. Others used battery-powered radios to find out what was happening. At Vasily's shop, the generator kicked in. It startled his customers at first, but then comforted them. Channel 6 went off the air, so he changed the station to Channel 5 to see what they had to say.

Vasily approached Jackie and asked, "Can I sit down with you?"

Jackie said, "Of course." Vasily sat on the other side of the table and they turned their attention to the TV.

"I am Jeremy Stillwell with Channel 5 Action News."

"And I am Sally Dexter, part of Channel 5's emergency news team. We're broadcasting from our emergency bunkers in Deer Park prepared for disasters like this one."

The studio had grey, concrete walls and emergency lights illuminating the news anchors. Manila folders covered the news desk in front of them.

Jeremy gave his story. "Hail, fireballs and blood. The City is in a panic. Fireballs raining from the sky created major fires across the region. Reports have come in from all areas of the City of homes and municipal buildings destroyed by gas explosions. Casualties are in the thousands, and many homes have been destroyed. Fire services could not respond until the horrific hailstorm stopped. Many fatalities have resulted from the grapefruit-sized hail."

A video of EMTs removing bloody bodies covered with sheets showed on the monitor behind Jeremy.

"Emergency services may not make it to your home today due to the nature of this emergency and the large volume of calls. Use your garden hose to extinguish fires in your home and extinguish fireballs that land in your yard. Do what you can until emergency services arrive. If you are able, turn off natural gas at the meter outside of your home."

Videos of firemen extinguishing neighborhood fires showed on the monitor.

"This disaster comes one month after the last earthquake. Scientists have no explanation as of yet about the storm covering the whole planet, which is a mix of hail, fireballs, and what appears to be blood."

A graphic on the screen behind Jeremy showed several dozen hailstones melting on the ground and homes with broken windows.

The camera switched to Sally Dexter. "The red substance falling from the sky that people call blood has not yet been analyzed. Please stay away from these blood-like blobs until we know what they are."

A video behind Sally showed blood running from neighborhood lawns into a sewer.

"Fireballs are brand new. President Callaghan is asking our scientists to determine the origin of this phenomenon. Scientists are analyzing samples of residue left behind by them as well as the blood-like blobs. Hopefully they can give us an explanation for this mysterious storm."

Behind Sally, the display showed a live satellite image of northern Brazil.

The camera switched to Jeremy. "The Amazon rainforest is on fire. Already one third of it has been destroyed. This is dangerous since this forest creates a large percentage of the planet's oxygen. Firefighters are waging a long and difficult battle to save the forest and the planet."

The satellite image changed to show fires covering North and South America.

Vasily shook his head. "Jackie, if this isn't fire and brimstone falling from Heaven, I don't know what it could be. I don't recall any disasters like this. We've had the Great Disappearance, two major earthquakes, and now this – all within a year."

***

In twenty-four hours, fire burned one third of all forests and all grassy fields. Not one home had a green lawn.

The Apostle John saw these sights and many others like it from the Throne Room. He noticed a few prayed to God for help, but not many. Fear prevented most people from doing anything.

John looked at the Elder and said, "I can't believe a disaster like this produced so little repentance. What will happen next?"

The Elder said, "There are six more trumpet judgments. Worse disasters will follow."

Twenty-One

The Second Trumpet – A Burning Mountain

In the Throne Room, the second angel blew his trumpet. To the Apostle John only a half hour elapsed since the first angel sounded his trumpet, but three months elapsed on Earth.

In the Queens borough of New York City, not too far from Vasily's coffee shop in Brooklyn, people waited for the traffic light to change so they could cross the street. It was January and people kept warm with overcoats and mufflers. They heard the loud blast of a trumpet and looked to the sky.

A Polish lady screamed, "Oh no. It's starting again. I don't know if I can take another disaster like the last one."

A Japanese woman said, "What's it going to be this time? What's worse than blood, hailstones and fireballs?"

A Jamaican vendor with handfuls of beads said, "I don't want to know."

A construction worker with a heavy jacket and hard hat said, "I don't know whether to run for cover or scream."

The Japanese woman asked, "Did I hear a tornado siren?"

The Polish lady said, "I thought it sounded like a trumpet."

The light changed and everybody crossed the street, but kept a watchful eye to the sky.

***

Deep in space, a massive fiery meteor shot out of Heaven and approached the Earth. Scientists detected it after it passed the Moon. News services broadcast the impact point, which was calculated to be four hundred miles west of Spain in the Atlantic Ocean. The speed of the meteor allowed a mere fourteen minutes of warning.

The meteor struck at 3:29 p.m., New York time. Vasily's coffee shop had three customers, so he turned the TV to Channel 6. Although the wire services reported the event, no video images of the impact were recorded. At 4:00 p.m., the story broke on TV.

"This is Mirek Trinka of Channel 6 News. A massive meteor struck four hundred miles off the coast of Spain, creating a powerful tsunami. Cities on coastal Europe suffered significant damage and great loss of life. Several coastal cities in these countries have disappeared."

The display behind Mirek showed a coastline of Europe before and after the tsunami.

"There is a little good news. The tsunami will not reach the shores of North America. Ronnie Einstein, our Science News anchor, has the latest development of the meteor's impact."

The camera switched to Ronnie Einstein.

"Satellite photos show an ominous red spot on the Atlantic Ocean at the point of impact, four hundred miles off the coast of Spain. The President has dispatched a research helicopter from a US Air Force base in England to obtain a sample of this red spot for analysis."

The display behind Ronnie showed a satellite image of the ocean where the meteor struck.

"The red spot is spreading and will reach our shores by noon tomorrow. FEMA has issued an advisory to coastal cities of the Atlantic Seaboard and island possessions of the United States. Please fill as many containers as you have with water in case this affects water purification plants. And now Melody Price, National News Desk."

"Other casualties in this most recent disaster are ships at sea. The meteor hit in the middle of military and shipping lanes. The Office of Naval Intelligence has estimated that one-third of all ships at sea have been lost. Of these vessels, most are military ships, tankers, merchant marines, fishing boats, and passenger ships. This disaster had no effect on vessels in the Pacific, Mediterranean and Indian Oceans. We will now to go our affiliate station in Washington, DC for the President's speech."

"Stan Reardon here with the Channel 43 News in Washington, D.C. The White House Press Secretary is announcing the President's arrival. In a few seconds, President Callaghan will update us on the current crisis here in the Press Hall of the White House."

As the President approached the podium, flashes from many cameras went off and the press secretary moved away.

President Callaghan adjusted his tie, shuffled papers, cleared his throat and said, "This is a time of national mourning. The disaster at sea has touched us all. Many families have lost someone close. That weighs on our hearts.

"As for the merchant and military ships sunk by the gigantic tidal wave, we do not yet have a complete count of the ships lost at sea. The number of lives lost will be in the thousands. A list of the victims will be made public when the final accounting has been made. The military is compiling their list of missing vessels as well as the merchant marines. There is no accounting available for private craft. Death touched many households today. Your prayers are requested for us all.

"We can get through anything if we try, and already have been through difficult times. We will survive. We mustn't give up."

A reporter shouted, "Mr. President, are there any rescue attempts in progress?"

"Yes, there are. Military ships, aircraft carriers and helicopters from the Pacific and Indian oceans race toward the Atlantic to search for survivors. Helicopters stationed in Great Britain and several ships from the Mediterranean have also joined in the search.

"Oil spill and environmental experts have been sent to the Eastern Seaboard to await the arrival of this red substance. We will advise any and all precautionary actions as we learn how to deal with this problem. Thank you for your attention."

The President exited the Press Hall of the White House.

Control returned to Melody Price at Channel 6. "And now our International News anchor, Jan Metz."

"Nist, the world leader, is safe in his New York Headquarters. He requests governments around the world provide aid to the countries stricken by this tidal wave."

The reporters continued their stories. Vasily talked to his patrons while he swept the floor of his shop. "What a mess. No end in sight for disasters. How many more can we take? I hope I can keep pace with the repairs to my shop from all of these disasters. I know you don't want to do without my coffee and pastries."

His patrons nodded.

Vasily used clean spring water for his coffee. Every day a delivery truck brought him more. He phoned his supplier and doubled his order of water for the next week and filled empty containers with tap water. He distilled water if he had to.

***

The next day, Ronnie Einstein of Channel 6 News Desk gave his report. "Scientists in the United States Air Force have determined that this red substance is chemically identical to blood and its origin is from the meteor."

A video behind him showed the Chief Scientist of the US Air Force speaking. She said, "This bloody spot is expanding and has shown no signs of abatement. Many dead fish have floated to the surface of the ocean and will have a severe toll on sea life and the environment of the planet. I have ordered teams of scientists to find ways to clean it after it stops expanding."

The camera switched to Mirek Trinka. "The red spot has reached our shores faster than expected and has covered the entire Atlantic seaboard with blood. It extends from Key West, Florida to the Bay of

Fundy in Canada. Independent scientists have taken samples for analysis. We have Myron Kelley on camera, who is a reporter from a sister-station in Daytona Beach, Florida. Myron, are you there?"

"Yes I am, and it sure stinks. The sea is red and so is the sand. You don't have to be a scientist to know what this is. Just put your finger in it to test it."

Myron leaned over and dipped his finger in the red water. "Yes, this is blood. Daytona Beach is one stinkin' place. Nobody is here except for reporters and scientists. Let's hope this goes away before Spring Break.

The control returned to Mirek Trinka of Channel 6. "The resorts and beaches along the Eastern Seaboard are deserted. Abandoned stores and motels line the beach because of the smell of blood, dead fish, and the lack of tourists."

The display behind Mirek showed images of the deserted shores.

"Not a single store is open. Environmental volunteers capture and wash seagulls and send them to the Pacific coast. Many cleanup workers have left, overcome with the stench of dead fish and blood."

***

The next day around 11:00 a.m., Vasily's customer, Nikola Silianos, complained while they sipped coffee. "I don't know how things could get worse. What's next? Will your coffee suffer from this? I've heard blood has gotten into the New York City's water supply."

Vasily said, "You are right. But I use either bottled water or distilled water for making coffee. That is how I keep my strong brew famous. At least you are here to talk to me while I make some needed repairs. I've got to paint my store's name on the new front window glass and mount this poster for this Russian stamp."

Nikola said, "What is that stamp anyway? Is it the Four Horsemen of the Apocalypse?"

"No, it is a stamp issued in 1939 commemorating the tenth anniversary of the Russian Cavalry."

While Vasily painted, Jackie, a construction worker from Harlem wearing a heavy winter coat, dirty jeans and a silver hard hat asked, "Why do you call this 'Vasily's *Stamp* and Coffee Shop'? When is the last time you sold a stamp here?"

Vasily thought and said, "About seven years ago, I think."

His patrons laughed.

Vasily grinned and said, "I get all this trouble for trying to make a living."

In spite of his humor, he wondered what the next disaster had in store.

Twenty-Two

The Third Trumpet - Wormwood

Adrian Morrison, a programmer in Myrtle Beach, South Carolina, worked in his cubicle when he heard the third trumpet. Out of the window he saw palm trees and the beach. The red water and sand worried him. He shook his head, and thought, "It has only been three months since the Atlantic turned into blood. What will happen now? How much worse can it get? Am I the only one with these thoughts?"

He grew up in Yonkers, so he decided to watch Channel 6 News via their web page. He put on his ear buds and adjusted his computer's volume.

"Merv Trammell with Channel 6 News Science Desk. The asteroid discovered by NASA after it passed the Moon will collide with the Earth. The impact point will be in Eastern Europe, and will happen at 2:07 in the morning, Eastern Time. While we sleep in the USA, untold damage will occur in Hungary. Residents of the impact area are being evacuated."

Merv pointed to an icon on the lower left of the screen. "Here is our countdown clock. There are less than eleven hours until impact.

We will keep you posted if anything changes. The impact of the object won't be felt outside of a seven-hundred mile radius in Europe."

A map of the target area appeared on the display behind Merv.

Adrian looked at the clock. It was 3:11 p.m., and he decided go home at 4:00 p.m. He decided to pick up a pizza on the way home, and watch the news about the asteroid all night.

***

Vasily closed his shop in Brooklyn, went home, and turned on the news. The countdown clock showed less than five hours. He rested in his easy chair. He looked at a photo of his wife on the table next to him. She passed away nine years ago. Her Bible lay open on her writing desk. He walked over to her desk and turned a page or two. She left a handwritten note to him, "Please get saved. I want to see you in Heaven."

He thought, "I'm a Russian Jew. How can I get saved?" Vasily thought about the recent disasters. "With all that is going on, I guess it won't hurt. I'll do this for my wife." He read the tract and decided to get saved. He prayed the sinner's prayer and gave his life to Jesus, his Messiah.

He went back to his easy chair, picked up her picture and kissed it. "I hope to see you again someday." He relaxed and went to sleep watching the news.

***

Millions of viewers stayed up all night to watch the big event. Telescopes broadcast real-time images of the asteroid to all news networks.

At 11:39 p.m., the noise coming from the TV roused Vasily from his sleep. "Ronnie Einstein here with a Channel 6 News Flash. The asteroid aimed at the Earth disintegrated into millions of fragments when it hit our atmosphere. Disaster has been averted. Now, to our mobile reporter at Times Square."

"John Detweiler here at Times Square for Channel 6. The news of the asteroid's destruction caused a celebration to break out here. When the news hit the Jumbotron, thousands cheered. New Yorkers use any excuse to party, and this is certainly a good one. It looks like New Years Eve here. Citizens of Earth do have a reason to celebrate tonight. Back to you, Ronnie."

"I have good news for stargazers. The asteroid's destruction caused an incredible meteor shower well worth going outside for. It is a warm, April night, and the sky is clear for New York City residents. And now, Jan Metz, our International News anchor."

"Nist, of the World Peace Organization, has expressed gratitude that the asteroid disaster has been averted since his goal is world peace and safety. He is still resolving conflicts around the globe and stays busy tracking terrorists."

Vasily turned off his TV and decided to go to bed.

***

Dodi LaCosta and her boyfriend, Kevin Golim went camping in Adirondack State Park near Utica, New York. They decided to spend a week relaxing in the woods. Both of them loved fishing and camping. They turned off their radios and cell phones during their trip.

Dodi woke up refreshed from a good night's sleep. She kissed Kevin on his forehead and his eyes opened. "Let us have coffee and fish for breakfast. I'll get the coffee ready and you cook the fish."

Kevin said, "I'll cook a few of the fish we caught yesterday. How many pieces to you want?"

"Two."

Kevin went around a tree to relieve himself. He stumbled to the stream and splashed water on his face to wake himself. The water had an odd smell about it, but the thought of frying fish occupied his mind. He returned to the campsite and took a couple of fish out of a cooler.

Dodi filled the tin coffeepot with water from the stream. She put it on the grill above their campfire. She cleaned their mugs and put some instant coffee in them.

The aroma of fried fish filled the air and the couple savored the smell.

Dodi said, "The smell of fresh coffee will make this complete."

Kevin agreed, "The fish will be done in a couple of minutes. Why don't you pour our coffee now?"

"Okay."

She poured the water over the instant coffee and the aromas of the fish and coffee blended.

Kevin took a sip of coffee and completed frying the fish. He placed a large portion of fish on two plates while Dodi took out two forks from their supply bag.

Kevin said, "This is almost perfect. The sun is up, and it is a beautiful April morning. No distractions, no cell phones, no radios, no nothing. Tasty fried fish and coffee to boot."

Dodi agreed. After breakfast, they decided to fish until noon. Kevin brought the fishing rods and the bait. Dodi brought two folding chairs.

About a half hour later, Dodi started feeling strange. "I am nauseated. My stomach is burning."

"Mine, too."

"I don't know about you, but I think you better take me to a hospital. I am feeling bad."

She collapsed to the ground, holding her hands to her stomach. Kevin felt bad, but had enough strength to get Dodi into their car. He used his GPS to locate the nearest hospital. During the drive, his girlfriend remained motionless.

Kevin worried she might not wake up. He tapped her on the leg. She came to and vomited onto the carpet. The sickening smell filled the car. Kevin rolled down his window.

Kevin asked, "Is there something I can do for you?"

"Keep driving."

With two miles to go, Kevin saw a slow train crossing the road and had to stop. Dodi regained consciousness for a minute and asked, "Why did we stop?"

"We are at a train crossing and I can't go around. We are two miles from the hospital according to the GPS."

"I feel like I might throw up again."

Kevin put his car in park gear, rushed around and opened her door. She threw up again.

Dodi labored to breathe. "I think I'm going to pass out."

She fell over limp onto the dashboard. Kevin leaned her against the seat and lowered it a little. He saw the end of the train, so he shut the door, raced back to the driver's seat, put the car in gear, and waited for the traffic to move. After he crossed the tracks, he sped around the slow train of cars ahead of him with his horn beeping and lights flashing.

He arrived at the hospital and entered the emergency driveway honking his horn. EMTs ran to his car.

The first medic to arrive asked, "What is happening here?"

"My girlfriend had some kind of attack while we camped at Adirondack Park. She has vomited twice and passed out while we waited on a train. I'm feeling pretty bad myself. We had fried fish and coffee this morning."

The ER tech checked Dodi's pulse and breathing. He nodded to another tech and his assistants whisked her away on a stretcher.

"The stream water you used to make coffee with is the culprit. We have had eighteen cases of this already. You and your girlfriend make number nineteen and twenty."

"What about my girlfriend?"

"She is not too far gone. The prognosis is good because we know what the problem is. And we know what your problem is, too. Come on in."

***

The next day, Vasily opened his shop. He mixed some batter to bake a fresh batch of bagels. He brought his wife's Bible to browse through when he had time. He turned on the TV expecting to hear good news.

"Hi, I'm Tina Levy, Channel 6 News, Special Edition. Nobody felt the impact of of last night's asteroid, but the Earth's water supply has been contaminated. Particles from the disintegrated asteroid scattered over the planet, falling into rivers and streams. The CDC in Atlanta says that one third of domestic rivers and streams have been polluted. They recommend that well water should be tested before drinking. So far, seventy-three people have died in the US from drinking polluted water. Hospital ERs across the country are full of campers who spent the night in the open."

A video behind Tina showed people in an Emergency Room being treated.

"And now, our Science News anchor, Ronnie Einstein, with his recommendations."

The camera switched to Ronnie. "Water treatment plants are in the process of neutralizing the acid content in your drinking water. Please wait one day before drinking tap water and test any outdoor water with pH strips. Drink only from bottled water. Soft drinks and bottled fruit juices are safe. And now, our International news anchor, Jan Metz."

"Good morning. I have an update from World Peace Headquarters. Nist has released new figures on the fight against the subversives. Soldiers have eliminated a total of 80,011 of them circling the globe preaching their message of death and destruction to the government. The new number is 160 higher than yesterday."

Vasily scowled. "What in the world is going on?"

***

John and the Elder in Heaven talked about the events on the Earth. The sundial near his desk displayed three numbers on its base. John didn't understand how they changed and the Elder didn't bother to explain. He did tell John the first number indicated how many of the original 144,000 have been martyred. The martyred evangelist number showed 87,011, then 87,012. The second number showed the total number of martyrs at 103,251. The third number, which indicated the number of people getting saved, exceeded ten million. The number of people getting saved looked blurry because it changed so fast. This pleased both John and the Elder.

John wrote of the burning mountain. When he laid down his quill, he asked the Elder about the blood. "Why was there so much blood with the first two judgments?"

"Because they have spilled the blood of His messengers, God is giving them blood to drink. And more *terrible* signs are yet to come."

Twenty-Three

The Fourth Trumpet – The Sun Dims

The fourth angel prepared to sound his trumpet. Two months elapsed since the burning mountain poisoned one-third of the Earth's water supply.

The Apostle John counted four more angels with trumpets. He thought the first three disasters would be enough to cause people to seek God for help.

John asked the Elder, "These signs are unmistakably from God. But where are the crowds of repentant people?"

The Elder responded by shaking his head.

***

Those remaining on the Earth heard the trumpet blast of the fourth angel and groaned again. People on the way to work heard the sound.

A female college student looked at the sky and said, "What's it going to be this time? These disasters come like clockwork every two or three months."

A businessman next to her said, "Did you see anything? Is anything falling?"

A policeman on his beat noticed the daylight decreasing. "It looks like it is late afternoon. What is happening? I don't see any clouds and this is the middle of June."

The sky was clear, but the daylight decreased. In about a minute the sky darkened and the street lights came on. The sun became a black disc. People stopped and looked at the sun. They did not know what to do.

The student asked, "What time is it?"

The policeman pointed to the clock on the street corner, "It is 7:56 in the morning."

A Russian lady asked, "Why does it look like night? I saw the sun a minute ago."

The student said, "I can see the sun, but it is a black disk. The stars are visible behind it. Isn't that weird? It looks like late afternoon. This is June, not October."

They looked at the image of God in the sky. It looked a bit brighter and changed from what it looked like before. It used to be white with dark lines outlining God's features. Now it had creamy colors in it: white, pink, blue and green.

The Russian lady pointed and said, "It looks more real than before. It is beautiful."

The businessman said, "Hey this kind of stuff happens in Queens all the time because of pollution, but this isn't the result of smog."

The student said, "I have to get inside. It is feeling cooler now since the sunlight is gone. And that thing in the sky looks creepy to me."

Others nearby agreed. The traffic light changed and the people proceeded to their destination. Many people decided to go home.

***

The patrons at Vasily's coffee shop didn't have to wait long to find out what happened. A news flash at 8:30 a.m. interrupted normal programming.

"I'm Ronnie Einstein with Channel 6 News, Science Desk. Today at 7:56 a.m., the sun became a black disk.

The display behind Ronnie showed a camera outside of the studio in Mount Vernon. The camera pointed toward the Sun and people could see the black disk.

Ronnie continued. "Panic has gripped the residents of the Greater New York City area. We advise our viewers to remain calm until scientists have assessed the situation. This has not escaped the attention of President Callaghan. To his credit, the President has taken quick action to solve this mystery. He has called the solar research team at Kitt Peak, Arizona, to investigate and has ordered NASA and other government agencies to cooperate with them. President Callaghan's assistant, Victor Borden, will fly there tomorrow to meet the best scientific minds on the subject."

Jeffrey Travis, another of Vasily's regular patrons said, "I'd like for them to solve his problem. It is 8:30 a.m., and the sky is dark. This gives me the creeps."

Jeffrey decided to call in sick, but stayed at Vasily's shop. At 10:00 a.m., he went to the front window with his cup of coffee to look outside. The sky went from dark to light. He said, "Hey, the sun brightened. It looks like 10 o' clock in the morning now. Well, almost."

Most customers crowded around the front window to see the sun.

Jeffrey said, "It doesn't appear to be full brightness. Is it hazy today?"

Vasily stepped outside and took a look. He came back inside and said, "There's no haze, but the daylight is not what it should be."

His patrons returned to their tables to sip coffee and watch more news. Vasily wondered about the duration of this plague and what its effects might be.

***

People worried about what happened to the sun. During the lunch hour at a sports bar in Chicago, a couple ate while watching a daytime baseball game. The Chicago Cubs were playing the Atlanta Braves. The diminished light from the Sun caused the lights at Wrigley Field to be turned on.

The wife poked at her chips and salsa. "I'm still in shock from what happened this morning. Even though it is noon, it looks like twilight outside. It reminds me of my winter vacation in Northern Canada when it looked like this around noon. And I am from South Texas. I wonder what is going on."

Her husband worked on a huge burrito. Between bites he said, "Yeah, and the image in the sky looks even stranger to me now that the sunlight has dimmed. It seems to look more real."

"Do you have any idea why all of this stuff is going on? I'm terrified at all this."

"I wish I did. This can't be far off from 'end of the world' stuff."

***

The next day, scientists at the National Solar Laboratory in Kitt Peak, Arizona, readied themselves for the President's assistant. They spent the last thirty hours at the lab performing tests.

The President's assistant, Victor Borden, flew there to meet with the scientists. He drove his car to the main entrance of the solar lab, and showed his badge to security guard. Victor gained access to the complex. Victor Borden parked and got out of his car. As he walked toward the front door, he noticed satellite dishes and radio antennas on the roof. Outside it looked like twilight, even though the clock on the face of the building showed 2:00 p.m. Security personnel admitted him to the building and escorted him to the lab.

The project leader, Brad Huron, saw the President's assistant approach via the security camera and unlocked the lab door to let him in.

Brad shook Victor's hand. "I'm glad to meet you, Mr. Borden. I'm Brad Huron."

Mr. Borden said, "Please call me Victor."

"I'm glad to meet you, Victor."

Victor looked around and said, "This is a nice facility. Can you show me around?"

"I'll be glad to." Brad pointed to the hall window. "Our network center is through this window and across the hall. Mike West and his team keep us connected to the outside world."

Brad waved at Mike through the window and Mike waved back. He led Victor to an array of telephones and computer equipment.

"Over here are our connections to various space agencies around the world. Each computer is video-enabled to allow our scientific team here more personal access with scientists at other agencies. Our CRAY computers take up the floor below us. We have three of them."

Victor said, "Wow. That's a lot of computer power."

"Yes, you are right. We use it day and night for weather studies here on Earth. Variations in solar radiation have a direct influence on Earth's weather, so we have to keep tabs on it all the time."

Victor shaded his eyes. "It sure is bright in this lab."

"We like light. You will get used to it. The theater on the lowest level is where we view images from the sun from the McMath-Pierce solar telescope. We also use the theater down the hall for special presentations. The electronic instruments you see lining the room analyze data from various satellites and planetary probes. There is more to see, but I want you to meet my fellow scientists."

Brad motioned for Victor to follow him and said, "I have five of the brightest minds in the world working here. Daily I am amazed with their knowledge and their hard work. I require lab coats to be worn in this area by my assistants. It lends an atmosphere of professionalism."

As they walked toward the other scientists, Victor said, "I'm impressed. But let us get to the point of our meeting. What have you been doing since the sun dimmed?"

Brad recounted yesterday's events. "It happened yesterday at 7:56 a.m. local time in Arizona. We discovered that it happened everywhere on Earth at the same local time. Because it was a very notable event, I did not allow anybody to go home. My associates and I spent yesterday, all of last night, and this morning searching for the source of this problem and running tests. I will give you my findings first. SOHO does not show any unusual activity. So the problem is not in the Sun itself."

Victor looked confused. "Talk in English."

"I'm sorry. 'SOHO' stands for 'Solar and Heliospheric Observatory'. SOHO is a satellite which is one million miles closer to the Sun. Its instruments give us data we can't get on Earth. Using that data, we discovered the sun's actual intensity has not decreased. This decrease in intensity has happened within our atmosphere. I'll show you images from that orbital laboratory."

Brad directed Victor to a computer and sent the images of the Sun from SOHO to a huge monitor. Radiation levels showed on the display's sidebar. Pointing to one of the meters, he said, "This indicator of solar output has been constant for the last eight weeks. The Sun has been relatively quiet for that period of time and solar storms have neither increased nor decreased."

Brad pointed and said, "Let's talk with my lunar expert over there."

Victor asked, "What does the Moon have to do with this?"

"You will see."

Brad and Victor walked toward him. Brad said, "This is Albert Weiss, our lunar expert. Albert, please meet Mr. Borden, the President's assistant."

Albert said, "Pleased to meet you, Mr. Borden."

Victor said, "Call me Victor."

Brad said, "Albert, show Victor what you have found."

He went to his computer terminal and sent satellite pictures of the Moon to the monitor. The display showed a different set of indicators. Albert pointed to them and said, "For this phase of the Moon, its brightness is normal outside of our atmosphere."

Victor asked, "What are you saying?"

Albert replied, "There is no problem outside of our atmosphere."

Victor asked, "What do you mean?"

Albert said, "Don't you know? The Moon has dimmed, too."

Victor didn't know about that.

Brad said, "Let's walk a few feet to meet Vadim Dmitrievsky, our deep space expert."

Brad and Victor approached Vadim's work area.

Brad said, "Vadim, please meet Victor Borden."

Vadim turned from his computer and said, "Hello, Mr. Borden."

Brad said, "Tell him what you have found."

"The luminosity of the stars is not affected outside of our atmosphere according to cameras on the Hubble Space Telescope. Space probes to other planets give the same reading."

Using the lab computer, he put images from the telescope on the huge monitor.

Vadim said, "The previous brightness of space objects has been recorded on this computer and they haven't changed. Notice this brightness indicator on the bottom of the screen when I switch from one week ago to today."

Vadim clicked with his mouse and the brightness indicator remained the same. Then he clicked his mouse and stepped through the days showing no change.

Brad said, "Let us move on to Ted Bennett, who is our atmospheric expert."

Victor said, "This seems like where the problem is. I can't wait to hear his test results."

Brad introduced Victor to Ted they shook hands. He said, "Please show Victor your findings."

"I've performed laser tests of the atmosphere and the opacity of the atmosphere has not changed. The opacity created by the volcano last year has dissipated. They sky has returned to pre-volcanic clarity, or in my terms, 'opacity'. I have done these tests when measuring industrial pollution for twenty-five years and cannot find anything in the atmosphere to account for the decrease in daylight."

Ted said, "Let me show you something else." He typed some commands at his computer and a false-color image of the earth appeared on his monitor. "The ozone layer filters out a large amount of ultraviolet radiation. The amount of ultraviolet light has neither increased nor decreased, so the problem is not in the ozone layer. And the ozone layer is bigger than it has been for twelve years."

Victor asked, "How can there *not* be anything blocking the amount of sunlight?"

Ted replied, "I don't know. I can't explain it."

Brad said, "Let us move on."

Brad and Victor walked to the next scientist.

Brad said, "This is Miko Tanaka, our solar and terrestrial weather expert. She graduated with honors from the University of Tokyo."

Victor said, "You must be familiar with Global Warming and keeping track of it, right?"

Miko laughed. Brad gave her a stern look and she sheepishly responded.

Miko said, "I am sorry. What you said is *very* funny."

Brad gave her another stern look.

Victor said, "Why did she laugh?"

Miko interrupted, "I have been keeping track of Earth temperature data for twenty-five years. We have been on a cooling trend since 1998."

"But many scientists working with the IPCC won't agree with you."

She laughed again. "I'm sorry I laughed. Their weather model omits influence of the sun's variations in solar radiation. It was either stupid or careless."

Brad wished he wasn't there for the moment. He spoke to Miko, "Please tell Victor what you have found."

"Yes. The amount of heat provided by the sun during normal days, or 'solar constant' is 1.94 calories per square centimeter per minute. It has been decreased to 1.28 since sunlight diminished. The SOHO satellite shows the amount of calories per square centimeter has not changed outside of our atmosphere. The solar constant falling on the Moon is still at 5.856. If this condition persists, the Earth will be on a severe cooling trend. This will affect crops, ocean currents, and will change weather patterns worldwide."

Miko smiled.

Brad hurried Victor away from Miko to talk with another scientist.

"I'd like to introduce you to Bärbel Eberstark, our chronologist."

Victor squinted at her name tag.

Brad knew his thoughts. "You pronounce it like 'bearable' without the middle 'uh'. She's from Germany. Bärbel, tell Victor what you found."

"Yesterday, the sun went dim at 7:56 a.m. local time in all time zones. It brightened up at 10:00 a.m., but not at full strength. The dimmed sun went dark at 4:00 p.m. local time everywhere. I discovered that by calling my contacts in every time zone. After 4:00 p.m., you can still see the sun, but it appears to be a black disk against the sky. This morning, at normal sunrise time, the sun rose. It remained a black disc until 10:00 a.m., but remains at two-thirds strength.

"At 10:00 p.m. last night, the stars and the moon became black discs, and remained that way until 2:00 a.m. I will be keeping track of these changes."

Brad knew Victor wanted a solution.

Victor said, "Well, how do we solve this problem?"

"We have to determine a cause before we can devise a solution. We can't find any atmospheric disturbances or changes in the opacity of the air. Solar radiation data from SOHO is normal outside of our atmosphere, and the Moon is getting its normal share of solar radiation."

"So you boys are telling me there isn't a problem?"

"No. What we are saying is we can't find a cause for it. The atmosphere is not blocking anything. We can't think of any other possibilities at the moment. As of right now, we have no explanation or solution."

"So you want me to tell the President that nothing is wrong? Do you know what that will do to your funding?"

"You can tell him what you like. We can't tell you anything more. We have hard data for the facts we have presented to you. We can't solve a problem we can't find a cause for."

Victor glared at Brad, but had nothing else to say.

Brad handed Victor a manila folder and said, "This is a document summarizing what we have found. I hope it helps."

Victor left irritated. He rehearsed in his mind telling the President what little he found out from the scientists.

After the President's assistant left, Brad said, "You did an excellent job on your presentations. I am proud of all of you. As for Victor, be easy on him, boys. Government people aren't expected to have manners or intelligence."

The small group of scientists laughed.

Brad said, "Now get back to work."

***

While driving home from work, Brad Huron called his wife on his cell phone.

When she answered, Brad said, "Hi there, Honey. I'm on the way home."

His wife, Elsa, said, "How close are you? I am getting ready to put steaks on the patio grill."

"Not too far, but I will be home a little later than normal. The roads close to us have repair crews working on them. Half of the road is blocked off. I guess they have to do that to fix all the cracks in the road from the recent disasters. I'll call you again if I encounter worse problems."

"Did you figure out why the sun went dim?"

"No, and we encountered a worse problem."

"What is that?"

"We had to tell the President's assistant we don't know."

Elsa said, "That doesn't make sense. The sun has dimmed and you can't find out why?"

"That's it. There is no good reason why the sunlight has dimmed. It is clear when you get into space, and there isn't any atmospheric blockage."

"Well, maybe it is because I'm a woman, but I think God is mad at us. Have you found out what that *thing* in the sky is staring at us?"

"No, I can't explain that either. I don't even like looking into a telescope with it out there. It gives me the creeps. But your comment about God being mad at us - well, it's the best explanation I've heard. I can't think of a better one."

Elsa said, "It is all I can think of. Our church-going neighbors have been missing since the Great Disappearance, so I can't ask them. That happened almost two years ago. What a mess. I guess we won't need sun block for our trip to the lake this weekend. That is, if the lake hasn't turned into blood. Maybe we should bring our sweaters even though it is June."

"I guess we will find out when we get there. We should take the sun block in case this is a temporary dimming of the sun."

Elsa suggested, "I think we should read our Bible and see if there is anything there that could help us."

"It doesn't sound like a bad idea. See if you can find it before I get home."

Elsa's voice brightened. "Okay. I will."

"Bye for now." Brad hung up his cell phone. He arrived home about fifteen minutes later.

After parking his car, he walked to the curb to check the mailbox.

"Good. All junk mail today. No disaster is strong enough to stop junk mail. No bills today. Hallelujah." He threw the junk mail in the trash. He went through the garage door to meet his wife.

Brad said, "Hello, honey. I've missed you today."

Elsa kissed him at the door, "I've almost got dinner ready. I'm cooking steaks on the patio grill and have potatoes in the oven. Why don't you slip into something more comfortable?"

"I think I will. I'll take me a couple of minutes."

He went into this bedroom and took off his lab coat and tie. He hung them up and put them in the closet. Then he looked around in his closet and found his favorite outfit.

When his wife saw him, she smiled, "Ah, you're wearing your favorite lab coat."

The sun blacked out at 4:00 p.m., an hour before Brad got off work. Even so, the warm summer evening invited dinner on the patio. A fresh pitcher of tea glistened with moisture. Citronella candles chased the insects away. Crickets chirped in the woods behind the house. Brad put his favorite jazz album, Dave Brubeck's "Take Five", on the patio music system. The darkened sky entranced the couple with its beauty. The dimmed moon and stars decorated the black sky.

The image of God glowed with iridescent colors in the night sky.

Elsa finished cooking the steaks and put them on their plates. The smoke added to their appetites. She took the potatoes out of the oven, set them next to the steaks and brought them out to the patio table. They sat down and ate their dinner.

When they finished, Elsa said, "I found something interesting in our New Testament."

Brad said, "New Testament? What happened to our Bible?"

"I don't know. It is probably in your study. I couldn't find it right away, but I did find this New Testament in one of the compartments of my writing desk."

"I'll have to look for the complete Bible later. But I interrupted you. What did you find so interesting?"

"The crazy events of the last few years sounded like 'end of the world' stuff, so I decided to read the Book of Revelation. There is a lot of wild and strange stuff in that book. What I found interesting is in chapter eight, and verse twelve.

Elsa took the New Testament from her pocket, opened it to the Book of Revelation, chapter eight, and read from it. 'And the fourth angel sounded, and the third part of the sun was smitten, and the third part of the moon, and the third part of the stars; so as the third part of them was darkened, and the day shone not for a third part of it, and the night likewise.'"

Brad's eyes grew big. "What did you say?

Elsa repeated what she read, "And the fourth angel sounded, and the third part of the sun was smitten, and the third part of the moon, and the third part of the stars; so as the third part of them was darkened, and the day shone not for a third part of it, and the night likewise."

"That sounds like what happened yesterday."

Elsa handed him the New Testament and said, "Read verses five through twelve. It's even more interesting."

Brad read it aloud. "And the angel took the censer, and filled it with fire of the altar, and cast it into the earth: and there were voices, and thunderings, and lightnings, and an earthquake.

"And the seven angels which had the seven trumpets prepared themselves to sound. The first angel sounded, and there followed hail and fire mingled with blood, and they were cast upon the earth: and the third part of trees was burnt up, and all green grass was burnt up."

A bat flew in, squeaking, and made several circles over their heads. Both Brad and Elsa jumped from their chairs and moved toward the patio door. The bat landed on a support of the patio roof before taking off again in search of insects.

Brad patted his heart. "That didn't do me any good while reading from the Book of Revelation." They both sat at the table had a good laugh. He continued reading.

"And the second angel sounded, and as it were a great mountain burning with fire was cast into the sea: and the third part of the sea became blood; And the third part of the creatures which were in the sea, and had life, died; and the third part of the ships were destroyed.

"And the third angel sounded, and there fell a great star from heaven, burning as it were a lamp, and it fell upon the third part of the rivers, and upon the fountains of waters; And the name of the star is called Wormwood: and the third part of the waters became wormwood; and many men died of the waters, because they were made bitter.

"And the fourth angel sounded, and the third part of the sun was smitten, and the third part of the moon, and the third part of the stars; so as the third part of them was darkened, and the day shone not for a third part of it, and the night likewise."

Brad's mouth hung open. "That's incredible. This is a list of the disasters that happened in the last year or so. And in the order they happened. I remember hearing those trumpet blasts, but tried to pass them off as sirens. I didn't want to believe it could be something else."

He thought about what he had read.

"Since the Bible has been around for over two thousand years, and these disasters occurred as they appear here, and in the same order, then it is logical to come to a certain conclusion."

Elsa smiled. She saw her husband's scientific mind working. "What conclusion?"

"The rest of this Bible must be true. And that this book is from God. It is impossible to think otherwise. Mathematically speaking, for someone to make such a prediction, and it comes true after two thousand years, it is no coincidence. If so, then there is another conclusion to be drawn."

"And what is the other conclusion?"

"We're in one hell of a mess."

Elsa replied, "No kidding. And there is worse coming. Look at the next chapter. There will be monster insects from hell. Chapter nine, verses one through ten."

Brad read chapter nine of Revelation. "It has an exception in verse four."

"What is it?"

"If you have the Seal of God on your forehead, the monster insects won't sting you."

"How do we get that seal?"

"I remember from watching Billy Graham on TV years ago, that we should be 'born-again' or something similar. It is dedicating your life to God and what he called, 'getting saved'. Maybe you get the seal by getting saved."

Elsa thought for a minute and broke her silence. "Do you think it will keep us from being stung?"

Brad shrugged and said, "I don't know, but it is worth a try. Even if it doesn't, we will be saved and won't go to hell. I've wondered all my life about this book but I've never taken the time to study it. Now I know it is all true. We'd better pay attention because it looks like we're living in the middle of it."

"Do you remember how to get saved?"

Brad smiled and said, "I don't have to."

Elsa eyes grew wide and said, "Why not?"

"It is written in the back of this Gideon New Testament someone gave us at the county fair several years ago."

She said, "Don't do that to me. You scared me silly. Now how do we get saved?"

Brad turned to the section in the back of the New Testament. "Let's see here. First of all, we have to admit we are sinners. I have no problem agreeing with that. Number two - admit there is none good on this planet. Well, I can heartily agree with that, too. Number three, confess Jesus as Lord of your life, and believe in your heart God raised Jesus from the dead. I'm sure repenting of our sins is assumed to be here."

Brad continued. "As far as God raising Jesus from the dead, I am pretty sure it has been verified. One of my associates at work used to talk to me about such things, but I always felt uncomfortable when he did. I knew if I acknowledged those things, I'd be responsible for my actions to God, so I avoided him. He went in the Great Disappearance, I'm sure. He acted differently than the rest of us did."

Elsa asked, "In what way?"

Brad reminisced. "Well, he had the most even temperament of anybody I knew. He told corny jokes that were funny but never dirty and always seemed upbeat. Even when bad things happened to him, he had a calmness which seemed a bit unnatural. I can't recall him ever being depressed. But I'm digressing."

Brad continued. "Number four, we need to confess Jesus as Lord of our lives. That means speaking it out in public. After today's meeting with the President's assistant, I am more than willing to do it."

Elsa said, "Should we pray or something?"

Brad responded, "Well, this doesn't say we have to, but it sure won't hurt."

Elsa said, "Let's do that now."

Brad took his wife's hands and said, "Let's close our eyes and pray. Dear God in Heaven, we admit we have ignored your Bible. We haven't lived a perfect life, so we ask You to forgive us our sins. We are sorry for our sins. We accept Jesus as our Lord, and we will live our lives by this book. We believe You raised Jesus from the dead. Thank You for saving us. Amen".

Elsa said, "I feel much better."

"So do I."

"I guess we'd better study the rest of this book."

"A logical conclusion. I think we have a whole Bible in our library somewhere. I'll find it when we go in for the night."

Elsa asked, "Do you see the Seal of God on my forehead?"

Brad said, "No. What about me?"

"No, not on you either. But I am glad we got saved. Maybe the Seal of God is invisible."

"Let us hope those monster insects will be able to see it."

Elsa looked at the image of God in the sky and said, "Brad, the image of God in the sky appears to be smiling."

Brad looked at it. "Yes, it does. I think He likes what we did."

They enjoyed the rest of the night watching the stars until they winked out at 10:00 p.m.

Twenty-Four

A Dreadful Announcement

The Apostle John saw another angel take off from the Throne Room of Heaven and fly toward the Earth. The angel didn't carry anything with him and trumpets hadn't sounded. The Elder pointed to the Earth, so John watched.

***

A week after the sun dimmed, all the people on the Earth heard a booming voice at noon local time. The angel made his rounds to every time zone and continent. "Woe, woe, woe, to the inhabitants of the earth by reason of the other voices of the trumpet of the three angels, which are yet to sound."

A painter in work clothes left Vasily's coffee shop after taking his lunch break. He stood at an intersection waiting for the light to change when he heard the angel make his announcement. After the booming voice faded, he looked to the sky and saw the angel fly away. He had never seen an angel before.

An African-American businessman standing next to him said, "I was on my cell phone when the angel spoke. Did you hear what he said?"

The painter said, "Yeah. Who cares?"

A well-dressed woman beside him had her hands loaded with shopping bags. She said, "I do. What did you hear?"

The traffic light changed and people walked across the intersection, but these three remained at the corner to talk.

The painter said, "A loud voice that said 'To all the inhabitants of the earth. You will all be dead in twenty-four hours.'"

The woman said, "That's not what I heard."

The painter said, "Okay. I'm exaggerating a bit. It said, 'Woe, woe, woe, to the inhabitants of the earth by reason of the other voices of the trumpet of the three angels, which are yet to sound.' I didn't exaggerate much."

The woman said, "Trumpets of three angels yet to sound? Does that mean there are going to be only three more disasters?"

The painter shook his head. "*Only* three more, she says."

She swatted him gently on his back. "Aren't you in a foul mood? I hope the next one gets you."

The painter thought before speaking. "Can you imagine how bad the next disasters will get? I don't want to even think about it."

The lady said, "What worse thing could happen? And what will the government do to protect us?"

The businessman said, "What can they do? Can they get a court injunction to stop God from doing what He is doing? Or tell whatever or whoever is making those trumpet noises to stop?"

The painter responded, "You know, if I took bets, I'd say God is giving us His final warnings. I've been thinking of dropping in on one of those preachers, I mean 'subversives' to see what they've got to say."

The businessman said, "You mean they're still around?"

"Yeah. The news broadcast last night said they've killed about 85,000 of them. They estimated there were 150,000 of them when they first swarmed around the planet."

The traffic light changed again.

The painter said, "Well, it's time to get going. I hope the next disasters aren't as bad as the previous ones."

The businessman said, "Be careful attending one of those meetings."

They said good-bye to each other before they crossed the street and went on their way.

***

Bobby Dennis, the Channel 6 scheduler, looked at the stories broadcast in the last two years starting with the Great Disappearance. He recorded the dates of the various disasters and what happened. He thought he recognized a pattern, but wanted to see if anybody else noticed it.

He saw Mirek Trinka, Jan Metz, and Tina Levy in the break room, so Bobby decided to get their opinions. "Hello, ladies and gentleman. I've got something to show you."

Mirek Trinka said, "Let's see it."

Bobby showed them a list he had printed. "The Great Disappearance happened two years ago. The Great Earthquake happened three months later, and the second major earthquake occurred eight months after that. Three months later, the meteor hit the ocean sinking ships, and the Atlantic turned into blood. Three months later, the acid water plague struck. And two months later the sun dimmed."

Jan Metz said, "So?"

Bobby said, "Don't you see? It is a pattern. Every two to three months another disaster strikes."

Tina said, "So, are you saying you think another disaster will strike in the next month or two?"

Bobby replied, "Well, it has been two months since the sun dimmed. I think another one will strike either next month or two months from now. Wanna make a bet on this month, next month, or the month after that?"

Mirek shook his head and said, "How crass. Taking bets on the next disaster."

Jan added her opinion. "That's the tackiest thing I've heard you say."

Bobby looked at the three news anchors and said, "So you don't want to bet on next month?"

Mirek laughed. "Put me down for fifty dollars. My guess is two months from now."

Jan said, "I'll bet fifty dollars for two months, too."

Tina said, "I can't believe what I am hearing." She turned to Bobby and said, "Put me down for a hundred dollars for one month from now."

Bobby recorded the bets and collected the money in an envelope. "Should I ask all the other anchors?"

Mirek said, "Yes, and don't forget the boss. He loves betting pools."

Bobby made his rounds to all the personnel at Channel 6. A disaster was on its way, but nobody knew when.

Twenty-Five

The Fifth Trumpet – Demon Insects

Three months elapsed since the sun dimmed.

The fifth angel blew his trumpet with a mighty blast. John saw a "star" that took off like a skyrocket, fell from heaven and landed on the earth. The creature stood like a man but looked like a yellow jacket. The creature emitted a nasty, buzzing sound that made John's skin crawl. The creature's hands were black and insect-like.

When the insect stood, a key fell from the sky and landed next to him. He picked up the key, flashed an evil grin, and flew off to a volcano in Iceland. The creature put the key into a crack in the ground and turned it. Smoke and ash rose out of the fissure. The volcano erupted with a loud noise and belched out lava, tons of ash and smoke. The earth shook from the force of the explosion.

Volcanic ash darkened the sky and rose for a few thousand feet. Out of that cloud millions of insects emerged. Swarms formed and scattered over Iceland, then headed off toward Europe.

***

The last major earthquake occurred thirteen months ago. France completed the rebuilding of its national symbol, the Eiffel Tower, two weeks ago on the last day of August. The French tried to complete the construction before Bastille Day in July, but the disaster of hail, fire and blood hindered them.

France planned a grand lighting of the Tower tonight at 7:00 p.m. The September evening chosen couldn't have been more ideal. The temperature was a mild seventy-one degrees at 6:00 p.m. and the sky was clear. Thousands jammed the downtown streets of Paris to see the Lighting of the Tower. Tonight, French citizens forgot their troubles and celebrated in the streets.

Michelle Chancy and Pierre Larue met for dinner. Their café had an unobstructed view of the Tower. They chose an outdoor table on the restaurant's second floor balcony so they could see above the crowds. French flags and models of the Eiffel Tower decorated the glass-topped tables. The wrought iron chairs had patriotic ribbons tied on them. The couple ordered a dinner of ratatouille, wine and baguettes.

While they waited Michelle said to Pierre, "I'm so glad you picked this restaurant. I've wanted to eat here for a long time. The view is thrilling. Look at the city lights. I can't wait for the Tower to be illuminated."

Pierre said, "I had to bribe the maître d' to get this table."

Michelle smiled and said, "How romantic. No telling how this evening will turn out."

"After dinner, let's take a walk along the Champs-Élysées and see what we might find."

"Those stores are so expensive. Do you think we will find anything we can afford?"

"Probably not. But, I've never been in any of them. It will be fun even if we window shop."

"How do you like my outfit?"

"Cute. The black beret, black skirt, and wide black and white stripes on your blouse are classy."

"I don't look like a mime, do I?"

"Of course not. Oh, here comes our dinner. I ordered ahead to shorten our wait time. I want to be ready when the Tower lights come on."

The waiter arrived with the wine bottle, glasses, and the food and placed it on the glass-topped table. They ate dinner while being illuminated by the lights of Paris.

After eating, they enjoyed one more glass of wine.

While they sipped on their wine, the Eiffel Tower's lights turned on. All of Paris cheered. The sky exploded with fireworks and bands played. Small booths dotted the park underneath the tower and vendors sold food and souvenirs. Admission for the elevator ride to the top of the Tower was free tonight and the waiting line stretched out a block and a half.

Michelle said, "How wonderful. The Tower is beautiful. This is a gorgeous and wonderful sight. Let's finish our wine and get in with the crowd. I want to get close to the Tower."

Pierre agreed. He paid the check and they melted into the celebration.

They shopped at many of the stores buying souvenirs. Pierre bought small pieces of jewelry for Michelle and flowers from a street vendor. They sat at park benches to talk and kiss.

***

Two hours later, a buzzing sound captured the attention of the crowd in Paris. Demon insects about the size of a small cat appeared in the sky and descended on the crowd. They flew with lightning speed. The buzzing emitted from the demon insects sent fear into the people and they ran for cover inside shops. Restaurants. Police stations. Apartment buildings. Any open door.

Pierre and Michelle ran to escape the insects. One landed on her back, crawled over her hair and looked at her forehead. Her face twisted with terror as she saw its human-like face and its mouthful of fangs. It shook its long hair and shrieked, arched its back, and revealed its stinger dripping with venom. Like lightning, it plunged its scorpion-like stinger into the young lady's back. She let out a blood-curdling scream and collapsed to the sidewalk writhing in pain. Tears covered her face. The insect released her and attacked Pierre, who tried to get away.

The insects attacked people in Paris for four hours. They disappeared as quickly as they arrived. Screams of pain filled the streets of the city. Victims lay in the streets for hours before EMTs dared to come. Nobody knew if or when the insects might return.

A welt the size of a cantaloupe formed on Michelle's back where the insect stung her. An ambulance took her to the hospital. Morphine failed to give her the relief she needed.

What should have been a national celebration for France turned into a night of horror.

***

Patrons at a Brooklyn sports bar saw the Mets' game interrupted by a news anchor. The anchor broke into the game and said, "I'm Melody Price from Channel 6 with breaking news. Monster insects have invaded major European cities."

A drawing of the insect appeared on the display behind Melody. People at the sports bar gasped with fright when they saw the creature. Its fang-like teeth protruded from its mouth. It had a frightening human-like face and long, yellow hair. Its stinger dripped with venom.

"Paris, London, Bonn, Frankfurt, Luxembourg, Copenhagen, Prague, and a myriad of smaller cities have reported attacks by monster insects. A scientist in Colorado says this is a newly evolved species caused by the combination of global warming and volcanic vapors. He also claims the insects have been living underground for millions of years until now. A news service from Iceland said they originated from Eyjafjallajokull volcano."

The display showed a video of the still-erupting volcano.

Melody continued. "Attacks are likely in all cities of the world. Please stay indoors until something can be done about them. Stay tuned to this channel. We will notify you when they are sighted in the area. Please use protective clothing if you must go anywhere. So far all efforts to kill one of these insects have failed. We will keep you posted if we learn of a method to get rid of them. And now a related story from our Medical News anchor, Dr. Kees Vorhees."

The medical anchor, a retired Dutch doctor, had a moustache, grey hair, and a lab coat. He looked like a physician. "The pain inflicted by these insects is intense. Painkillers do not seem to be effective and many victims have attempted suicide. A doctor from The Hague treated several victims who tried to commit suicide but could not. Something in the venom of these insects prevents uncontrolled bleeding and maintains blood pressure even with severe loss of blood. In the future, we may find this new substance useful. And now back to Melody."

"Please stay tuned and we will keep you informed if and when those monster insects come into the area. I'm Melody Price with Channel 6 News. And now, we return to the baseball game in progress."

Patrons of the sports bar paid their checks and sped home.

***

Vasily arrived at his shop at five o'clock in the morning. After getting the coffee brewing and the bagels cooking, he opened his store at 5:30 a.m. He received a phone call for a large to-go order, so he had to prep another batch of bagels.

Vasily stopped his mixers when he heard screams in his shop. He looked into the dining area and saw patrons gathered at the front window. Wondering what they saw, he emerged from the kitchen to look with them.

He asked, "What is wrong?"

Nobody answered, so he looked through the window. At first, he didn't see anything, so he decided to step outside. When he opened the door, dozens of monster insects swarmed in.

Screams of terror and pain filled his shop while people fled from the demon insects. Vasily ran into the kitchen and shut the door. In the safety of the kitchen, he peeked through the keyhole while his heart raced and his hands shook. Several patrons were on the floor screaming with pain. Others battled the insects while others ran out of the front door.

He heard a buzzing sound in his right ear and felt insect legs on his back. It sent a shudder down his back. He turned his head and saw a monster insect perched on his right shoulder with its human-like face staring at him. He screamed, but the insect saw the Seal of God on his forehead and released him. He slid to the floor as the insect flew through the kitchen window looking for victims.

***

Two Special Ops soldiers in Texas formed a plan to capture one of these insects. They placed a realistic dummy in a public park inside a large, heavy-gauge wire trap. After much waiting, an insect entered the cage and the soldiers sprung the trap.

They traded high fives and emerged from their hiding place. They placed poles in special loops outside the cage and placed it in the truck.

The insect's rage captivated the younger soldier. The sound of its buzzing intensified. He said, "Now it is helpless. Let's take it to the lab. I'll ride in the back to keep an eye on it." He jumped into the back of the truck while his partner started the truck and drove toward the lab.

The soldier banged on the cage, which enraged the insect. The insect's teeth wrapped around the heavy-gauge wire and snapped through them. As it forced its way out of the cage, the soldier shouted to the driver, "The insect is escaping. I'm out of here." The soldier jumped out of the truck and ran for cover. The insect escaped.

***

Back in Heaven, John breathed a sigh of relief.

The Elder asked, "Why did you do that?"

"I felt the people's fear of those demon insects. I had to remind myself I wasn't in their reach. But I did notice many people getting saved. Look at the numbers on the sundial."

"Yes, but many are angry at God because of those insects. You'd think by now they'd realize God is trying to get their attention. There are more things coming that may get them to seek out God."

John wondered how much worse it could get. He was about to find out.

Twenty-Six

The Sixth Trumpet – The Death Riders

The sixth angel sounded his trumpet. The Apostle John heard a voice come from one of the Altar's horns. In spite of all that John had seen, this was a new level of weirdness. The voice called out to the sixth angel and said, "Loose the four angels bound in the great river Euphrates."

The angel took off toward the Earth and landed near the Euphrates River. He found four chained angels with leathery wings bound there. He released them and returned to Heaven.

For a year, a month, a day, and an hour they had free reign to kill one-third of mankind. One of the killer angels hit the ground with his fist and cracked the surface of the Earth.

Smoke came out of the crack and formed into millions of demon riders with small, but powerful flying horses. They had a terrifying appearance. The rider's eyes glowed like small fireballs and their chest armor looked like fire. The horse's heads looked like lion's heads, and they exhaled smoke and sulfur. They had huge wings and their tails looked like snakes.

About fifty million of them followed each of the four killer angels, provoking people to kill one another and to kill people with their deadly fumes. They enjoyed killing.

The memory of the demon insect plague lingered among the people since it ended only three months ago. People stayed on the edge of rage, and the Death Riders didn't have to provoke them much. They flew through populated areas, using their influence to incite murder, anger and violence.

***

In Toronto, people crowded together in a subway station waiting to go home. Many people still had visible welts from the demon insect plague.

A band of demon riders entered the subway above the crowd of jittery people. They couldn't be seen, but their influence could be felt. The riders irritated the crowd of people waiting for the subway train to arrive. A few of them got behind a couple of men to provoke them into an argument.

A well-dressed businessman spoke to a burly man next to him. "I heard another trumpet sound an hour ago. Have you heard anything about it?"

He sneered and said, "Who cares? I'm tired of people complaining. All day long, that's all they do. Complain, complain, and complain."

The businessman said, "Well, I simply asked if you heard anything."

The burly man said, "Look, jerk. I work in a foundry for ten hours a day. I'm hot, I'm tired, and I don't give a flip about anything at the moment. I missed five months of work because of those stinkin' insects and I'll have to work a double shift for three months just to catch up.

You know nothing of that kind of pressure sitting in your stupid air-conditioned office with your executive pay."

The businessman tried to calm him. "Look, I'm sorry you're having a tough time. I truly am."

The foundry worker poked the businessman's chest with his index finger and said, "Why don't you shut up your ugly face and go away."

With the influence of the demon riders, the businessman threw the first punch. A fist fight broke out, and one by one people in the crowd got into the fight. Someone pulled out a knife and stabbed random people.

After the fight, many people lay in pools of their own blood, moaning with pain. Blood-covered knives lay among the victims. Bloody handprints and splatters marred the bright yellow walls of the subway.

The Death Riders hovered above the crowd and breathed sulfurous fumes on them. Many choked and died from the fumes.

They turned their horses, flew to another location, and continued their work.

***

At 5:30 p.m., Vasily sat and had some coffee with an old friend, Bradley Klein. It had been years since they had seen each other at the synagogue. While they rehashed old times, the TV news came on. Vasily told Bradley he wanted to listen, so they both turned toward the TV.

"Hi. I'm Dean Braxton with Channel 6 News. Mass killings have been reported all over the New York City area. People seem to on a killing spree for no reason. The memory of the stinging insects is still with us, and people are on edge. Governor DeWitt called the National

Guard to restore order, but even they are getting into fights with each other. There is serious bloodshed going on. You are urged to go home as soon as possible and wait out this reign of terror. And now, Jan Metz, our International News anchor."

"New York is not alone in this killing spree. We have obtained reports from our correspondents in major European cities as well as other parts of our country and the news is the same. A psychologist in London, Dr. Newton Lewis says that this killing spree is a release of tension from the recent demon insect plague and shouldn't last long. Our National News anchor, Lawrence Powell, has his story from the President."

The camera switched to Lawrence Powell. "The government has asked all people to stay at home and off the streets if possible. President Callaghan signed an executive order requesting businesses to allow people to work from home if at all possible. This executive order is effective today and will continue until further notice. The President is hopeful that cooler heads will result in less bloodshed. Jan Metz has another story."

The camera switched back to Jan Metz. "This latest killing spree has even affected the World Peace Organization. In Great Britain, France, Russia and Mexico, fighting erupted in their offices leaving everyone in them dead."

Vasily looked at Bradley and said, "Maybe you should go home and take care of that lovely wife of yours. Come back when this is over. I've missed talking with you. Be careful on the way home."

Bradley said, "Thanks. I haven't far to go and my car is parked in front of your shop. I will be back."

"Say hello to Lynn for me."

***

Vasily decided to close his shop, but one couple remained. He decided to wait until they left.

The husband said, "Evette, I'm glad I called in sick today."

His wife replied, "Aramis, for once, I'm glad you didn't go to work today."

"What's that supposed to mean?"

Tears streamed down Evette's face. "You've been coming home drunk. Now you can't get drunk. We don't have enough money for booze. At least I can enjoy you while you are sober and I love coffee, which is better for both of us. We can afford coming here."

She buried her face in her hands as she cried.

Aramis hung his head, "I know. I'm so sorry. Things have me on edge. I'm still watching the sky for those insects. I wish I knew what to do next. This planet is falling apart and there doesn't seem to be any hope left. Even Nist is having problems in his offices."

He moved across the table and sat next to his wife and hugged her. She wrapped her arms around him. He asked, "If you think there is hope for me, I will go to church with you on Sunday. Maybe we will find something good there."

She said, "I'd love for you to go with me. Since Vasily has provided us a safe place, let's come here often. I love his coffee shop."

Aramis agreed. "I promise you, I won't be going to the clubs anymore."

They spent two hours talking and hugging at the coffee shop and went home. As they left, Vasily asked them to go straight home.

Vasily took a quick look at the sky before he shut the door. He saw the image of God and smiled.

He spoke to the image and said, "I'm glad You are still there."

***

Back in Heaven, John and the Elder witnessed these events. John said, "I do hope that couple finds eternal life next time they go to church. I am glad when married people get back together."

The Elder said, "They will find eternal life soon. Their hearts are hungry for God."

Tears rolled down John's cheeks. "I didn't know you could cry in Heaven. I enjoyed seeing soft hearts."

The Elder said, "Yes, but I am still amazed more people haven't repented of their immoralities, drug usage and dealing, thefts, idol worship and pride. It is amazing how hard most people's hearts are."

John said, "I will write these things on my scroll. These demon riders are scarier than the insects to me. Imagine that – one third of people on Earth will die from them in a little over a year."

"And God has a few more mysteries to reveal to you soon."

Twenty-Seven

Between the Trumpets

<u>The Little Book - Bitter things yet to come</u>

The Elder directed John to leave the Throne Room. Once outside, they saw a mighty angel leave Heaven. The angel wore a cloud and had a rainbow around his head. His face equaled the Sun in brilliance, and his feet shone like fire. He planted his right foot on the sea and his left foot on the Earth and carried a little book in his right hand.

The angel roared. Seven thunders sounded in response. John understood the message of the thunders. From his vantage point in Heaven, he dipped his quill in ink, and prepared to write. The angel commanded him not to write, "Seal up those things which the seven thunders spoke, and do not write them." John laid his quill aside.

A voice came out of Heaven and spoke to John. "Go and take the little book which is open in the hand of the angel who stands on the sea and on the earth."

John walked toward the angel and said, "Give me the little book."

The huge angel leaned over and gave him the book. He felt like an ant compared to the angel. It said, "Take it, and eat it up; and it shall make thy belly bitter, but it shall be in thy mouth sweet as honey."

John ate the book. It tasted like honey, but made his stomach hurt.

"You must prophesy again before many peoples, and nations, and languages, and kings."

He thought, "These are terrible things which will happen. I hate even having to write these things. But the righteous will be made glad. Maybe more people will repent."

Measuring the Temple

John walked toward the Throne Room. An angel stopped him at the door and said, "Take this rod and use it to measure the Temple Mount in Jerusalem. Do not include the Court of the Gentiles. Jerusalem will be dominated by Gentiles for three and a half years."

Without warning, the angel picked him up, and took him to the Temple Mount in Jerusalem. The flight thrilled John. The sights of deep space and our solar system amazed him.

John saw the Third Temple as the angel approached Temple Mount. John had not seen it from the air before. When he landed, the angel released him. John measured it with the rod the angel gave him.

He greeted people walking on the Temple Mount, but they didn't respond. The angel said, "They can't see you. You are a shadow here. They are real."

After John measured the Temple, the angel returned him to the Throne Room where he recorded the measurements.

The Two Witnesses

The Elder directed John's attention to two people descending to the Earth. They landed beside the Temple Mount. Many people saw them come from Heaven, but either ignored them or ran away not knowing what they might do.

The Elder said, "Take a look at these witnesses. You will know who they are. Watch what they do and write."

John replied, "I see them. They are Moses and Elijah. I remember them when they met Jesus on the mount. Peter and James were with me."

"They have power to protect themselves using fire, water, and plagues."

"Good choices. Both of them have experience using plagues."

John noticed the way people in the crowds dressed and asked, "This isn't the past, is it?"

"No. It hasn't happened, but will. Now watch these events."

***

The Two Witnesses, Moses and Elijah, arrived five months after the Great Disappearance. Upon arrival, they positioned themselves a few feet east of the Golden Gate of the Temple Mount. They dressed in sackcloth, had beards, long hair and wore sandals like the prophets of old. From their vantage point, they could see the door of the rebuilt Temple. Large crowds of people came to hear them, and listened to their fiery preaching.

Day and night, the Two Witnesses preached Jesus as Lord and Savior. They demonstrated through the Law and the Prophets – and the New Testament – that Jesus is the Christ. They commanded repentance of all who heard them. Tourists kept their distance, but took pictures of them while they preached and sent the photos around the world. Some heeded their message and were saved.

A lot of people didn't. Many people ridiculed and threw rocks at them. If the listeners blasphemed God or otherwise provoked the prophets, fire came out of Moses and Elijah's mouths and destroyed them.

Sometimes the prophets commanded a flash flood to take hecklers away. Other times, fire and drought hit the country they represented.

After one month of preaching and few people repenting, Elijah declared, "By my word, it will not rain anywhere on the planet until people as a whole respect the prophets of God." Clouds formed, but no rain fell while they preached.

***

In their second month of preaching, several onlookers threw rocks and rotten food at them. The prophets decided to do something different.

Moses looked at Elijah and said, "Since nobody is taking us serious today, I'll give them an itch to hear us."

Moses picked up a handful of dry dust and tossed it into the air. He blew it toward the crowd.

They fell silent as they watched as the cloud of dust approach them. The dust turned into lice, hives, shingles and psoriasis as it settled on the hecklers. Jeers turned to screams as the mockers ran off looking for emergency medical treatment.

A week later, a tourist threw cherry bombs at the prophets while they were preaching. The explosions startled the prophets.

After recovering his composure, Elijah looked at Moses and said, "Let me try something."

He picked up two handfuls of pebbles and held them up high and looked at the tourist. He leaned to the ground and rolled the pebbles in his direction. The rolling pebbles turned into lobster-sized scorpions and scurried toward the crowd. The assembled crowd turned and ran.

Elijah yelled at them while they were within earshot. "What's the matter? Don't you get along with Scorpios?"

During the hot part of the day, John saw angels bring the Two Witnesses water and fruit to eat. One angel with a flaming sword glared at the spectators and protected Moses and Elijah while the other angel served them.

✳✳✳

Three months after the prophets came, UN soldiers erected concrete barricades to limit the number of people exposing themselves to damage. They didn't stop tourists from seeing the Two Witnesses, but warned them not to provoke them. The soldiers refused to take action against them because they were afraid of what might happen.

On a warm June day, a tourist named Steve Hubbard approached the soldiers. His clothing consisted of a tacky "Florida" shirt, sock and sandals. He had a camera in his hands and asked to see the Two Witnesses.

He said to the soldiers standing guard by the concrete barriers, "I'd like to see these two, uh, whatever they are."

Steve held up his camera to show the soldiers he was a tourist.

The gate guard asked, "Why do you want to see them?"

"I'd like to hear what they preach and I want to take some pictures."

One of the soldiers shrugged, "Okay, but take my word for it. Don't say anything to them that might rile them."

"Why?"

"Let's say you will not live long enough to regret it. Please show me your identification and I will let you through."

Steve showed his passport. He came from Orlando. That explained the tacky outfit.

"Everything looks okay here. Permission granted."

The soldier opened the gate and Steve went around the concrete barrier. He walked toward the Two Witnesses.

***

Moses noticed the tourist and said to Elijah, "Look what comes in this direction."

Elijah grinned. "Yes. Here comes another victim. This one is dressed tackier than most. Should we flame him now?"

Moses restrained Elijah. "Don't be too eager to do damage. This one might be a serious inquirer."

Elijah rolled his eyes. "Oh that will be the day. Come on, let me flame him."

Steve drew closer. He stopped about fifteen feet away and looked at the pair.

Moses asked, "What do you want this fine day?"

"My name is Steve Hubbard and I've heard about your preaching. What is it all about?"

Elijah rolled his eyes. "Were you born yesterday? Haven't you heard?"

"I've also heard that you two have done some pretty severe things."

Elijah responded, "Yes, we've done them. What of it? Do you dare reprimand us?"

"Why are y'all doing these things?"

Moses looked at Elijah. He detected impatience so he said, "I will answer him."

Moses cleared his throat. "We preach the Gospel of Jesus Christ, Son of God, who lived a sinless life, died on a cross, and rose from the dead. We preach repentance to sinners. We have the words of eternal life, if you will hear them. Most people are unrepentant. They mock God and ridicule the Gospel."

"But I've heard you roasted quite a few people. Isn't that mean?"

"To ridicule the Gospel, display arrogance, and jeer when God has taken the time and effort to send us here deserves something. God is doing all He can to get people's attention and commands repentance. But if they are slow to repent, God will take extreme measures to warn them before the final judgment falls."

"Well, I'd like to hear your message."

Moses said, "Come closer."

Steve approached until he was only three feet away.

Moses looked at Elijah, nodded and smiled. Then he looked at Steve. "We will be more than pleased to do so. God promised Adam and Eve He'd send a Savior. He kept His promise through Abraham, who listened to God and obeyed Him."

A heckler behind Steve threw a rock at Moses. The rock boomeranged back to the heckler and Moses didn't even look at him. Elijah was tempted to do something, but Moses motioned him to keep quiet. He saw Elijah glaring at the heckler but doing nothing.

Moses continued. "The Savior came, and Jesus was His name. He lived a perfect, sinless life and gave Himself as a sin offering. Anyone who repents from his sins and makes Jesus to be his Lord and believes God raised Jesus from the dead will be saved. God will forgive that person's sins. That person will be taken to live with God for eternity. On top of that, God will live in him right now. Now, isn't that good news?"

"It is great news, but how do I get saved?"

Moses heard a chuckle coming from Elijah and tried to be patient.

"I told you. Repent of your sins, confess before men that Jesus is your Lord, believe in your heart God raised Jesus from the dead. It is as simple as anything can get."

"Okay. I'll do that now. I say it to all present here: Jesus is my Lord and I believe God raised Him from the dead. I repent of my sins."

An invisible angel put the Seal of God on his forehead.

Steve said, "Well, I do feel better now, but I have to go now. I hope I will see you two soon."

Elijah smiled at last and said, "You will. You will. Tell your friends and family, too. It will make our job easier."

Steve asked, "Can I take your picture before I go?"

Moses said, "Sure you can. Get our good sides."

At that remark, Elijah burst out laughing and said, "If you show me how to work that thing, I will take a picture of you and Moses."

"Okay. Look at the back of this camera until we are both in the center. Stand far enough back to include our heads. Then press this button. I'll show you what it looks like afterward."

They moved about six feet away. Moses put his arm around Steve. They smiled and Elijah took their picture.

Moses said, "I want to see what it looks like."

"Okay, Elijah, give me the camera and I'll show you the picture."

He gave the camera to Steve and looked at the image of Moses and Steve.

Elijah said, "Take my picture, too."

Steve gave the camera to Moses and stood beside Elijah. They moved into the same spot about six feet away.

Moses said, "One, two, three…" Then he pressed the camera button.

Elijah grabbed the camera and gave it to Steve. "Show me my picture."

Steve showed him the new image.

Elijah's face fell. "I blinked. Let's take another one." He gave the camera back to Moses and posed with Steve again.

Moses snapped another picture.

Steve took the camera from Moses and showed Elijah the new picture.

"I am pleased. It shows my best side."

Steve took his camera. "I will go now. I will share your message to my family for sure. They will envy these pictures. Thanks. I'll see both of you later."

Moses said, "Without a doubt you will."

Steve turned around and went through the gate and concrete barrier.

The soldier said, "I can't believe you survived. You almost acted chummy."

Steve replied, "I don't know what worried you. They are nice."

***

John laughed at the interaction between Steve and the Two Witnesses. He said, "I needed that."

The Elder said, "There are more mysteries to be revealed. Keep your quill ready."

Twenty-Eight

The Seventh Trumpet

<u>Celebration Time in Heaven</u>

In the great Throne Room of Heaven, the seventh angel sounded his trumpet. John heard voices singing praises rise from the Throne Room and from the City of Heaven. The voices said, "The kingdoms of this world are become the kingdoms of our Lord, and of his Christ; and he shall reign forever and ever." The excitement in those voices spread to John. He couldn't wait to see the upcoming events.

All the elders fell on their knees and worshipped God again.

After that, the doors of the Temple in Heaven opened and a bright light caught everybody's attention. The Heavenly Ark became visible.

The elders said in chorus, "We give thee thanks, O Lord God Almighty, which art, and wast, and art to come; because thou hast taken to thee thy great power, and hast reigned. And the nations were angry, and thy wrath is come, and the time of the dead, that they should be judged, and that thou shouldest give reward unto thy servants the prophets, and to the saints, and them that fear thy name, small and great; and shouldest destroy them which destroy the earth."

John looked toward the Earth. He heard many strange voices and saw a lot of lightning, thunder, hail. A smaller (but planet-wide) earthquake occurred, which frightened the remaining population of the Earth.

The Woman, Israel

An angel beckoned John and the Elder to a place outside of the Throne Room. The angel said, "Come this way." Then he pointed to the sky. John admired the beauty of the beautiful blue sky. John saw an image start forming in the sky.

When the image became sharp, it was of a pregnant Jewish woman wearing a crown of twelve stars. She sat on a rock in the wilderness. A red, Chinese-type dragon approached her. Labor pains came on her and the angels helped her escape the dragon. She stayed hidden for three and a half years while God took care of her.

The dragon ascended to Heaven and fought with God's angels, but lost the battle. The angels threw it to the Earth. Since the dragon lost the fight with the angels, it became angry and decided to fight the woman.

The dragon searched and found her. God gave her wings of an eagle and she escaped from the dragon, but it found her again. The dragon cornered her in a canyon and spewed out water instead of fire in an attempt to drown her. But God made the earth open up and swallow the water. Losing that fight, the dragon searched out her children in order to persecute them.

John had a puzzled look on his face after the image faded away. He asked the Elder, "What is the meaning of the woman and the dragon?"

The Elder replied, "Why, John, I am so surprised. You should know this woman is Israel. Remember Joseph's dream of the sun, moon, and eleven stars bowing before him? Well, Joseph and his brothers – the tribes of Israel – are the stars in her crown, and the woman is Israel. What you saw covers the history of the Jewish people since the beginning. Israel produced the Savior, the Child you saw the woman give birth to. God will protect her, even by supernatural means.

"God will have a meeting in the wilderness with her while there is relative peace for three and a half years. He will meet with Israel and they will turn to Him as a nation. The covenant between Israel the Beast will last for three and a half years. The devil will persecute Israel, and will fight the 144,000 sealed evangelists from the tribes of Israel."

Twenty-Nine

The Antichrist and the False Prophet

The Elder faded from John's vision, and he found himself standing on the shore of a sea. He didn't know how he got there, but stranger things had happened.

He felt a warm, ocean breeze on his face and the waves lapped at his feet. He was by himself. While he puzzled out his situation, a large beast rose out of the sea. John's eyes grew while the beast approached him. The large, seven-headed beast was ugly in appearance. Its fearsome paws shook the beach when it walked and its growl made John shiver. John retreated several steps.

A few of those heads had two horns. John counted ten horns. He noticed each horn had a crown. The heads had terrible words written on them like "Pride", "Blasphemy", "Murder", "Idolatry" and "Lust".

The beast had bear's feet, but could move like a leopard. Its mouth had large teeth like a lion's. John noticed scar tissue on one of the heads of the beast. It looked like it had recovered from a near-fatal head wound.

John noticed other people with him.

The raging beast fascinated them. When the dragon approached, people standing near bowed down to it. Later, they bowed to the beast. They said, "Who is like unto the Beast? Who is able to make war with him?"

The Beast spoke like a man and uttered great blasphemies. He cursed God on high, cursed God's tabernacle, cursed God's saints on Earth, and cursed the saints in Heaven, too.

John thought, "What will this Beast do?"

He saw the Dragon give the Beast permission to rule for forty-two months and to wage war against the saints on Earth. The Beast hated anyone with the Spirit of God in him.

The Beast overcame the saints of God and extended his rule over all the people of the Earth. This Beast required all on the Earth to worship him as god. And all the people on the Earth did worship him, except those whose names were in the Lamb's Book of Life.

Seeing these things made John afraid for the people of God on the Earth. He didn't know what could be worse than what he saw.

He heard a guttural noise behind him. He turned around and saw another beast rising up from out of the Earth instead of the Sea. He looked different from the first beast. This one had two horns coming out of his head like a lamb's, but had the voice of the dragon.

This beast appeared to be a magician, doing wondrous illusions, even making fire come out of the sky. He had many tricks, all of them to convince people to worship the first beast.

He used magic to trick people into worshipping the first beast by making a statue of the first beast come alive. He caused all people on Earth to receive a mark on either their forehead or right hand to participate in financial transactions.

John heard a voice saying, "Here is wisdom. Let him that hath understanding count the number of the beast: for it is the number of a man; and his number is Six hundred threescore and six."

✱✱✱

John's vision at the seashore ended and he found himself in the Throne Room at his writing desk. The Elder asked him, "What did you see?"

"A horrible vision. I must write it before I forget what I saw."

He sat at his desk and wrote what he had seen. He knew he would soon see these events happen on Earth.

Thirty

Nist Settles In

At the World Peace Organization headquarters, one could hear the sound of computer keyboards, and ringing phones. Advisors made phone calls and faxed agreements all over the planet. Nist walked through his building and saw how busy his workers were.

Nist went back to his private office, one twice as big as the Oval Office, and on the top floor of his building. He had many computer displays showing maps of the world and various news outlets. One of the monitors showed countries accepting his financial arrangements in red and non-accepting countries in blue. Blue marble adorned his file cabinets. Several red telephones directly wired to different capitals lined the left edge of his desk. Across the room, Nist had a large conference table surrounded by oversized wing-back chairs. The luxurious drapes and lighting made desk lamps un-necessary.

He worked his world-takeover plan with diligence. Most nations caved in to his demands and gave their sovereignty to the United Nations. A new international currency took over old, failing currencies. The World Bank monitored all transactions to prevent money-laundering, drug deals, and other financial crimes. The World Bank system owned ninety-five percent of all banks.

Nations exchanged sovereignty for financial relief. When a nation signed Nist's agreement, peace seemed to settle in. Prices of food and gasoline dropped in a week or two. These benefits came with a price: individual freedoms.

Nist received a call on his personal cell. He greeted his caller and listened. His smile grew.

"Thanks. I'll let you know what you need to do next." He ended the call, pumped his fist and said, "Yes."

He called his secretary, Stile Vastens, on the intercom. "Please bring in two wine glasses and the best wine we have. I've got something to tell you."

"Yes, sir."

A couple of minutes later, Nist saw Stile come through his door with a silver tray, an expensive bottle of French wine, and two wine glasses. She placed the tray on an empty space on his desk.

Nist said, "Here is the good news. The UN vote occurred this morning. I am now the absolute ruler of the world. No one has ever been the ruler of the entire world before. What I say goes. Isn't that wonderful?"

He leaned back in his chair and his smile grew. Nist pointed to the calendar on the wall.

"Only three Septembers ago I put my plan into motion and now my dream has come true. You know, it took Hitler a lot longer to get significant power, and he only took control of Germany and a few surrounding countries. I have had the vote of the entire world to assume command. This calls for a toast to me."

Nist held his arm into the air and spun his chair around in glee.

Stile poured their drinks and raised her glass and said, "Hail to the Ruler of the World."

They clinked their glasses and drank their wine.

Stile sat on the corner of Nist's desk.

Stile sipped a little wine and asked, "How did you get by China and the other Far East leaders who didn't want to have anything to do with you at the UN?"

"Oh, I invited them to a conference in Turkey. Once I had them occupied, I had them detained for a couple of days while my liaison at UN Headquarters in New York brought up the vote".

Stile smiled. "Just like in the old days at the UN. I love stuff like that."

"It is business as usual at the UN."

"I remember the last time something like this happened. Red China kicked Taiwan out of the UN and had itself voted in. It cuts through the red tape, doesn't it?"

"Yes, it does. Now that I have achieved this goal, I can implement the last phases of my plan which will increase my control over the world."

"As long as I am there to help you."

Nist stood and gave her a gentle hug. "Stile, don't you worry. I will always take care of you."

***

After a few more glasses of wine, Stile rose to leave and paused at the door. "Oh yes, Jack Delson, your financial advisor, wants to give you a status update."

"Okay. Send him in."

Stile shut the door on the way out and took the tray, wine, and glasses with her.

A minute later, Jack entered Nist's office.

Nist leaned back in his chair and had his feet on the desk. He gestured to a chair on the other side of his desk and said, "How are you, Jack?"

Delson sat in the large, overstuffed chair. "Good. What's the big smile about?"

"The UN promoted me to ruler of the world this morning."

"Awesome. All hail to the ruler of the world." Jack raised an imaginary glass in a toast to Nist.

"Thank you. Now give me a status update on the Far East countries."

"I wish I had better news. They won't sell their banks yet. Part of the resistance is their overcautious and independent culture. Conducting worldwide business will force them to join our network if we set up our rules right."

"How are the rules being set up?"

"According to your plan. For a transaction to reach in any destination that we control, it has to go through our computers. If they don't have an approval code, the transaction will be cancelled."

Nist sat up and picked up a pen and tapped it on a pad of paper. "How soon will that be effective?"

"In six months."

"How are they managing to make transactions now?"

"They have a near monopoly on Rare Earth metals that the Western nations need, so the rules have been bent. Until we come up with something else, that will continue."

"What are Rare Earth metals?"

"Thirty or so years ago, they were nothing. Nobody can even name them, they are so rare. But satellite, computer and cell phone technology has made them hot commodities. Outside of China, they are extremely rare."

Nist looked at the ceiling as if he were doing some calculations. "Okay. We will have to come up with a better plan. Thanks for the update. Keep up the good work."

Delson left Nist's office.

Nist considered what his next step should be.

Thirty-One

Recovery Time

Kevin Golim rented an apartment in Utica, New York. The small-town hospital in Gloversville transferred his girlfriend, Dodi LaCosta, to a larger hospital after being treated for acid water poisoning. She contracted hepatitis along with other complications and endured several operations on her digestive system. Her stay in the hospital lasted a year and six months. Even though she had a TV in her room, she couldn't pay attention to world events.

Kevin's endured a brief stay in the hospital. After his discharge, he found a job in Utica and visited her every day after work. He suffered from guilt since he took her camping. One night, he watched the local TV station news while in her hospital bedroom.

"Good evening. I'm Andrej Nowak with Adirondack News, Utica, New York. Today, Nist of World Peace Organization gave President Callaghan new restrictions on travel, religion, and celebrations.

"Restrictions imposed on individuals cover road and air travel. Citizens will have to submit dates, times, and point of origin six weeks before they take any road trip. Once it is approved, they will be given travel papers. People travelling without these papers will be subject to jail and heavy fines.

"Airline travel will also have to be approved six weeks in advance. Reservations will be analyzed to prevent terrorist activity. And now to Muriel Katz for other restrictions."

"Citizens must apply for a permit if they wish to attend church. The name of the church and reasons for attending must be stated on the application. This is not to imply that attending church is illegal. Pastors must also apply for a permit to preach.

"All permit applications will be available on your local police headquarters' website. President Callaghan has ordered these changes to be implemented six months from today. This will create new jobs for at least 300,000 individuals across the United States.

"The celebration of national holidays like the Fourth of July, Memorial Day, and Flag day is now forbidden to lower international tensions generated by displays of nationalism.

"Nist insists these changes will result in peace and safety throughout the world. Terrorists will be tracked with more efficiency."

Kevin wondered at the reasons for this kind of government control.

✳✳✳

In September, three years after the Great Disappearance, the day of Dodi's discharge from the hospital arrived. Kevin took the day off to bring her home. The hospital staff completed her release paperwork around noon. Nurses wheeled Dodi to the front door and helped her get into Kevin's car.

On the way to his apartment, Dodi asked, "Can we stop for a hamburger and fries? I want real food. I don't know how much I can eat, though."

Kevin agreed. "Sounds like a good idea. You have lost thirty pounds during your treatment. How about Bob's Monster Burgers and Barbeque? We are almost there."

"Yes. I can smell the food already."

Kevin parked the car and guided Dodi into the restaurant.

After being seated, a waitress came by. "My name is Taffy. What can I get you to drink?"

Kevin said, "Two Cokes, please."

Dodi said, "I don't want Coke. Please bring me tea."

Taffy said, "One Coke and one tea coming up."

Kevin said, "We already know what we want to order."

"Okay, I'll take your order." She took her pen and order pad out of her apron.

Kevin said, "Two well-done half-pound burgers with curly fries and lots of barbeque sauce."

Dodi added, "I'll have a salad, too."

Taffy said, "Okay. I'll put you down for a salad. I'll get those burgers cooking right away."

When the waitress left, Kevin noticed Dodi's tired expression. She buried her face in her hands. Kevin asked, "Do we need to go home now?"

"No, but I am tired. I wanted to get out in the real world and go shopping, but I can't. I need to go to our apartment and sleep. I will be okay in a few weeks, maybe a month. I intend to do a lot of serious shopping when I recover. None of my clothes fit me anymore. These shorts I wore when I came to this hospital are falling off of me."

Dodi noticed the news on the TV in the far corner of the restaurant. "What's been going on in the world? Has anything happen since the acid water plague?"

"Dodi, there've been so many changes during your hospital stay, you don't want to know."

"Look, I slept most of the time while in the hospital. A year and a half is missing from my life. I missed two birthdays and I don't even remember. I need to know what has happened."

"Okay. I'll bring you up to date. Two months after we drank the acid water, the sun dimmed and scientists still can't find out why. The sun goes dark at 4:00pm."

"Do you mean twilight starts at 4:00 p.m.?"

"No, the sun goes dark and it looks like night. You can still see the sun, but it looks like a black disk. It happens every day at 4:00 p.m."

"Weird."

"Then the attack of the demon insects came three months later in September."

"That sounds like a 1950s horror movie."

"I wish it were just that. Wicked insects like flying scorpions the size of small cats descended on the planet from who knows where. Iceland I think. I saw a swarm of them coming and managed to get away from them. They were this big."

Kevin held his hands two and a half feet apart.

"And their eyes were as big as CDs."

He made a circle with his thumbs and index fingers.

"They had yellow hair on their heads and bodies that were as tough as metal. And teeth that looked like shark's teeth."

Kevin grimaced and showed his teeth. He ran his fingers through his hair and pulled it straight back to illustrate.

"And their claws were nearly as big as my hands." He gestured with his hands as if they were claws.

Kevin heard people in the next booth giggling. He knew they were amused by his antics, so he ignored them.

"Their stings were so vicious that the pain lasted five months. The insect invasion lasted six months. Soon after that people everywhere went on a killing spree. That's still going on. That reduced the Earth's population by one-third according to the news. And the UN made Charti Nist the ruler of the world."

"Wasn't he the man who negotiated peace a few months after the Great Disappearance?"

"Yes, the same one."

"What is the meaning of these things?"

"Terror by day because of the government, and terror by night with plagues."

Dodi asked, "What is the government doing to us?"

Kevin replied, "Imposing heavier taxes, issuing restrictions on driving, and monitoring our movements. The kind of things world rulers do."

"And the plagues?"

"We never know when the next disaster will hit or what form it will take. It seems there is no end to them."

"That's not good, is it?"

"No, it doesn't. We will have to find a way to deal with it."

Dodi stared into the distance trying to absorb the impact of what she heard. "We have a lot of catching up to do. Why did you stay? You could have left me for all the trouble I caused."

"I've been thinking of marrying you."

Her eyes welled with tears. "I'd be glad to marry you."

"You have made me a very happy man."

They held each other's hand across the table and stared at each other.

Their food arrived and they ate.

Thirty-Two

Search the Planet

A week after being made ruler of the world, Nist called one of his researchers via the office intercom.

"Sean, come to my office now. I have a job for you to do."

"Yes. I'll be there in a sec."

A few minutes later, Sean Prussia entered Nist's office. Sean wore jeans and a graphic t-shirt. He seemed to be the most relaxed and confident man in the building.

Nist said, "Hello, Sean. Please sit. This is what I want you to do. Find an expert, the top expert in the world who will lend persuasion to my actions. I will need help in selling a loyalty test. Don't limit yourself to one country or continent. Are you up to it?"

Sean smiled. "I sure am. As a matter of fact, I have two men in mind already."

"Good. I'm pleased. Find me that someone and I'll reward you handsomely. You'll get a big promotion and pay raise if you can get the right person."

"I'll get back with you soon. I've have phone calls to make and a bit of research to do."

"Keep me posted."

"You bet."

With his new assignment, Sean left Nist's office.

***

Vasily put fresh bagels into the display rack. After that, he saw someone who looked familiar. After a few seconds, he recognized him. His signature horn-rim glasses, bald head, suspenders, and tacky sport coat made him stand out.

"Sam Reuben. Where have you been, buddy?"

Vasily shook his hand across the counter.

Sam said, "Why don't you have a cup of coffee with me? My table is over there."

"Sit and I'll be there in a minute. I've got to take my last batch of bagels out of the oven and let them cool. I'll get a cup of coffee and chat with you in a few minutes."

Sam sat at his table and read his newspaper.

Vasily looked at his clock. It was 9:30 a.m., and the breakfast rush had subsided. He got a cup of dark roast coffee and sat with his old friend. "How long has it been since we've seen each other, Sam?"

"Eleven years."

"That's too long. What have you been up to?"

"Well, I retired eight years ago. I've been in and out of the hospital for the last two years. I have a small tumor in my lung that doesn't want to go away. How's your health?"

"Can't complain. I haven't had time to get sick."

"Have you heard from any of your family in Russia?"

"Not in twenty-five years. Maybe they're all dead by now. I'm in my late sixties you know."

Sam asked, "Aren't you ever going to retire?"

"When I die, perhaps. This business isn't that hard to run and it keeps me busy. I like coffee and bagels."

"You miss your wife, Leyla, don't you? I saw the notice in the papers several years ago when she died."

Vasily stared up to the sky and his eyes welled with tears. "I do. I have her picture beside my easy chair at home. I really miss her. How is your wife doing?"

"Betsy is okay as long as she remembers to go for dialysis twice a week. She's got a touch of Alzheimer's, too, I'm afraid."

Sam changed the subject, "What do you think of the man who became ruler of the world a week or two ago?"

"I don't like it. It reminds me of when I lived in Russia. Bad things happen when a man gets too much power. I've never seen good come out of this."

"But he has settled many disputes and united many nations. He's given relative peace to Israel."

"Yes, but at what price? I'd rather solve our own problems than have someone across the ocean tell us what to do."

Sam said, "His office is thirty miles north New York City."

"Okay. Let me clarify my last statement. I *wish* he was across the ocean."

Vasily paused to get a sip of coffee. "What if he turns out to be a power-hungry politician who taxes us to death and starts running our lives? Look at what he has already done. Isn't that how Hitler started? If so, who is going to stop him? Unless his organization is corrupt to the core, it will take an outside influence to defeat him."

Vasily extended his arm straight up and pointed with his index finger. "It will take God to defeat him if he turns out bad."

Sam scoffed and said, "Are you getting religious?"

"No, but I did make *Yeshua* my Messiah."

"That's not going to win any points with your friends at the synagogue."

"I haven't been there in years and they haven't come to see me either. I've been reading my wife's Bible. Old *and* New Testament. I didn't realize how Jewish the New Testament was until I read it."

Sam and Vasily were quiet for a couple of minutes after that last exchange.

Sam broke the silence. "Vasily, you are a big talker, but look at you. You run a coffee shop."

"A successful coffee, bagel, *and* stamp shop. The best one in all of Brooklyn."

"For fifteen years straight, I had the best insurance agency on Long Island."

Vasily paused and sipped on his coffee. He smiled and said, "Have you enjoyed retirement?"

"You haven't changed a bit, and I love you for it."

Sam and Vasily talked for two hours.

Vasily looked at his watch and said, "Customers will be coming in for lunch soon. I have to get back to work, pal. Don't make yourself so scarce. I don't want to wait another eleven years for another conversation. Please say hi to Betsy for me, please?"

"All right. I'll see you soon."

Vasily watched Sam leave and wondered if he'd ever see his friend again. He wasn't very healthy. He was seventy-three years old with a tumor on his lung, high blood pressure and diabetes.

***

Two weeks later, Nist still had not heard from Sean and his patience wore thin. He decided to call Sean and threaten him to get him moving. He reached for his phone and right before he picked up the receiver, his phone rang. The caller ID showed "Sean Prussia".

He picked up his phone and said, "I almost called you. What has taken you so long?"

Sean said, "I'd like to come to your office and tell you. I have good news for you. I'll be in your office in a couple of minutes."

He entered Nist's office a few minutes later with a big smile.

Nist's mood changed. "You do look like you have good news. Tell me what you've found."

Sean sat in the large chair in front of Nist's desk.

"I located a strange character, Eftas Helpphor. He is a Jew living in Iraq, in the city of Babylon. He can help you sell your loyalty test."

"What happened to the two men you had in mind?"

"They were both committed to long-term projects. I spent most of my time playing phone tag with them. Their secretaries weren't much help. But the second person recommended Eftas Helpphor to me. I located his office in Iraq and talked with him a couple of hours. I spent a week's time checking his references after our conversation. None of them responded by e-mail and I spent the second week playing phone tag again. But I did manage to check them out. He's good, but he is strange."

"Strange?"

Nist noticed the hesitancy in Sean's voice.

Sean said, "Well, he's into the Black Arts."

"Black Arts? Do you mean he's a warlock?"

"Yes, but I think you will like him. I warn you – he looks a bit bizarre."

Nist found that amusing. He leaned back in his chair and grinned. "What do you mean by that?"

"He creeped me out on the videophone when I spoke with him. He looks like you would imagine the Devil to look like. His résumé is impressive for the kind of things you need. Many Middle Eastern countries use him as a consultant."

"When can you get him here?"

Sean checked his tablet. "He can be here in our New York headquarters in a week."

"Okay. Make an appointment for him to come here at his earliest convenience. Let me know when you get the appointment."

"Yes, sir. I'll fly him in."

***

Brad Huron and his team of scientists at the solar laboratory continued to monitor the sun's reduced output and its effect on the Earth.

Brad, being in his late fifties, only had a little hair. He had glasses he used for reading and resisted getting contact lenses. He stood 5'8". His calm demeanor and purpose of mind enabled him to assimilate his diverse group of scientists into a tightly-knit unit.

Miko Tanaka and Bärbel Eberstark couldn't be more different, but were the best of friends. Miko stood 5'9" and had long, black hair and pale skin. Her black glasses accented her features. Bärbel stood 5'1" and had sandy blonde hair, braided into a long ponytail.

Brad approached Miko and Bärbel and asked, "Do either one of you know how the diminished sunlight has affected agriculture?"

Miko said, "Yes. I checked with the Department of Agriculture in Washington, DC, as well as our own state of Arizona. There has been a slight decrease in crops, but we don't have enough data to blame it on the diminished sunlight. We have only a year and a half of data."

"How long before we have enough data?"

"I might say five years. I'm glad food production is not off because of the decreased sunlight. I will say we are on a larger cooling trend than before this event. There is nothing we can do about it except to see what trends emerge in the Earth's weather patterns."

Brad turned to Bärbel and asked, "Have you been keeping track of sunrise, sunset, and when the sun changes from a black disk to its current strength?"

"Of course I have. You ask me at least twice a week. It has been like clockwork. The same events happen at the same time every day. The sun shines at 67% strength at 10:00 a.m. local time and goes dark at 4:00 p.m., local time. I have kept track of it every day."

Miko looked at Brad and said, "You don't seem to be concerned about the diminished sunlight or the more recent disasters. As a matter of fact, you seem to be rather cheery. Are you so scientifically detached that you don't care?"

Brad took his glasses off and put them into his lab coat pocket. "Of course not. I don't like what these disasters portend, but I can't worry about them."

Miko replied, "Well, I do. How can you *not* worry about them?"

"I trust God to take care of us. He has honored my prayers and protected all of you."

Bärbel thought for a minute and said, "He's got a point. Do you realize nobody on our team got stung by those monster insects?"

"I prayed for you in advance of their coming. That is why you didn't get stung."

Miko asked, "Prayed? How did you know in advance about them?"

"I read about those monster insects in the Bible."

Bärbel's mouth fell open. "The Bible? I can't believe you read the Bible."

Brad's team stopped working when they heard that and assembled beside Miko and Bärbel.

Brad waited until he had everybody's attention. "Yes, the Bible. Haven't any of you read the Book of Revelation?"

Ted Bennett, Brad's atmospheric expert said, "I read it many years ago when I was a kid, but I don't remember anything."

Brad went to his desk, picked up his Bible and opened it to chapter eight. "Miko, read verses five through twelve."

Miko said, "I don't want to have anything to do with your Bible. Let somebody else do it."

Brad asked, "Bärbel, would you read this?"

"No. I don't want to read it either."

Brad asked, "Who wants to volunteer?"

Ted said, "I'll read it for kicks. Besides, I used to do theater work when I was in college."

Ted took the Bible and read. "And the angel took the censer, and filled it with fire of the altar, and cast it into the earth: and there were voices, and thunderings, and lightnings, and an earthquake."

Ted added a little bit of drama to his reading by waving his hands around to accent the thunder and lightning.

"And the seven angels which had the seven trumpets prepared themselves to sound. The first angel sounded, and there followed hail and fire mingled with blood, and they were cast upon the earth: and the third part of trees was burnt up, and all green grass was burnt up.

"And the second angel sounded, and as it were a great mountain burning with fire was cast into the sea: and the third part of the sea became blood; And the third part of the creatures which were in the sea, and had life, died; and the third part of the ships were destroyed.

"And the third angel sounded, and there fell a great star from heaven, burning as it were a lamp, and it fell upon the third part of the rivers, and upon the fountains of waters; And the name of the star is called Wormwood: and the third part of the waters became wormwood; and many men died of the waters, because they were made bitter.

"And the fourth angel sounded, and the third part of the sun was smitten, and the third part of the moon, and the third part of the stars; so as the third part of them was darkened, and the day shone not for a third part of it, and the night likewise."

Ted stopped reading and his face paled. He said, "I don't want to read anymore."

Miko said, "This is interesting. I'll read it." She took the Bible from Ted's hands.

Brad noticed that Ted's hands trembled.

Brad said, "Miko, read chapter nine, verses one through five."

"And the fifth angel sounded, and I saw a star fall from heaven unto the earth: and to him was given the key of the bottomless pit. And he opened the bottomless pit; and there arose a smoke out of the pit, as the smoke of a great furnace; and the sun and the air were darkened by reason of the smoke of the pit. And there came out of the smoke locusts upon the earth: and unto them was given power, as the scorpions of the earth have power. And it was commanded them that they should not hurt the grass of the earth, neither any green thing, neither any tree; but only those men which have not the seal of God in their foreheads."

Vadim Dmitrievsky, the deep space expert, broke in and said, "That sounds like what has happened in the last two and a half years by my accounting."

Brad said, "Keep reading, Miko."

"And to them it was given that they should not kill them, but that they should be tormented five months: and their torment was as the torment of a scorpion, when he striketh a man."

Brad said, "Read verses seven through ten."

Miko adjusted her glasses. "And the shapes of the locusts were like unto horses prepared unto battle; and on their heads were as it were crowns like gold, and their faces were as the faces of men. And they had hair as the hair of women, and their teeth were as the teeth of lions. And they had breastplates, as it were breastplates of iron; and the sound of their wings was as the sound of chariots of many horses running to battle. And they had tails like unto scorpions, and there were stings in their tails: and their power was to hurt men five months."

Brad said, "That is enough. What do you scientists think of what Miko read?"

Ted said, "It is enough to scare you. That is what happened to the sun a year and three months ago. Those things happened in the same order as Miko and I read. How did people two thousand years ago know this? It is like Nostradamus on steroids."

Bärbel said, "And the demon insect plague *did* last for five months."

Brad noticed the pensive look on the faces of his fellow scientists. He said, "You have to arrive at the conclusion that whoever wrote the Bible knew of these events ahead of time and recorded them to warn us."

Albert Weiss asked, "Warn us about what?"

"Read it for yourself and decide. It appears God wrote this book. It is beyond coincidence for someone two thousand years ago to make wild predictions like these and get it right. Albert, you have skill in probabilities. What are the chances of this happening by coincidence?"

Albert looked at the ceiling and said, "Too high to calculate."

Brad asked his team, "What conclusion does this force?"

Miko admitted, "The Bible must be accurate in what it says."

Brad answered, "Correct. And what does it demand of you?"

Albert said, "It demands we take responsibility of our actions to God. I'm in big trouble if that is the case."

Brad said, "I have a task for you. I want you to read a paper I've written on this subject and let me know what you think. I value each of your opinions and judgments."

He printed several copies of a PDF document he created and gave it to each of his fellow scientists. "This document contains the verses we read and the time and date each of the disasters occurred along with other details. I will discuss this with each of you individually when you are ready."

Brad said, "I appreciate your attention. I wish for all of us to make it through this time of terror alive. I pray for each of you every day."

The group fell silent. Bärbel broke the silence. "We appreciate you doing this for us. I apologize for making fun of you earlier."

Brad said, "No problem, Bärbel. I expected to take some heat."

Within a week's time, one by one, Brad's team came to him and gave their hearts to the Lord.

Thirty-Three

Meeting of the Minds

On the first week of October, Eftas Helpphor arrived in New York, but his luggage didn't. He waited three and a half hours at the airport before they arrived.

The limo Nist sent for him stalled in the middle of Manhattan. Steam came out of the hood and the driver phoned for a backup vehicle. An hour later, another limo picked him up and took him to the World Peace Headquarters thirty miles north of New York City.

Nist spent time pacing the floor in his office and looking at his watch. The wait irritated him. The multiple delays wore his patience thin.

Nist's intercom buzzed.

He answered, "Yes?"

Stile said, "Eftas Helpphor is here."

"Finally. Send him in."

Eftas Helpphor entered Nist's expansive office.

Nist looked him over. He thought, "Sean was right. This is one weird-looking person. I hope he is worth the wait."

Eftas had cabalistic symbols embroidered on his suit. He dressed the part of a modern-day wizard.

Nist shook his hand and motioned for Helpphor to sit.

Helpphor sat and said, "Congratulations on your most recent achievement – becoming the ruler of the world."

"Thank you. I heard you had a few difficulties from the time you landed until you got here. I am sorry it happened."

Helpphor said, "Anyone who travels a lot has these difficulties every now and then. It is nothing to be upset about."

Nist leaned back in his chair. "My advisor, Sean Prussia, talked with you. I am curious about what he told me. You are Jewish, yet you live in Babylon. Don't you fear for your life being there?"

Eftas sat on the edge of his chair, leaned forward and answered, "It is the *others* who fear for their lives. I am well-respected – and feared – in Babylon." Then he relaxed.

Nist was surprised – and impressed – by his answer. "Good. I did wonder about that. Let's get to the point of business at hand. I assigned Sean to find a man with specialized knowledge. He told me you have the answer to my problem. I am looking for someone to help me sell the perfect loyalty test."

"I have the answer to whatever you need."

"What do you have? I know you are a great illusionist. What else?"

"I'm a public relations expert, an illusionist, and much more. I also practice the Black Arts as well."

"I don't care about demons or the devil. Can you to show me something that isn't an illusion?" Nist put his elbow on his desk and rested his chin in his right hand. He raised his eyebrows and threw his left hand in the air. "Get on with it."

Eftas glared at Nist and his appearance changed. His face turned from sinister to evil-looking. After two minutes, he noticed two horns growing out of Eftas' forehead. An overwhelming feeling of evil filled the office.

He leaned forward and pointed to one of his horns. "Now touch me here if you dare." Eftas showed his fang-like teeth and growled at Nist.

Nist's mouth hung open and his eyes grew wide. His hands shook. He thought of pressing a button to call security. "Wow. This is real."

Nist screamed, "*Now, make it go away.*"

In a couple of minutes, Helpphor returned to his "normal" creepy appearance.

Nist played with a pen to calm himself. He used his handkerchief to wipe the sweat off of his face. He leaned back in his chair when he recovered his composure and took a couple of deep breaths.

Eftas said, "Now tell me about your loyalty test and why you need me to help sell it."

"I want every person to have a tattoo of me on their foreheads or right hand."

"Is that all?"

"Well, it won't be a mere tattoo. It will be my image with a thirty-nine digit account number. The machine that transfers these tattoos also will implant a RFID chip with a lithium battery. I need to sell the whole world on the idea of taking this mark to show their loyalty. And I don't want them to realize the control I'll have over them."

Eftas raised his eyebrows. "I see. But, you don't think people will go for it right away, do you?"

"No, I don't. All the selling points fall short of acceptance." Nist sat up and pounded his desk with his fist.

Eftas said, "You will need to convince people you're worthy to serve. I know how to do that."

"Surprise me with what you have."

Eftas leaned forward and held up three fingers. "It will be a three-part deal. For the first part, I will need to make you a god, and I can do that. The second part is this: I will make an image of you come alive in front of a large crowd and TV cameras. That will give me credence, too. I will command people to worship it. You will be their god. If they don't worship the image or worship you, they will be at your mercy. This is religious part of the loyalty test you requested."

"I hate the very mention of God. I hate Christians and Orthodox Jews in particular. And I don't have any use for religion."

"Yes, you do. If I need to make you a god, there will have to be a religious component. Besides, other conquerors have used religion as a tool."

Nist sighed and drummed his finders on his desk. He agreed even though it displeased him. "What's the third part?"

"I will raise you from the dead."

Nist's eyes grew big. He looked hard at Eftas and said, "How are you going to do that? Are you going to kill me?"

Eftas chuckled and leaned back in his chair. "No, not at all. As to how, leave it to me. I have a few ideas, but it will take me a few weeks of planning to get it right. If my show succeeds, you won't have any trouble selling your mark. But your offer will have to sound attractive. Or at least, look like a good offer on the surface. Remember, it will take a number of years for the entire population of the planet to take your mark. You will have to maintain a good ad campaign to keep interest from waning. Don't act like you are in a hurry."

Nist raised one eyebrow and said, "Why not?"

"Your eagerness will raise suspicions. If you take your time, you will soften any resistance. People will find it easier to accept new ideas after a while."

Nist picked up a pen from his desk and played with it. He said, "You're right. I have the time and the money."

For the first time, Nist smiled. He said, "How right you are. I must show you something." He went to his marble file cabinet and took out a folder. He removed a photo and handed it to Eftas. "Here is a picture of the mark. The account number is across the bottom."

He took out a plastic bag and emptied the contents on a piece of paper. A single chip about the size of an insect egg fell out. "This RFID chip will go in at the same time the tattoo is imprinted."

"I know about this chip. Several corporations already use this chip for security purposes. The Royal Family of Great Britain have these chips implanted in them so they can be tracked in case of kidnapping. Several years ago, the United States enacted something like this by way of a phony healthcare law. Two selling points obtained passage for it. The first point claimed to keep track of sex offenders, and the second point claimed to prevent identity theft. What a laugh. The writers of that law had the same idea as I suspect you have – total slavery."

Nist grinned and said, "Isn't it grand?"

"What is your offer to lure them into slavery?"

Nist revealed his plan. "I will offer them complete debt cancellation if they take the mark. Later, of course, they will be right back in debt, but to me. They will be under too much financial stress to pass up an offer like that. And yes, it will be total control. And they will willingly give it to me after you make me a god."

He went to the refrigerator near his desk and took out a bottle of cold water. "Would you like a bottle of cold water or wine?"

Eftas said, "Water, please."

Nist handed him a bottle of cold water and sat at his desk.

Nist said, "It will be perfect. You will command them to worship me. I will be like the Roman Emperors. If they do not have my mark on their bodies, they will be allowed to starve to death. It will be easier than hunting them, and it will be a much slower death than a gunshot wound. Peer pressure alone will make most get my mark. That's a lesson I learned from Karl Marx. If they outright refuse my mark or make a scene, I could have them beheaded."

He whacked a pen on his desk with a letter opener to accent his last statement.

"Once they submit, I will control their money by computer. I will be able to freeze their account at any time anywhere in the world. They will be forced to eat out of my hands. I will be able to track everyone on the planet. I will be able to find out who anybody supports. No one will be able to hide anything. I will be able to control entire countries. Nobody will be able to move without me knowing."

Nist laughed, leaned back in his chair, and put his feet on the desk. His smile couldn't get any bigger. "What do you think about it?"

"It's a great idea. Other conquerors have used similar items. This is the first time something like this is achievable on a world-wide basis. My advice is this: get control over Europe first. Sell them by telling them they are the revived Roman Empire. Europe is the most financially insecure continent at the moment. After you get control of Europe, then go for the rest of the world."

Nist asked, "How are you going to make that image come alive and raise me from the dead? Where will you do it?"

"Leave all those details to me. Remember, a good wizard never reveals his secrets."

"I look forward to seeing you make me a god and raising me from the dead. Are you sure you aren't trying to kill me?"

"No. I'm just after your money."

They both looked at each other and laughed.

Eftas added, "But, it will cost you."

"Don't care. Just do it. The UN is funding me and I have an unlimited spending account. The UN is collecting money from almost all nations for me."

"I'll send you my bill tomorrow. When it is paid, I will commence operations."

"It will be paid the day I receive it."

Eftas checked his calendar, "Good. I'll get back to you in about five months. Expect to be impressed. Call me anytime."

Nist beamed and said, "I can't wait."

"By the way, you need to move your headquarters to Jerusalem. It will be closer to me and it is where you need to be. Take it from me. It is center stage of the world at the moment. You will be close to where the action is. I have a Jerusalem office ten kilometers north of the city. The building next to mine is available and will suit your needs."

"I've been thinking of moving there. Give me the address of that building. I think I will make that move."

Eftas asked, "Are you married?"

"No. Why do you ask?"

"We are alike in this matter. Our mistress is power. There is little room in our hearts for anyone but us. We seem to be two of a kind. I wanted to know how free you might be to move around. Let us dare to do great things."

Eftas stood to leave. He said, "One more thing. What is your middle name?"

"Why do you want it?"

"If I can evaluate your name, it could mean a stronger following."

"Okay. If you must have it, then I'll send it to you by e-mail. It is a Greek name and I don't want you to misspell it."

Eftas nodded. "Good. I'll be in touch."

"Okay. Have a good flight home."

Nist shook Eftas' hand and watched him leave. He went to a mirror near the file cabinets to check his appearance and to adjust his tie. Looking closer, he saw a glint of light in his pupils.

***

The demons inside of Charti Nist danced with delight. Their plan to bring Nist and Helpphor together succeeded. The devil in Nist gained more control. The dragon demon exhaled volumes of smoke in excitement.

***

Nist laughed and a small puff of smoke escaped his lips. He thought, "How did that happen?" Nist did not smoke. The dragon demon gained strength and Nist felt its influence.

***

The next day, Nist announced to his staff his plans to move to Jerusalem. He offered to manage the sale of their homes and buy houses for them in Jerusalem if they made the move with him. Most of his staff decided to make the move. The next day, he decided to take a flight to Jerusalem and look at the building Eftas mentioned.

Thirty-Four

Marketing

Nist completed his move to Israel two months later in December. Nist's building stood next to Eftas' building. A secure underground walkway connected the two buildings with World Peace Organization troops guarding it. The expanse of his new office surpassed the old one in New York.

About 10:00 a.m., he decided to call his advertising manager, Vadim Marolov, on the intercom. "Vadim? This is Nist."

"Sir?"

"Are you ready to show me your ad campaign?"

"Yes. Do you want me to bring the materials to your office?"

"No. I will come to your office. I want to see what you've done to the multi-media lab."

Nist went to Vadim's office on the third floor. The multi-media lab had large conference desks in it as well as a small theater for viewing the ads.

Nist greeted Vadim and shook his hand. "Good to see you. Where is your presentation?"

Vadim pointed. "Over there at the presentation table. We will be able to spread out these ads."

They both sat and reviewed the signs and posters.

Vadim said, "We will put up these signs after the Big Reveal. Do you like them?"

Nist took his time looking over them. "Yes, I am pleased. I like this series altogether. It makes the new mark look like fun. You developed the security features I asked you to include. You and your team did an even better job than I envisioned."

"We decided to sell the GPS chip as a safety feature for children and individuals. The ad campaign will encourage moms to get the mark for their family members by eliminating kidnapping as a viable crime.

"Also, 'Where is my child?' is another campaign we will promote. Moms will be able to track their kids on a computer and locate them at any time. No more missing kids. The kids will hate us, though."

Nist smiled.

"We will stage six kidnappings in major countries. The criminals, that is, our actors, will be caught within an hour using the new tracking technology. Phony stories will be released about their executions a few weeks later. This will encourage others to get their marks."

Nist's grin grew. "I like this a lot. This will soften many objections."

Vadim agreed. "Yes. Over a period of time, this will be accepted if we don't push too hard. It will take a little time to get used to, but our ad campaign will erode most mental blocks. Let's go to the theater and I will show you the TV ads we created."

"I can't wait to see these."

Nist sat on a front row seat. Vadim turned on the theater projector by pressing a button. A curtain moved back to reveal a huge TV screen on the wall. He went to his computer and clicked on the presentation.

Nothing happened.

Vadim's face turned red in embarrassment. "This stupid thing worked an hour ago. What is wrong? I can't believe it." He worked on his laptop for ten minutes with no results. He banged his fist on the computer in anger. "I don't know why this thing isn't working. I'll have to get back with you later to show you the videos we will broadcast."

Nist said, "After the Big Reveal, I want these signs everywhere in the world. Each culture will have its own message, but with the same results. Centers for making these marks will be called, 'Identity Verification Centers'. Advertise a lot for the next three years and make the mark and these identity chips a cultural icon. Make them more popular and desirable than mp3 players and smart phones."

"Well, it looks like I have my work cut out for me for the next few years anyway."

"It looks like you have things under control. Well, except for this computer." He pointed to the non-working unit on the table. "I know about temperamental computers. I'll see your presentations when you tame that beast. I have to go now. Let me know when I can see the TV ads."

***

On the way back to his office, Nist called Stile on his cell phone. When she answered, he asked, "Do I have any appointments before lunch?"

"Yes. You have an appointment with Sajeeb Berra. He wants to give you his progress report on the massive computer network."

"Is he coming to my office?"

"Yes. He will be there in thirty minutes. I'll get things ready for you."

He ended the call to return to his office on the top floor.

***

Sajeeb Berra arrived at the appointed time.

Nist greeted him and asked, "How are the financial computer networks coming along? Will they be able to handle the new account numbers?"

"Yes, and they will be ready soon. It is in its final stages of testing and should be fully operational in six weeks. We have several backup systems and our own generators in case there is a power failure or another disaster. It is such a huge system. The people who work there call it 'The Beast'."

Nist leaned back in his chair and said, "Have you contacted vending machine manufacturers yet?"

"Yes, I have. New machines will be ready for the new account numbers and the old machines will be retrofitted with scanners. Store cash registers will be programmed to scan them. Things will be ready two weeks before the Big Reveal."

Nist leaned forward in his chair and said, "Very good. Keep up the good work."

"Thank you. My crew is working double shifts until we resolve all issues." Sajeeb left Nist's office.

***

Nist spent the next three months continuing his takeover of the world's banks. Things went well. He and Eftas talked by phone often to discuss the Big Reveal.

In March, he received the call he was looking forward to.

"Hello? ... Yes, Eftas. Wonderful ... What's the plan? ... Okay. I'll meet you at your office." Then Nist hung up.

Nist called Stile on the intercom. "I'm going to Eftas' building next door. Notify the corridor guards."

He went to the first level below the ground and entered the underground corridor. His personal Segway took him to Eftas' building in seconds.

***

Nist arrived at Eftas' building accompanied by several security personnel. After passing though security, they went to the top floor.

The Jerusalem secretary, Judith Polanski, directed Nist to Eftas' office door.

Eftas greeted saying, "Welcome to my world."

Nist responded, "I haven't seen you for a few months. You have a nice office, a desk almost as big as mine, and excellent furnishings. It is a lot quieter than my office."

"How do you like your new location?"

"I like it a lot. I've had a sense of excitement ever since I moved here."

Eftas nodded. "I have much to go over with you. I'm ready to show you the details of my plan. I think you will like it. Once we approve the details, we will carry it out. I intend to execute this plan two weeks from today."

"Let's get started."

"After our session, I have a little meditation time set aside for us."

Eftas motioned for Nist to follow him to a door on the opposite side of the office. He showed him a room prepared with cushions on the floor, a hookah and several incense burners.

Nist grinned. "Yes, I like that kind of meditation. I get a lot of ideas that way."

"Let's get to work. We can enjoy ourselves later."

They went into a large conference room, shut the door and discussed Eftas' plan. They spent hours fine-tuning the steps he created.

Eftas said, "I will handle the media for this event. I haven't told them what will happen, though. But I did tell them it will be big news. You need to bring troops to support us."

After they completed the work Eftas said, "It is meditation time."

They both took off their coats, ties, and shoes. Eftas lit incense and turned on some New Age meditation music. They inhaled the powerful drugs in his hookah. While meditating, more demons entered Nist. The demons of mass murder, hate, and blasphemy grew in power.

Thirty-Five

Image Problems

One week before the Big Reveal, Eftas worried about the image of Nist. It wasn't ready and Eftas called his contact at the factory. "You promised me an earlier delivery date. I need this image to be here in seven days. What can you do to expedite this?"

The factory rep said, "I'll call you back while I check on this. I'll be back in a less than a half hour."

Eftas stared at the palm trees outside of his office while pacing the carpet.

After forty-five minutes, his contact returned to the call. "Sorry about the delay. I had a hard time locating the project manager. He released the files to me, so I'm forwarding them to his assistant."

"When will my project be ready? I can't be late on this one."

"How much time do you have?"

"Seven days."

"Your shipment will arrive at your destination address in three days. I will make sure there are no more delays."

"It's about time. Notify me when it ships."

"I will. Thank you for your business."

Eftas ended the call. He decided to calm his nerves with a drink.

***

Four days later, Nist received a call from Eftas. He said, "Do you have any news about the image?"

"Yes. It arrived yesterday. We have three more days before the Big Reveal. Come over and we will drive to the warehouse where it is stored."

He ended the call and went to Eftas's building. They entered a limo and rode to a warehouse forty kilometers away. When they arrived, a security team allowed them into the parking lot. They drove through a large door and parked inside the warehouse. They got out of the limo and saw the thirty-foot tall image covered by a tarp.

Eftas spoke to the crew, "Unveil the image of Nist."

The crew pulled the tarp from the image and Nist stared at the cast-iron marvel. His jaw dropped. "Wow. It looks just like me. I'm impressed."

Nist walked around the image. "He looks good from all angles. He has my jawbone, my eyebrows, and my good looks."

The crew chief pointed to a snorkel truck and said, "Do you want me to give you a closer look in this cherry picker?"

Nist said, "Yes. I'd like that."

The crew chief turned on the snorkel truck and lowered the hydraulic platform to the floor. Nist entered the compartment and the chief closed the door. He lifted Nist to the image's hands.

Nist pointed at the detail of the image's hands. "You can almost see my fingerprints on this. How did you get these details?" He looked at his own hands and compared them to the image's hands.

He said, "Lift me up to the face."

Nist stared at the image's face. "He's a handsome devil, don't you think?"

He rode around the image several times admiring it.

Eftas let him admire it for thirty minutes. Then he said, "It is time to go now."

Thirty-Six

My Gut Is Talking

Vasily mopped the floor after a customer knocked over a coffee urn. He said, "Spilled coffee is something to cry about."

While mopping up the spill, thirty medical employees from the King County Hospital entered his shop. He saw a familiar face among the nurses and asked, "What is going on, Katie Taylor?"

She answered, "Somebody came to the ER with the Bubonic Plague. Management ordered us to leave while the HazMat people decontaminate the emergency room and the waiting area. It will take about two hours, so we decided to come here."

"Is there a certain kind of coffee or bagels you might like?"

"I'm in the mood for an 'Everything' bagel and dark roast coffee."

"The dark roast coffee will be ready in a few minutes. I'll get your order in as soon as I get everybody's orders."

Vasily visited each table and took orders.

He turned on the TV to Channel 6 News.

"Paz Meyerheim here with Channel 6 International News. Charti Nist, the new world ruler, appointed Eftas Helpphor, a Middle Eastern consultant, as his spiritual advisor. Helpphor will assist Nist with handling different cultures and their local religious values. He has an office building next to World Peace Headquarters in Jerusalem. And now, Rebecca Schmeltz with Channel 6 Financial News."

"The International Currency has been unveiled by Nist's Financial Advisor, Jack Delson. Your bank statement will show your transactions in US dollars, and in International Currency Units, or ICUs."

On a display behind Rebecca, the International Currency Symbol appeared.

"The US dollar sign will be phased out along with currency symbols of other nations. The conversion rate will appear on your bank statements. Next month, all stores will feature price tags in US dollars and ICUs. In two years, the ICU value alone will remain."

The news anchors continued their report, but Vasily didn't want to listen anymore. He sat with the nurse and let off a little steam.

"Katie, I don't like people that high up with so much power. Nothing good will come of it." Vasily put his elbow on the table and rested his jaw on his right hand.

Katie said, "Don't you think you are a little judgmental? Remember, you are in your sixties and you like the old ways."

"Old ways or not, when I grew up in Russia, this was always a bad thing. I lived through it and still don't like it."

Katie looked a little shocked.

Vasily said, "I'm sorry for talking harsh to you. I have seen this before. Believe me, it isn't good. I hope I'm wrong. I'll bring you a free bagel to go since I talked your ear off."

Katie thanked him. Vasily didn't want to see any more news, so he went into the kitchen area to put up the mop and looked over his receipts.

***

Moses and Elijah continued to preach in Jerusalem near the Temple Mount. Busloads of tourists came to see them on a regular basis. The soldiers on duty brought in bleachers to accommodate them.

One day in March, three and a half years since the Great Disappearance, a bus filled with college students unloaded near the soldier's gate. The soldiers warned them not to provoke the prophets.

A student approached them. He appeared to be about twenty years old, and had black, curly hair and a beard. Moses greeted him and said, "What is your name and what can we do for you today?"

"My name is Charlie. What are your names?"

"Don't you know?"

"Well, those soldiers over there say you are Moses and Elijah, but those are probably stage names."

"I am Moses and he is Elijah." Moses pointed at Elijah.

"I'll buy it for now."

"Why don't you believe us when we tell you our own names?"

Charlie ignored Moses' question and asked, "What are you here for? Are you making a movie or something?"

"No, we are here to preach the Gospel of Jesus Christ, the Savior."

"So you are one of those narrow-minded, Bible-thumpers, aren't you?"

Moses looked at Elijah and saw him grinning. He knew Elijah's thoughts.

Moses said, "We are preaching the truth."

"Yeah, I know. What is truth anyway?"

"It is something that never changes. Like right and wrong, good and evil. God's Word, the Bible."

"You sound awful intolerant of anything different. My teachers tell me good and evil are relative as well as right and wrong. You are so 'Establishment'."

"What do you mean by that?"

"You are just like my old man. He always talks about stuff like that, but I know better. If something is right for you, it is right."

"Old man?"

"Like, wow. You are out of touch, Pops. I'm talking about my father."

Moses' desire to flame this kid grew. He counted to ten under his breath.

A girl approached and said, "Charlie, what are you doing? Remember what the soldiers told us." Moses waved her off.

The student continued. "Your message is so offensive. Don't you know you are preaching in the middle of thousands of Muslims? Why are you so intolerant of other religions?"

"Who says we are intolerant?"

"My professors at the university do. They teach Comparative Religion and say all religious people think their way is the only way."

"Charlie, you are ignoring what is written in the Holy Bible. God's Word is filled with prophesies of Jesus and how He fulfilled them."

"Yeah, right. My teachers tell me that the Bible is full of mistakes and that other religions claim the same thing. So don't waste my time telling me all of your bull."

"What do you mean, 'bull'?"

"It is all the crap you're doing. Dressing in these weird get-ups and passing off your religion to gullible people who see you do these tricks."

Moses said, "That's enough." Fire came out of Moses' mouth and blasted the student.

Charlie's girlfriend screamed and ran toward the gate. The other students ran out with her.

Moses turned to Elijah. "I tried to be patient, but he earned that punishment."

Elijah agreed. "You were. I'd have done it much sooner."

Moses blew the student's smoldering ashes out of sight.

***

John the Apostle shook his head. He turned to the Elder and said, "That student was so close to hearing the Gospel. If he could have controlled his arrogance, he could have gotten saved."

The Elder nodded but said nothing.

Thirty-Seven

Offenses in Jerusalem

The day of the Big Reveal arrived on the fourteenth day of April, three and a half years after the Great Disappearance. Nist picked up Helpphor in his limo and they drove to the Temple Mount. The flatbed truck with the image of Nist followed.

In spite of the police escorts, a man threw an IED at their car and the explosion overturned the limo. Police assisted the two leaders out of the wreckage. They had a couple of bumps, but nothing serious.

Nist said, "I have been world ruler for six months and already someone has tried to kill me. I hope this doesn't change our plans."

Eftas replied, "No, but it is making me mad. I can't have any more delays at this point."

Another limo arrived and took them the final three blocks.

Nist came to the Temple Mount and approached the Temple with his troops clearing a path for him. The troops displaced the Temple Guards at gunpoint.

Orthodox Jews approached Nist when they saw this.

The Chief Priest said, "You can't do this. You signed an international treaty with us guaranteeing us this property."

Nist replied, "Don't care. Get back."

Troops removed Jews from the Temple and the Temple Mount area, but allowed them to watch.

Nist and Eftas walked to the altar and stood in front of it. Nist commanded the crew with the crane. "Put my image in front of the door of the Temple." Workers hoisted the thirty-foot cast iron image out of the truck and placed in front of the Temple door. Guards prevented anybody from removing it. Horror and anger filled the Jews who watched. They knew this had happened in 150 B.C.

Nist took advantage of the TV news crews present and shouted. "I am your God. Worship me."

He pointed to the image of God in the sky and shouted at it. "I defy anybody up there to strike me dead." Nist waited a couple of minutes. He broke the silence by mocking. "I didn't think anything would happen."

Eftas patted Nist's right shoulder with his left hand. Nist winced for an instant at the slight sting on his right shoulder.

A Jewish guard ran past the soldiers. He drew his sword and hacked at Nist's head. Soldiers rushed in and captured the guard but Nist was dead.

Blood covered his body and the pavement where he lay.

TV cameras recorded the gruesome event. The men and women in the crowd charged the Temple area but the troops restrained them.

The soldiers beat the Jewish guard and put him in a straight jacket. They covered his bloody head with a burlap bag and took him away.

Nist's body lay in a pool of his own blood. People cried because their world leader was dead. The angry crowd demanded justice and came close to rioting.

Medical First Responders came to the Temple area to take Nist's body. Before they got too close, Eftas shouted. "Stand back. Watch your priest work a miracle."

The crowd grew quiet. The wailing diminished to a lone murmur.

Eftas looked hard and laid his hands on Nist. "I command you to come to life now."

Nist opened his eyes. "What happened? Am I dead?"

The crowd cheered. People jumped up and down, and gave each other high fives. The ladies who wept saw the miracle and hugged each other. The reporters' mouths hung open. The TV crew recording this event could not hold their cameras still because of the excitement of this huge event.

Nist propped himself on his elbows, then sat. He felt his head, neck, and stomach. He saw blood covering his body and said, "What happened?" Silence fell over the crowd when they saw him move.

He stood and danced around a bit. He sobbed because of the emotion welling up in him.

The crowd roared with excitement.

In the midst of the celebration, Eftas motioned to people standing near the Temple Mount and said, "Bring the sacrifice and place it on this altar." They placed a dead pig on the altar.

The crowd grew quiet and their mouths fell open. A pig on the altar shocked the Israelis.

Eftas looked into the sky, spread his arms and said, "I call down fire from Heaven to consume this sacrifice."

Fire came from the sky and devoured the sacrifice. Even though this took most people by surprise, many of them suspected a trick.

One person near the front of the crowd whispered to his friend, "Is this a David Copperfield kind of trick, or is it real? What do you think?"

His friend whispered back, "I think it is a trick. I wonder what they are up to?"

Eftas could see the disgusted look on the faces of the Orthodox Jews. He defiled their Temple and watched them spit before leaving the Temple area.

He held up his hands demanding attention. He shouted, "Watch while I demonstrate my powers." Eftas turned toward the image of Nist and waved a wand. "I command LIFE to come into this image."

The image came alive. It opened its eyes. It looked at its hands and then looked at Eftas. It asked, "Who are you?"

Eftas said, "Don't you know who I am?"

"You are my Creator."

"Who are you?"

"I am Charti Nist."

A helicopter flew overhead and the image of Nist looked up at it. It said, "What is that?"

Eftas said, "That is a helicopter. Don't be afraid of it. It won't hurt you."

The image turned its head and looked around. It walked over the Temple Mount area and looked at people in the crowd. The TV cameras focused on the image that came to life.

One person in the front of the crowd whispered to his friend. "When it looked at me, it sent chills down my spine."

His friend whispered back. "A look from either Nist or Helpphor sends worse chills down my spine. I don't know whether I should stay for this event or run away."

Eftas said, "Know this. I raised Nist from the dead. I am his high priest and I have the power of life and death. I gave life to this image. Now I confer on Nist the power he wants."

The wizard waved his wand and hands in Nist's direction. "Receive the powers of the universe." Nist held his hands high to receive his new powers.

Eftas said, "I am going to reveal to you now the loyalty test I will require of every citizen of the Earth. It is a simple one."

He picked up a poster of the new mark. "Take this mark on either your forehead or right hand to show you are a loyal world citizen.

Worship this living image of Charti Nist at least one time. This living image will be on a world tour and people in other countries will have an opportunity soon to worship it in person. Do not miss your opportunity."

He paused for effect.

"Once you have worshipped this image, you will choose the location of your identity mark. It will be either your forehead or right hand."

Eftas pointed to his right hand, and to his forehead.

"Included with this mark, an identity chip will be inserted at the site of your mark for your personal safety. With this identity chip, kidnapping will be a thing of the past. Your children, or your spouse can be found anywhere on the planet. Lost children can be found in a matter of moments on your computer. Runaways can be found in a matter of moments. Crooks can be located in an instant. Safety will flourish."

His words couldn't have been smoother.

He pointed at Nist. "He is here to bring you peace, safety, and later, prosperity. This new identity chip will be available worldwide soon, insuring your safety.

"In two year's time, with this identification, you will be able to participate in any financial transaction anywhere on the planet. Non-citizens will not be able to buy or sell. Cash, credit and debit cards will be phased out for your protection. We ask so little of you and will provide much. Nist will be telling you the other benefits of this mark."

Eftas gestured to Nist.

Blood covered Nist's clothes and face. "When you take this mark and ID chip, *all debts to all your financial institutions will be cancelled. Every citizen of Earth who takes my mark will be free from all debt.*"

Nist paused to let his words sink in.

"You will be able to start with a clean slate. My computers will keep you out of financial trouble. You will not be able to overextend yourselves. Direct deposit will be provided for all. Your taxes will be calculated and deducted. No more cash. No more checks. No more deposits. No more debit or credit cards. No more tax returns."

The crowd cheered at his last statement.

"Medical expenses will be free. Loans will be calculated and taken from your pay. Robberies will be all but impossible. Kidnapping and related crimes will vanish. Locating lost children will be easy. Security will be increased. There will be peace and safety.

"World citizens will have many benefits. You will get travel discounts, exemption from travel papers, discounts on food, cars, gasoline, and services.

"Centers for getting your personalized mark will be constructed soon. In twelve months time, you will be getting your appointment card in the mail for this purpose. Please keep your appointment. Your appointment card will have a box to check stating you have worshipped my image. This will be required before you can take my mark. You will have a choice of getting your mark either on your forehead or on your right hand. You will have a few choices of colors. Details will be available soon. In two year's time, it will be required for all financial transactions.

"Let us work at developing a world where peace and safety exist."

The crowd applauded.

Nist and Helpphor left in the limo they arrived in.

Armed guards positioned themselves on the Temple Mount. The living image of Charti Nist walked around the Temple area. Soldiers placed a chain and padlock on the doors of the Temple.

***

Yitzchak Tovim, the Jewish High Priest called a meeting in his home in Jerusalem. He said, "Today our Temple has been defiled. Nist, at first glance, has been raised from the dead. I don't think he was dead."

His cousin, Marvin Kimchi asked, "Did you recognize the guard that tried to kill Nist?"

"No, and that is what makes me wonder about it. Does anybody here know him? I don't."

Gerta Meyer said, "I've seen him around, but he is not religious at all. He is an actor."

Yitzchak said, "What do we do now? I'm sure we are on Nist's 'bad' list."

Marvin said, "Why don't we camp out at Petra and figure out what to do. We can pray undisturbed there."

Yitzchak said, "I like that idea. Let's pack up and leave Jerusalem now."

They all agreed and went to their homes to pack.

***

Helpphor and Nist's motorcade left the Temple Mount area, heading north until they came to Sultan Suleiman Street. They merged into Sderot Hayim Barlov highway, which became Derech HaAluf Uzi Narkis. Their office buildings were eight kilometers further.

After getting out of the business district Nist said, "You didn't tell me about that man charging me and hitting me with that fake sword. That blow to my head gave me a bad headache. I will probably have a scar from this cut on the side of my head."

Eftas replied, "I thought it added a nice touch. A scar and a headache is a small price to pay for being raised from the dead. I drugged you moments before he charged you so you would appear to die."

Nist's mouth fell open. "You drugged me?"

Eftas laughed. "Yes, the ring I tapped onto your right shoulder injected a small bit of drug into you. You were probably ready to pass out when you received that phony blow on the head."

Nist complained. "It didn't feel phony."

Eftas had the same calm, sly grin. "I'm glad you didn't know. You looked surprised."

Nist's anger cooled. He said, "Really? How real did it look?"

"Real enough."

He asked, "How is your fake guard?"

"He is doing well and on his way to Babylon. I will be take care of him and keep him out of sight."

"How did you get him into the Temple Guard?"

"I didn't. I had his outfit made. Did you notice where he came from?"

"No, I didn't."

"I kept him hidden until the right moment. I also ordered your soldiers to rough him up, but only a little. He did get beat up, if it makes you feel any better."

They both laughed.

Eftas said, "Did you see the look on their faces when I called fire from heaven?"

Nist said, "Yes, I did. It was priceless. How did you do that?"

Eftas winked and said, "A good wizard never reveals his secrets."

Eftas remembered his research on Nist's name. "By the way, I did a little research into the value of your name. Your original name is Greek, isn't it?"

"Yes. My father moved from Greece to Turkey. I was born in Istanbul."

"Your name, in terms of numerology, signifies great power."

That statement piqued Nist's curiosity. "Go on."

"The value of the letters of your name comes to 666. And six occurs three times in your name. This indicates you are the acme of mankind."

Nist sighed. "I expected something a little more mysterious. Does it get me any money? No. So I don't care what the letters in my name add up to."

Eftas raised his eyebrows. "Don't worry. It will be useful in the near future."

The motorcade arrived at Helpphor's building. Before Nist got out of the limo, he had a new thought. "I want you to write the heads of all religious groups requiring them to move their headquarters to Babylon. Tell them they will be on my payroll from now on."

Eftas looked pleased, but curious. "Why do you want to do that? I thought you didn't like religions."

"I don't. I want these people where I can keep a close eye on them, and I don't want them in Jerusalem. I want *you* to direct them into creating a custom-made, one-world religion. It will be easier if they are all in one place."

"Babylon is a good choice. I like Babylon. It's a magical city. It has its own mystique."

"Maybe so, but I need you close by. You need to spend more time in Jerusalem."

Nist turned and stared at Eftas. He said, "I really don't like this religious aspect. If I had my way, I'd destroy them all now."

Eftas took that comment in silence and nodded. He said, "Well, I have to return to my headquarters in Babylon now. If you have any questions, I'll be at my headquarters for a few weeks. If you need any more tricks, I am the man you need."

Nist got out of the limo and returned to his office. Eftas went to the airport.

***

Eftas landed in Babylon two hours later. He admired the city while he rode to his office building. Babylon's wealth showed everywhere. Palm trees and beautiful building adorned the roads. The street markets, golf courses, swank hotels, trade centers and parks are what made Babylon attractive.

Eftas entered his headquarters. People knelt when he walked by.

He greeted his secretary, Farrah Jaffari, and gave her an assignment. "Write to the heads of all religions requiring them to meet with me in Babylon. Make it two months from today. Nist has ordered them to move their headquarters to Babylon within six months. We will work together to create a new world religion. Remind them of the lavish resorts nearby."

She said, "I will be glad to."

***

Vasily's coffee shop enjoyed much business the day after the Big Reveal. The medical team at Kings County Hospital were the bulk of his customers. Today, he sat with Ike Jackson, an x-ray technician.

The news anchor on Vasily's TV energetically announced, "I'm Wally Mason, Lifestyle News for Channel 6. The hot news today is the new World ID mark. Last night at Rockefeller Center, photographers took pictures of the world-famous Czech model, Riza Chovanec with her new identity mark."

Behind Wally, the display showed several close-up photos of Riza's face. She chose to have her mark of Nist on her forehead using iridescent colors.

Wally continued. "It's the key to your car. It's the key to your house. It's your PIN number and all your credit cards. It's your driver's license. It's your passport. It's your security key at work. And it can be next to invisible. And now to my partner, Jenna Ashford, also with Lifestyle News."

"No cash will be needed when everybody has their mark. In two years it will be phased out. All vending machines and cash registers are being retrofitted to scan the new ID mark. Surveillance scanners will be installed in many places. This will make the world safer and criminal activity go down. Kidnapping will be impossible. Crooks will be found. And it will be available soon. Look for your appointment card in the mail."

Vasily shook his head. He said to Ike, "It is a sad thing to happen in America. I never thought it could happen here."

Ike said, "I can't believe how bad things have gotten. Don't people realize what is happening? I can't believe the level of privacy that has been invaded and nobody is complaining. Well, except for you and me."

"I'm sure others do, too. I wish there were enough of us to make a difference."

***

The Apostle John noticed a crowd gathering in the Throne Room. Each of the 144,000 evangelists had been martyred and Jesus called them in for a special celebration. The number of original evangelists martyred on the sundial read 144,000. John and the martyrs met on Earth at Mount Zion. Jesus walked among them. Beautiful harp music came from Heaven. Later they returned to the Throne Room. They sang a song written for them: the martyrs who gave their lives preaching the Gospel of Jesus Christ.

The Elder described these people to John. "These are they which were not defiled with women; for they are virgins. These are they which follow the Lamb whithersoever he goeth. These were redeemed from among men, being the firstfruits unto God and to the Lamb. And in their mouth was found no guile: for they are without fault before the throne of God."

Thirty-Eight

Testing His Powers

Three months after the events in Jerusalem, Nist wished to test his new powers. He wanted to make an example of the Two Witnesses so he called one of his advisors, Mallon Karth into his office.

Mallon was forty-nine years old and showed signs of aging. What little hair he had was gray, and his facial skin was rough. He wore a white shirt and tie and wore expensive shoes. He stood 5'9", and weighed 195 pounds.

Nist said, "Tell me something. Are those pesky magicians near the Temple area still there? You know, those weirdos who call themselves Moses and Elijah or something like that?"

"Yes, they are still there."

"How long have they been there?"

Mallon checked his tablet. He said, "They arrived a few months after the Great Disappearance. They've been there almost three years and six months ago. They seem to be a kind of local tourist attraction and have a large following, but they are dangerous and have certain powers. We've tried to photograph them, but the photos come out blurry. Fire, water, lice, giant scorpions, and other plagues seem to be in their arsenal. My report says fire can come out of their mouths when they are threatened."

Nist replied, "Well, it's time to do something. I will deal with them."

Mallon said, "Won't that generate negative publicity?"

"Don't care."

Nist picked up his phone and dialed a number. When someone answered, Nist said, "Give me commander of the Jerusalem militia. ... General? Can you get rid of those two troublemakers near the Temple? ... Yes, those are the ones. Have you tried anything to get rid of them? ... No, don't use a tank on them. Simple gunfire will be sufficient. ... Well, I'm giving you the authority right now. ... Yes, you have my permission. Call me when they are gone." Nist hung up.

Nist spoke with Mallon about other public relations issues. After eighteen minutes, Nist's phone rang.

Nist answered his phone, "Yes? ... Well, good. Spread the news to the networks. ... No, no, don't bury them. Let their bodies be shown to the world on TV. ... How about a week? ... Okay ... Yes, three and a half days will do. One day for each year they have been a pain to us. I like that."

Nist hung up. He said, "Mallon, see how powerful I've become? I got rid of those two nuts near the Temple who have been causing all the problems. I guarantee you the whole world will cheer me."

"Let us hope so. In the future, you should be more subtle."

"I'll do what I want. You may go now."

Mallon left Nist's office.

***

Three and a half days passed.

A reporter came to the scene where the Two Witnesses preached to cover the cleanup story. The reporter said, "I'm Bruce Wellington with CNN News in Jerusalem. It has been three and a half days since the death of these so-called prophets. The planet has been on a huge block party since. Reports have come in from the whole world and people are exchanging presents to celebrate their deaths. Also, rain has been reported in almost every continent of the world in the last twenty-four hours. The plagues these two conjured have stopped, and the world is celebrating. A cleanup crew is on the way to get rid of these bodies."

While the reporter spoke, smoke came from Heaven and entered the bodies of Moses and Elijah. The dried blood on them disappeared. Tears in their flesh vanished. Their eyes opened.

The camera operator screamed and ran away when the Two Witnesses stood. Bruce turned around and saw Moses and Elijah looking at him. He dropped his microphone and ran like mad.

A cloud formed around Moses and Elijah. It picked them up and took them into the air. When the cloud disappeared, the reporter and the camera operator came back. Bruce picked up his microphone.

"Well, you saw what happened. I've never been so scared in all my life. Good or bad, they are gone. And that's good news. Bruce Wellington, CNN News."

***

Vasily watched Bruce Wellington's story as he sat at a table with Denise, a secretary in the Kings County Hospital business office.

He said, "I'm sorry to see them go. They did make things interesting in Jerusalem. What do you think?"

"I tend to agree with you. But they did cause lots of damage. We have had a severe drought for the last three and a half years."

"True. But I will miss them."

While they chatted, breaking news came on. "Jan Metz with Channel 6 news. A massive earthquake has hit Jerusalem. The 6.2 Richter scale earthquake had its epicenter a half of a kilometer east of the Mount of Olives. Ten percent of the city is in ruins and the number of casualties has been estimated in the thousands. Many First Responders are on the scene to give medical attention to the injured. Rescue teams are in search of people trapped. Most of the damage occurred in the business district along Jaffa Street."

The camera switched to another reporter. "Tina Levy, with Special Edition News. This earthquake occurred within one hour after the prophets Moses and Elijah rose from the dead and went into Heaven. Talk of them is trending high on social media throughout the world. And now a story from our religious editor, Lillian Gibson."

The camera switched to Miss Gibson.

"Many in Jerusalem accuse Nist of murdering the Two Witnesses. They claim this earthquake is God's retribution for their deaths. Many people in Jerusalem are afraid of a new disaster at any moment. Tonight at 7:00, there will be a three-member panel discussing Nist's handling of this incident. They will be, Charles Whitley, a professor of Comparative Religion from Columbia University, Dr. Dawid Lutz, a rabbi from Poland, and Cardinal O'Malley from the New York diocese."

"This morning, a new page appeared on our website featuring pictures and videos of the Two Witnesses. Today it has had over 118,000 hits. Look for the link entitled, "Moses and Elijah." If you have any photos or videos of them, please upload them to our website. Lillian Gibson, Channel 6 news."

***

That night, Nist heard TV reporters criticize him about the way he handled the two prophets. They also blamed him for the earthquake. Nist called Mallon Karth on his office phone. When Mallon answered, Nist didn't even greet him. He shouted at him. "Why are the media outlets broadcasting bad news about me?"

"What do you mean?"

"They are blaming me for the earthquake since I eliminated those two prophets. Why did they get away with broadcasting that?"

"Do you want to clamp down on them?"

"By all means. Do what it takes. And be harsh with them. Threaten. Have a few people fired. Make some heads roll. *Now.*"

Nist slammed his phone.

***

Mallon Karth felt Nist's wrath and might feel more if he didn't stop the criticism. He called the World Peace Organization's legal advisor Clute McKenzie to discuss ways to restrict the media.

***

The day after the Jerusalem earthquake, about half of Nist's office staff did not report to work, so Nist had to clean his own office.

He picked up items from the floor the earthquake had shaken from his desk. While picking them up, he noticed photos taken on the day of the Big Reveal. He saw photos of the Orthodox Jews spitting at him.

Nist called for Sean Prussia on his cell. He asked, "Where are you? I need you in my office now. Can you be here by 10:00 a.m.?"

Sean replied, "I'm three floors below you. I rode my bicycle this morning."

"Come to my office, I need you to find out something for me."

"I'll be there in a 'sec'."

A few minutes later, Sean entered Nist's office.

Nist shook the photo in his hand. "Here is a little bit of unfinished business. These are the Jews who mocked me at the Temple when my image came alive. Where are they?"

"I don't know, but I can find out. I have contacts who knew them."

Nist glared at Sean. His eyes burned in anger. "Do that *now*. And when you find out, let me know right then. I want to know where they went and I want to make an example of them. *Now*."

Nist emphasized his statement by slamming his fist on his desk. Sean, who hadn't seen this side of Nist, hurried back to his own office.

Four hours later, Nist got a call from Sean.

Nist said, "Yes?"

"I have it on good word they went to Petra."

"Good." Then he hung up and dialed another number.

"General Kane? This is Charti Nist. .... I've heard the Jews who defied me are hiding at Petra. Do you know where that is? ... Good. I want you to wipe them out today. Got it? ... I want them to spend a long time dying. ... Good. Let me know when the job is done. I want this on the late evening news." Nist hung up.

***

The Jews at Petra spotted General Kane, ten trucks full of soldiers, and six tanks approaching them. They prayed for a miracle. A voice from Heaven spoke out to Rabbi Solomon at Petra and said, "Be calm and watch. You are about to witness that miracle."

The rabbi shouted, "I received a good word from the Lord. He told us to be calm and watch for a miracle."

Rabbi Solomon's son said, "We need one about now."

They watched the troops approach.

Before the tanks got in range, the earth opened up and swallowed the six tanks and the ten trucks. Then the ground closed. The Jews cheered.

***

Nist called the general but didn't get an answer. He called the army base, intending to fire the general. "Give me General Kane now. ... No word? ... You can't find him? Well, find him and let me know within an hour."

Thirty-five minutes passed and Nist received a call.

Nist answered, "Hello?"

His eyes grew big.

After a couple of minutes, he said, "Well, send out more troops to Petra. Call me back when the job is done."

Nist called Stile and asked her to come into his office.

She entered and saw his face. "What is wrong?"

"I don't know. General Kane is gone and so are the six tanks, ten trucks and all the soldiers in them. No one can find them. I told them to send out more soldiers and to report back when the job is done."

Nist stared out into space with a puzzled look on his face. Stile brought glass of wine into his office to calm him. She talked to him while he waited on the phone call.

Two hours passed and Nist received another call.

Nist answered, "Hello? ... Oh, never mind. Just forget them." Nist shoved his phone off the desk.

Stile asked, "What happened now?"

"Major Balboa followed behind them to watch. He said the second set of troops disappeared. The earth opened up and swallowed them. He almost fell into the same crevice. I don't believe it."

Nist continued griping. "Well at least those rebels are out of my face. As long as they stay where they are I'm fine. They better not show their faces here in Jerusalem."

Stile picked up Nist's phone, put it on his desk, and returned to her office.

Nist stared into space and tapped a pen on his desk. He did not know what else to do.

Thirty-Nine

The Three Angels and Their Messages

<u>The First Angel preaches the Gospel to the entire Earth</u>

An angel motioned for John and the Elder to follow him. He led them outside of the Throne Room. It was the same place they saw the image of the woman with the twelve stars. From there, they could see all the way to the Earth.

The angel looked at them and said, "Witness the three angels and their messages for those who remain on the earth. The merciful God is giving fair warning to them in a way they can't miss. Watch it and write what you see and hear."

Another angel took off behind them and flew toward the Earth.

The first angel shouted like thunder. "Fear God and give glory to him; for the hour of his judgment is come: and worship him that made heaven, and earth, and the sea, and the fountains of waters."

John said to the Elder, "Wow. No one on Earth can say they didn't hear him. Will they be able to understand his language?"

"People will hear his message in their own language. And he is giving his message to everyone during the noon hour."

Second Angel proclaims Babylon destroyed

Then John saw the second angel fly toward Earth. He also proclaimed his message in each time zone at noon.

The second angel shouted, "Babylon is fallen, is fallen, that great city, because she made all nations drink of the wine of the wrath of her fornication."

John looked at the Elder and said, "Is Babylon already destroyed? Did I miss something?"

The Elder explained, "No, but it will happen soon. It has been declared in the heavens. Babylon's destruction has been prophesied."

"These angels left ten minutes ago. Did the people on Earth hear these two messages in the same hour?"

"No, the angel visits will be a day apart from each other. 'Time' is not the same on Earth as it is in Heaven. These angel visits will happen a week apart instead of a few minutes apart like you saw. By spreading out the messages, people will have time to grasp the importance of these messages."

The Third Angel Gives His Warning

Then John saw a third angel take off toward the Earth.

John thought, "What a merciful God we have. He is giving them every possible chance to repent, giving every warning needed."

The third angel made his announcement throughout the Earth.

"If any man worship the beast and his image, and receive his mark in his forehead, or in his hand, the same shall drink of the wine of the wrath of God, which is poured out without mixture into the cup of his indignation; and he shall be tormented with fire and brimstone in the presence of the holy angels, and in the presence of the Lamb: And the smoke of their torment ascendeth up forever and ever: and they have no rest day nor night, who worship the beast and his image, and whosoever receiveth the mark of his name. Here is the patience of the saints: here are they that keep the commandments of God, and the faith of Jesus."

After the third angel delivered his message, a voice from Heaven spoke to John. It said, "Write, Blessed are the dead which die in the Lord from henceforth: Yea, saith the Spirit, that they may rest from their labours; and their works do follow them."

John went back to his desk and wrote what he saw and heard. He wondered how many of them would heed the last angel's message.

Forty

Decisions, Decisions

In mid-September, four years since the Great Disappearance, people at Chicago's Buckingham Park enjoyed a warm, summer day. Kids played in the spectacular fountain while their moms enjoyed watching them have fun. Because of the sun's reduced output, the heat was pleasant.

Two young ladies sat on a park bench near the fountain watching their children play. They were neighbors in Oak Park.

A large electronic billboard flashed its messages to people in the park. The message alternated between several ads: One "Where are my kids?" ad, and six "Got Mark?" ads, and one 'SafeChild Plus' ad.

The first "Got Mark?" ad showed a model smiling and with the mark on her forehead, and her escort had it on his right hand. The next ad showed the reverse: the woman with the mark on her right hand and her boyfriend's mark on his forehead. The next ad showed the "American Gothic" couple. Both of them had their mark on their foreheads. The next ad showed a couple and both of them had it on their right hands. The next ad showed a couple and both had their marks on their foreheads. The 'Where are my kids?' ad showed police rescuing a kidnapped child. The next ad showed, 'SafeChild Plus: Find

Your Children by our child location program, available on your home computer for only ×9.99 international currency units (ICUs) a month'. The last of the series of ads showed a person so full of tattoos he only had room on his forehead for his mark.

The ads on the electronic billboard made them laugh.

Joyce said, "What a nice day. It is pleasant to be outside today. It's a little cooler than usual, but I guess that will change when the sun decides to shine as it should."

Her friend Marta said, "Yes, and thank goodness there haven't been any monster insects for about two years."

"You can say that again. I hurt for five months when I got stung and wanted to die because of the pain. That will always be in my memory."

"I remember the pain, too."

"Those bugs plagued us for six months. This is the first time I've ventured outside with my kids since."

Joyce asked, "Have you heard any more about those unexplained killing sprees?

"No, I haven't. I think the last of them occurred two months ago in Kuwait. Thank goodness that has stopped, too."

The ladies stared at the kids playing in the fountain for a few minutes.

Marta broke the silence and asked Joyce a question. "Have you gotten your appointment card?"

"For what?"

"Your identity mark."

"Oh, *that* appointment. Yes, it came in the mail last week. I thought you were talking about my OB-GYN appointment. I might be pregnant again."

"That's wonderful. But when is your other appointment?"

"In December, I think."

Marta asked, "Where are you going to get yours done? Are you going to choose your forehead or right hand?"

"My right hand. It might get in the way of my hair style if I had to get scanned from my forehead. Where are you going to get your mark?"

Marta crossed her arms and said, "I don't want to get it at all."

Joyce looked at Marta. "Well, you'd better get it. You will starve if you don't. You will be considered unpatriotic to the world community. Besides, you will be able to track your kids."

"I don't care. I've been worried about the angel who told us not to get the mark. I don't want to go to hell. I'm creeped out even when the county fair wants to stamp our right hands with their temporary pass."

"Well, I don't know about Heaven or Hell. But I do know you will be in trouble, and so will your kids. Do you want your kids to go hungry? Do you want them banned from schools?"

"Of course not. But I want to think about my options. I've heard of survivalists who refuse to get the mark. They're hiding in the woods with four years of supplies. They have underground homes, lots of guns and ammunition, medical supplies, and are ready for almost anything. Don't you remember the people who bought underground shelters in 2012?"

"Why did they do that?"

"It was the Mayan 'end of the world' thing."

"Oh, yeah. Now I remember. But why four years of supplies?"

"They have measured time since the Great Disappearance. They say the world will end in seven years from that event. There is less than four years until that time. Maybe closer to three years."

Joyce rolled her eyes. "You don't believe that, do you? Those 'end of the world' people have never been right. We are still here, aren't we? You'd better get with it and keep your appointment. You might be able to hold out for yourself, but you'd better not put your kids in danger."

"But it won't do any good if we all go to hell."

Joyce looked irritated. "Look, I've had it with this hell talk. Sure, the last couple of years have been terrible. But don't jeopardize your future and your kids' future with this religious hogwash."

"Well, I'll think about it. That angel sounded pretty serious. We all heard it, you know."

Joyce wanted to change the subject. She looked at her watch. "Well, it is about time for me to gather my kids and head home. I've got to prepare a special dinner tonight."

***

John the Apostle watched this scene from Heaven. When it was over, he heard another voice from Heaven. It said, "Write, Blessed are the dead which die in the Lord from henceforth: Yea, saith the Spirit, that they may rest from their labours; and their works do follow them."

John dipped his quill into the inkwell and wrote what the voice told him. He wondered what life would be like for those who disobeyed the warning messages and received the mark.

Forty-One

So Much Better

Dorian Janus was a native Southern Californian. He worked at a saddle factory in East Los Angeles. He had curly black hair and a handlebar moustache, measured 6'5" in height, and weighed 156 pounds. Before he left his home, he brushed his hair in front of the bathroom mirror. His smile revealed a missing front tooth. He wore his best worn-out jeans, and a white round-neck T-shirt.

The appointment for his identity mark arrived in March five years after the Great Disappearance. He chose to get his mark on his forehead. The employee at the Identity Centers entered his social security number, bank information, and other identity information into the new system. The computer generated his new identity number. They put his driver's license into a shredding machine.

A week later, the government retrofitted his car and his house to respond to his mark. He no longer needed keys.

The following Saturday, he went grocery shopping. He left home with no wallet, no car keys, and no house keys. The front door locked after he left, and his car door opened for him as he approached it. He pressed the button to start his car and punched in the store's destination code. His car drove him there and parked in the closest available space.

When Dorian exited his car and shut the door, it automatically locked.

At the front of the store, he selected a buggy from the outdoor rack. An LCD display on the handle showed his total amount in dollars and International Currency Units.

He walked through the aisles in search of his weekly needs. He bought a bag of oranges, rye bread, cereal, cheese crackers, a salad mix, light bulbs, frozen yogurt, two pizzas, shaving cream, orange juice, eggs, barbeque sauce, hamburger patties, buns, and a case of bottled water. When he placed items in the cart, the LCD display showed the cumulative amount of his groceries.

The store had no cashiers. A scanner read his mark and a monitor above him displayed his name, his picture, and the total amount of his groceries. It also thanked him for his business. Because the computer kept a record of his purchases, he didn't need a receipt if he needed to return any items.

His car unlocked when he approached. He still had to press a button to open his trunk. He unloaded his groceries. The buggy gently beeped until Dorian returned it to the rack.

He sat in the driver's seat of his car, entered his home's destination code and his car drove him home. When he arrived home, his front door unlocked. He unloaded his groceries and watched TV while he planned his activities for the rest of the day.

He could go where he pleased without carrying any cash with him. Even vending machines scanned his mark, so he didn't need a card or cash to buy a candy bar.

He knew the option for debit cards, credit cards, and cash expired in another year and didn't care. He couldn't do a bank statement anyway.

Forty-Two

Dealing with Rebellion

A year's time passed since the "Big Reveal". Back in Jerusalem, the people who worked at the World Peace Organization headquarters had plenty to do. Phones rang, and people had deadlines to make.

Nist called Mallon Karth into his office for a status update. When he entered, Nist saw the look on his face and said, "What's the matter?"

"We have a rebellion on our hands. One nation in particular: Germany."

"I know. What are they doing?"

"They don't like your control over them and are demonstrating against you. They are hanging effigies of you and the whole country is in a mood to do away with you. Rumors are afloat that they are printing their own money again and making coins."

"We can't have them doing that, can we? What percentage of Germans have my mark?"

Mallon checked his paperwork. "About 97.5 percent. It is the highest percentage in Europe."

Nist grinned. "Great. Now it is time to kill one of the heads of Europe." He picked up the phone and dialed a number.

Nist said, "Cancel all of Germany's authorizations. Cut off all citizens of Germany no matter where they are. Cut their electricity and stop fuel shipments there right now."

Nist hung up. He looked at Mallon and said, "We shall see how long this little rebellion lasts."

Mallon said, "Call me if you need me."

He left Nist's office.

Nist focused on the CNN feed in his office. He leaned back in his chair and put his feet on the desk. He asked Stile to bring him two glasses and some wine.

A few hours later, he heard the story he had waited for.

"Xiang Wing, CNN news, Frankfurt. Germany is in rebellion and Nist has ordered the country shut down. All of Germany is in a panic. Business transactions have been stopped. No goods can be purchased, and water and electricity have been turned off. Also, banks have closed, ATMs shut down, and transportation services stopped. Every computer network in the country is down. Citizens of Germany are rioting in the streets and demanding action from their government."

The buzzer on Nist's intercom sounded. He answered, "Yes?"

Stile said, "You have a call from the Chancellor of Germany."

Nist smiled. "Put him through on line 1." He pressed line 1 on his phone and said, "Hello?"

After listening for a couple of minutes, he laughed. "No, you can't get out of the system once you get in. Why do you even ask? ... Yes, I can bring you back into existence in about five minutes. I can if I want to. ... Okay. Go on TV and tell the world who your savior is. And stop your little rebellion. Printing money is a serious offense. You'll have to stop that, too. Then I'll bring Germany back into existence."

He hung up his phone and continued watching the news. The news bulletin he waited for came through three hours later. Nist picked up his phone and dialed a number. When someone answered, he said, "Put Germany back online now. They've learned their lesson." Then he hung up and continued to watch TV.

After a little thought, he dialed another number and said, "Send more troops to Germany and find their coin minting and money printing presses. Destroy them and kill the people running them. Also kill everyone who has been in those buildings in the last three months."

Nist called Stile back into his office.

She asked, "What have you done?"

"I killed a nation, and then brought it back to life. Am I great or what?"

"Did you need to order the deaths of the people printing the money?"

"Of course. People have to learn what it means to cross me."

***

Another year passed. Five years and six months had elapsed since the Great Disappearance.

Nist looked at his calendar and said, "Stile, get Mallon Karth back in here. I have something for him to do."

"Right away, Charti."

Nist couldn't wait for Mallon to return to his office. He put his feet on his desk and played with a letter opener until he heard the intercom buzz. He answered Stile's call. "Yes?"

"Mallon is here."

"Send him in."

Mallon entered and Nist pointed to the chair in front of his desk. "Sit there. I've got a new task for you."

"What is it?"

Nist put his feet on the floor and stared at Mallon. "Isn't my mark required for business now?"

"Tomorrow."

"Good enough. What percentage of people worldwide has my mark?"

"Not as high as you'd like. Only 27 percent."

Nist growled at Mallon. "I thought you told me Germany had 97 percent. What's wrong with the rest of the world?"

"In Europe, your mark is popular, but it isn't that way in the Americas, Asia or in Australia. In those regions, many people have set up bartering networks to get around your requirement. They cashed in their money a day before your deadline for precious metals or desirable items to exchange for food and services."

Nist's face grew redder. He waved his finger at Mallon and said, "That percentage is way too low. I need to put some fear into not having it. I know what to do. Hire some killers as enforcers with broad swords capable of chopping off heads. Have them go out in teams of six men, roving the malls and streets of every country seeking people not loyal to me. Instruct them to behead disloyal people in public. Leave the dead bodies in the streets or malls or wherever. Have the videos played every night on the news. I'm tired of being Mr. Nice Guy. Send out the teams tomorrow. Start with the capital cities first and then spread out."

Nist stared at Mallon without saying anything to make his words have a stronger effect.

Mallon said, "I see. I know who I can enlist. It won't be a problem. And it will accelerate the number of people taking your mark. I'll give those fanatics passes for airlines and other forms of transportation."

"Good. Now get out of here and get busy."

***

Channel 6 News appeared on the Jumbotron screen at Times Square at 7:00 p.m. The opening story consisted of the first execution of people without Nist's mark.

Jan Metz, the Channel 6 International News anchor gave her story. "As of today, marking is required by Nist's World Peace Organization. Today's victims, who failed to comply with the new law, were shoppers at the Shops at 2000 Penn. It is a mall five blocks from the White House. They were the first victims of the roving fanatics sent by Nist.

They are authorized to execute anyone not having his mark on either their forehead of right hand."

The video of the beheading of the entire family played. The fanatics seized a family of four at gunpoint and examined their hands and foreheads. When no marks were found, they were executed, beginning with the youngest to the oldest. The fanatics held the young girl by the head and lowered her onto a chopping block. The mother's screams filled the mall as she begged for the lives of her children. The fanatics ignored her. It took several hacks to sever the girl's head while the rest of the family watched. The boy was next, followed by the mother and the father. Their bodies were left in a pool of their own blood.

The fanatics had their heads and faces covered, and showed the blood on their broad swords to the camera as they walked off in search of their next victims.

Jan continued her story. "These executions will continue until the entire population of the planet complies with this rule."

The camera focused on Jan's forehead, the site of her identity mark.

Shoppers without their marks fled Times Square. Many of the shoppers threw up on the street while watching the video. All left feeling sickened.

The video continued to broadcast on a loop for the rest of the night.

The next day long lines of people waited outside of the Identity Centers to get their marks.

***

John felt sick after watching the execution. He was sad for the people who would be killed, but angry that more people took the mark of Nist. He knew that not all people who refused to take the mark were saved.

Forty-Three

The Second

An angel led John out of the Throne Room again. An awesome sight awaited him. He saw Jesus sitting on a huge throne. No, He sat on a *cloud*. And this cloud nearly filled the sky. Jesus wore a gold crown and had a sharp sickle in His hand.

An angel came out of the Temple, flew over John's head and approached Jesus. He shouted to Jesus, "Thrust in thy sickle, and reap: for the time is come for thee to reap; for the harvest of the earth is ripe."

Jesus passed His sickle over the Earth and reaped it. People saved since the Great Disappearance shot into the air from the Earth. They moved like lightning past the moon and the planets at an incredible speed and arrived in Heaven in seconds.

John saw the new arrivals. He recognized many: the Indians from South America, Vasily, Steve Hubbard the tourist, Brad Huron, his wife Elsa, and the team of scientists Brad worked with, and Tara from the Space Needle.

He also saw Abraham approaching the new arrivals.

***

This Disappearance also caused much panic in the world. Millions disappeared leaving the planet full of crashed planes, trains, and cars. The panic wasn't near as big as the one caused by the Great Disappearance a few years ago.

The event occurred at 3:32 a.m. New York time. People not asleep at that time woke up to news that kept them at home glued to their TVs. Scenes of disaster filled the planet and the casualty count mounted.

***

Retirees George Royal and Wayne Brown met for coffee several times a week. Since they lived a mere four blocks from Vasily's store, George would meet Wayne at his apartment and walk together from there. They arrived at 9:00 a.m., but Vasily's shop wasn't open. Other regulars came by, but didn't wait long before leaving.

George asked Wayne, "I wonder what has happened to old Vasily? Did he die? I haven't checked the obituaries today."

Wayne said, "I haven't read them either. I read them when I get a cup of coffee. Vasily is entitled to a sick day every now and then. He runs the whole store by himself. I don't know how he does it. I've often told him he needs to hire some help. 'Get a cute girl to help you ring up sales', I told him. But does he listen? No."

"Do you know of another coffee and bagel shop?"

"Yes, and it is a few blocks away. It is not near as good as Vasily's. It's called The Big Apple Deli."

George said, "Let's go anyway. Maybe Vasily will be back tomorrow."

"Okay. Let's walk. It is not too far away and the day seems pleasant. Even for August."

They walked toward the Big Apple Deli.

After walking a whole city block, George stopped and said, "Hey, listen to the noises of the city."

Wayne strained to hear something. "I don't hear anything. Maybe I need a new battery in my hearing aid."

"No, that's it. There *isn't* any noise. I wonder what happened."

"I don't know. I haven't turned on my TV or read the paper yet. Maybe something is going on we don't know about yet. We will hear about it on the news when we get to the Big Apple Deli. They have a TV, too."

"Let's go."

When they arrived, they placed their order and sat. Wayne was right. The Big Apple Deli's bagels were tough and their coffee tasted bad.

Ray said, "I'm going to get something else. This bagel is too tough. See if you can find the obituaries in this paper."

Ray ordered two cappuccinos while Wayne cleaned his hearing aid. The TV news came on when Ray returned.

"Good morning. I'm Tina Levy with Channel 6 News, Special Edition."

A large poster appeared behind Tina. It said, "The Great Disappearance" with a hand-painted red "2" across the letters.

"Yes, another Disappearance happened while we slept this morning. Millions of citizens from all nations have disappeared. Accidents resulting from vehicles without drivers and planes without pilots have occurred again."

"Because there were fewer people traveling, there were fewer plane crashes, train wrecks, and car accidents. Because of FEMA training, we were more prepared for this disaster. Still, casualties in the thousands occurred here in the New York City area.

"The township in Greater New York City area with the greatest damage is Flushing, near LaGuardia airport. Several planes failed to land properly and crashed into the surrounding neighborhoods. EMTs and rescue workers are taking care of the injured and transporting bodies to local morgues. Area hospitals are at full capacity. If any trained medical person is able to travel to this area, they can be put to work. And now to Dean Braxton with Channel 6 Local News."

"New York City's three major airports are closed. JFK, LaGuardia, and Newark are all in shambles. Damaged aircraft litter the runway. Smaller airports have been closed for twenty-four hours. Several subway trains collided last night bringing the Metro system to a standstill."

The monitor behind Dean showed the runway at JFK airport littered with crashed planes, fire trucks, and ambulances. Covered-up bodies lay near the wreckage.

"Many roads are impassible because of the accidents that occurred last night. The mayor requests non-emergency personnel stay home today to reduce confusion and keep the roads clear for emergency vehicles. And now, Ronnie Einstein, our Science News anchor."

"No good reason for the missing millions has been given by our governments. Scientists are at an equal loss to explain it, too. One scientist, Professor Jack Danby at Oregon University suggests that aliens abducted the missing millions. Dr. Danby, who experienced an alien abduction twenty-eight years ago, says they have returned with a vengeance and may return soon to populate the planet. He claims they took the people off the planet to make room for themselves. One prominent person has a different explanation of this event. With that story, Jan Metz with International News."

The camera switched to Jan. "Eftas Helpphor, spiritual advisor to Charti Nist, has his explanation of the millions who disappeared last night."

A video of Eftas appeared. "I am the one responsible for the disappearance. My magic sent them to Hell. If you know someone who vanished, you will realize they were one of those religious zealots. We have been eager to remove such people. You know my magic is effective, because nobody opposes us now. The world will soon see what we can do without these people. Be reassured all is well, in spite of the current difficulties. Within a few weeks, this will be all but forgotten."

Jan Metz returned to the screen. "Do you think his explanation is believable? Please visit our website and take our survey. Let us know if you believe either Dr. Danby or Eftas Helpphor. Perhaps you think nobody has a good explanation. Vote, and at 5:00 p.m., we will show the winner of today's 'Golden Bull' award. And now to our weather…"

Ray and Wayne shook their heads. Ray said, "I guess I've been out of touch since I retired. I didn't even think anything was wrong when I didn't see any traffic this morning. I must listen to my radio or TV more often."

***

The Elder said to John, "There are now no more followers of God left on the earth. Great and terrible judgments are coming quickly, with an emphasis on 'terrible'.

John asked, "Why did God remove all believers from the planet again?"

"I told you. It is judgment time. But not for God's family."

"Do you mean all the things I've seen *weren't* judgment?"

"I should have said time for *wrath*. You will understand what I mean soon." The Elder motioned for John to follow him.

Forty-Four

Preparation for Wrath

John noticed an angel coming out of the Temple and another one coming from the Altar. The second angel had power over fire. Both angels took off together and flew toward the Earth. They flew with great speed. When they approached the earth, they slowed.

The angel who controlled fire shouted, "Thrust in thy sharp sickle, and gather the clusters of the vine of the earth; for her grapes are fully ripe."

The other angel flew off and harvested the grapes of wrath from the Earth. After harvesting, he placed them in a winepress and squeezed them. Great drops of wrath fell on Earth.

John eyes grew big as he saw blood rise in a deep valley two hundred miles long to the height of a horse's bridle.

The Elder pointed and said, "What you have seen is a dreadful sign. Those who live on the Earth will taste God's wrath in full strength. There will be enough death to fill this valley with blood. The judgments so far have been bad. Now they will get much worse."

John wrote what he saw and heard.

Forty-Five

The Bowls of Wrath

John noticed fire underneath the crystal floor of the Throne Room. God gave the arrivals from the Second Disappearance a harp to play.

They sang out the song of Moses, and the Song of the Lamb. "Great and marvelous are thy works, Lord God Almighty; just and true are thy ways, thou King of saints. Who shall not fear thee, O Lord, and glorify thy name? for thou only art holy: for all nations shall come and worship before thee; for thy judgments are made manifest."

John saw the door of the Tabernacle of the Testimony open, and a brilliant light came from it. From that light, seven more angels emerged wearing white robes with a band of gold around their chests. Each of them carried a gold bowl, each of which contained a judgment from God.

Two angels brought in a table and placed it in front of God's Throne. The angels placed their bowls on the table.

The "Eagle" beast stood, and walked to the table. He picked up the bowls, one by one, and gave them to the angels. John still was not used to these strange creatures having human behaviors.

After the angels received their bowls, John noticed that the Temple filled with smoke and the glory of God.

John heard a great voice out of the Temple shout out to the seven angels. It said, "Go your ways, and pour out the vials of the wrath of God upon the Earth." He wrote what the voice uttered and waited to see what the bowls of wrath contained.

Forty-Six

The First Bowl – Sores

The first angel took off with his bowl and flew toward the Earth. Pus and bacteria filled his bowl. After he passed the Moon, he tossed the contents of his bowl toward the Earth. When it hit the atmosphere of the Earth, it scattered into a brown mist and covered the whole earth.

***

On a warm, September morning, six years after the Great Disappearance, Gene Gregory in Brooklyn prepared himself for work. In the bathroom mirror, he noticed a slight stinging and redness on his right hand. His mark was infected.

Later he left his home and took a bus to the subway. The subway car had "Got Mark?" ads on the inside. He noticed redness on other people's marks. A few people had pus oozing out of their marks. Others had blood-stained bandages covering theirs. He decided to stop at the Big Apple Deli since Vasily's shop closed.

Gene ordered dark-roast coffee and an onion bagel and sat at his table to watch the news. He winced after taking one sip of his coffee and spit it out. He thought, "Varnish remover tastes better."

He waved to the manager and said, "What am I going to drink with this bagel? I can't drink this coffee."

The manager asked, "What's wrong with it?"

"It seems to be a bit strong."

"Do you want something else?"

"I'll have a caramel macchiato."

"Okay. It will take about two minutes."

Gene looked around and saw other patrons with the same sores. Grimaces of pain were on many faces.

Two minutes later, his macchiato arrived and he had something to go with his bagel. He tried to relax as he watched the news on the TV.

The Channel 6 news was on and Jan Metz was in the middle of her story. She had a small bandage over the mark on her forehead. Gene could tell she was in pain.

"Charti Nist's massive, thirty-foot image is touring the world. Carried on a military cargo plane, he has gone to India today to be worshipped. His two-week stay will include the cities of New Delhi, Calcutta, and Bombay. Later, he will be moving on to Bangladesh, Thailand, and several other Asian nations."

The display behind Jan showed masses of people in India bowing in worship to the image.

"In three months, he will make his tour of the United States and Great Britain. And now to Nate Perkins, our weather anchor…"

Gene decided to leave and go to work. He also decided to seek out a better coffee shop.

***

Katish Raut, the chief engineer hired by Eftas Helpphor, flew out from Simi Valley, California to Nagpur, India. He had routine maintenance and repairs to do. After his arrival there in the middle of the night, he drove a rented car to a converted airplane hangar. Nist's security team had secured the area and restricted entry. He arrived and the soldiers at the gate verified his identity before he entered.

A large flat-bed truck surrounded by troops entered the complex. The warehouse doors opened and the truck drove in. The thirty-foot image of Charti Nist lay covered on the flat-bed truck. A crane hoisted the image into place on the floor. It lay on its back. Technicians gathered around.

Katish saw the team of technicians and approached them. Among them, he recognized his friend Asok. "Long time, no see. How are you doing, Asok?"

"Great, except that my mark is infected. And you?"

"I'm doing okay. What's on the list today?"

"It is the image's 10,000 mile service job. The seams near the left elbow joint are starting to come apart. I will repair them."

Jagadish said, "I will clean the servos and oil the joints."

Gopi said, "The eye movements are a little off. I'm going to upload the latest bug fix to correct those eye movements."

He removed a plate under the right armpit of the image and plugged wires into the exposed USB ports. He connected it to his laptop and uploaded the software fix. His laptop tested the eye movements. The test sequence opened and closed the eyes and updated the blink interval to something more realistic.

Katish said, "This is one expensive robot. The service fees alone are making us rich. It should last another four years before it needs replacing."

Jagadish said, "It sure looks like Nist."

Gopi replied, "It should. He paid plenty for it."

***

Gene Gregory left work at 5:00 p.m. The street lights came on at 4:00 p.m. even though the black disk of the sun was visible.

He entered a drug store and looked for salve to soothe infected mark on his right hand. He found the shelf empty. He searched the store and found an employee. Her name tag said "Tasha". The mark on her forehead was covered by a bandage.

Gene asked, "Do you have any antibacterial cream in the back?"

"No. We are out for now. We have been cleaned out since 3:00 p.m., but we should get some in on the truck tomorrow."

"But I need it now."

"I'm sorry we don't have it. I'm not a doctor, and our clinic is closed for a couple of weeks. Maybe you can try something like isopropyl alcohol."

"What?"

"Rubbing alcohol. It may sting a bit, but it will clean it out. I hope. At least, I think it will."

"What about the pain?"

"Try ibuprophen. It worked for me."

"Okay. I'll buy some. I'm not sure I have any at home."

Gene purchased the ibuprophen and a Coke to chug the pills.

***

At midnight in Manhattan, two friends, Drew and Carl, waited at a street corner for the light to change. The street lights cast their shadows on the pavement. They both looked at the scanner above them that recorded their movements.

Drew said, "I hate those scanners. They are everywhere now. They are on every street corner, every city building, every store, every gas station, every restaurant, and every bar. It is like *1984*."

Carl saw a puzzled look on Drew's face. "1984? What do you mean by that?"

"You know, the book by George Orwell."

"No, I don't know."

"Never mind."

Drew asked, "Doesn't the government have anything better to do than spy on us?"

"I think that is the business they are in. I don't know how I got talked into getting this mark on my forehead in the first place. Things haven't gotten any better, have they?"

"No, they haven't. Not only that, I'm getting angry at paying ×10 ICU a month for a 'monitoring fee'. It's not enough they track my movements over the planet, but then charge me ×10 ICU a month to boot. I bet it is a real money-making racket. I pay them to snoop on me. How wrong is that? Along with my wife and two kids, it takes ×40 ICU's a month out of my budget."

Carl said, "Yes, I found that on my monthly statement, too. Burns you up, doesn't it? To think how much money they are making on, let's for say for the two billion people still alive, that's 20 billion ICUs a month, and 240 billion a year. I didn't even ask for it. It just appeared on my bank statement. There isn't a number to call to even ask about it, thanks to Nist."

Drew and Carl saw several gaunt and bearded men on the opposite corner. They had posters saying, "The End Is Near", "Repent", and "The End of the World is NOW". People looked at them as they passed by. These survivalists refused to take the World ID mark and lived by their wits and careful planning.

Drew pointed, "Look at those idiots with the posters."

"Yeah, but look at us. We're in pain and they aren't. They refused to take the mark."

"Lots of people still refuse to take the mark on religious grounds. The Orthodox Jews are the largest group. Those guys with the signs are "survivalists". In all likelihood they have food, guns and ammo hidden somewhere."

"Shouldn't we report them?"

"Why? I say leave them alone. They've got guts to stick it out. I shouldn't call them idiots, I envy them. These last few years have been hell with or without the mark. I'm also tired of seeing people beheaded in my neighborhood by those thugs Nist hired."

"Don't you know."

"I'd have a drink now if I could find a good club."

Drew responded, "You stink."

Carl said, "You do too."

They both laughed.

Carl said, "My mark is oozing pus. I need to clean it and get some pain relief."

Drew pointed across the street. "Why don't we get a drink at the Paris Café Club?"

"No, there is one two doors down, The Algerian Connection. I like it better."

Drew noticed a new club across the street, "Look at the name of that club, The Gaza Strip."

"Yes, let's go there and get a drink. At least liquor is a commodity that hasn't become scarce since this whole mess started."

They entered the Gaza Strip and sat at the bar.

The bartender approached. He looked like a retired wrestler - bald, with gray stubble on his cheeks, white shirt, suspenders and a bow tie. He asked, "What do boys want?"

Carl said, "Scotch."

Drew added, "Me too."

The bartender sniffed, "You know you both stink. There is a dispenser with antibacterial soap over there you can use on those sores."

Drew asked, "Have you tried it?"

"Yeah. It keeps you from stinking. But it still hurts. Clean off your foreheads so I can scan your marks."

Drew and Carl cleaned their marks and the bartender scanned their foreheads. The flashing lights made the men wince.

Carl said, "Don't you hate that thing in our eyes night and day. It makes me wish for the old days of keys, credit cards and coins. At least you didn't have to get flashed in the eyes ten times a day. Scanners give me a headache."

Drew said the bartender, "Where are the girls?"

"What girls?"

"You know, the name of this club is The Gaza Strip."

"I know the name of this club. It is the name the owners gave it. Other than the girls you see at the bar, there aren't any."

"Why not?"

"With the way TV and the Internet are these days, the owners felt there is too much competition. They didn't want to deal with it."

Drew and Carl shrugged at each other and drank.

Forty-Seven

The Second Bowl – Bloody Seas

The Atlantic turned into blood almost five years ago. Blood had spread to Antarctic (Southern) Ocean and the western edge of the Indian Ocean.

John saw the second angel leave Heaven with his bowl of wrath. The angel flew toward the Earth, entered the atmosphere, and hovered over the Pacific.

The angel poured out the contents of his bowl into the ocean. All of the world's oceans turned into blood in four hours. Millions of dead fish floated to the surface.

***

In a West Side apartment, a Ray and Nellie Franklin turned on their TV for the seven o'clock news.

Ray said, "The news anchors look awful tonight. Look at their outfits."

Nellie said, "Their outfits look awful because you are in your late sixties and they are not. Don't you want to watch reruns? I know what the news does to you."

"I'll tell you what. If there is another disaster, I'll change the channel." He tuned in Channel 6.

"Good Evening. I am Wally Mason, and my partner is Harry Guest. We are sitting in for vacationing Mirek Trinka and Ronnie Einstein. Overnight, the Pacific Ocean has turned into blood. Millions of dead fish are floating on the surface of the world's oceans. If our scientists don't find a solution for this, an important part of our food supply may soon be extinct. We have no official cause of this latest disaster and many opinions abound. Harry?"

"Many scientists blame this on global warming and the world's changing weather patterns. Pollutants are thrown into the ocean by all nations, oil spills from the large number of sunken ships, and the acid poisoning from five years ago may have caused the chemical reaction that created this red fluid. The truth is our world leader has relaxed business rules for dumping waste in the world's oceans and this is the result.

"In another story, scientists haven't yet found a cure for the identity mark sores. The doctors need more time because the plague seems to defy analysis. They have been working at it night and day for two months now. Many people have removed their marks and RFID chips by visiting unauthorized doctors, in spite of severe penalties from the World Peace Organization headquarters. And now, back to Wally."

"Channel 6 has two recommendations. The first is to carry antiseptic wipes in foil packages for your sores. Second, buy as much bottled water as you can. Since the world's oceans have turned into blood, it may be a matter of time before other sources of water such as springs become polluted. Scientists have petitioned the world government to allow mining the fresh water reserves frozen in the polar caps."

Ray looked at Nellie and said, "Okay, okay. I'll change the channel. But first, how many containers do we have that we can fill with water?"

Nellie said, "I don't know right off the bat."

"Well, find what you can and I will fill them with water and store them in the hall closet. When we fill all we can, we'll watch some reruns."

"I'd rather watch the night sky. There won't be any advertisements. Come to think of it, that *thing* in the sky is still there. I want it to go away."

"Me, too."

They filled any usable container in their apartment with drinking water.

When they looked out of their balcony window, they stared at the image of God. Both of them wondered what might happen next. They didn't have to wait long.

Forty-Eight

The Third Bowl – More Blood

John looked at the bowl prepared for the third angel. A brown, smoky vapor came out of it. John also noticed this bowl had a dropper apparatus on the side. The top cover prevented the contents from spilling out.

He thought, "I'd hate to be holding *that* bowl."

Like the others before him, the angel took off from the Throne Room and headed toward the Earth. He landed on the ground and squeezed a drop into a sparkling spring. Blood poured out of the spring. Moving rapidly, he made his rounds to the rivers and springs of the entire planet. A drop in the Mississippi, a drop in the Potomac, a drop in each of the Great Lakes, a drop into Lake Okeechobee, and a drop in the Great Salt Lake. They all turned into blood. The angel hurried off to Canada, Europe, Russia, Asia, Australia, Central and South America, then to Africa. The polar caps turned red as they became frozen blood. This occurred two months after the oceans turned to blood.

After this angel completed his job, he flew into the sky in sight of all people. "Thou art righteous, O Lord, which art, and wast, and shalt be, because thou hast judged thus. For they have shed the blood of saints and prophets, and thou hast given them blood to drink; for they are worthy."

John, in the Throne Room, heard a voice from out of the Altar saying, "Even so, Lord God Almighty, true and righteous are thy judgments." John picked up his quill and wrote what he saw and heard.

***

In Topeka, Kansas, Debbie and Lynn encountered each other in the grocery store parking lot. The chilly January winds whipped around them as they loaded their trunks with bottled water.

Debbie said, "What a mess inside the store. We fought for water bottles. I can't believe we did that."

"My neighbors warned us before they disappeared about these disasters and we didn't believe them. Now, this is all the water we can find. I dare not say to anyone else that I have twenty cases of water in my basement."

"We do too. But I seem to stay thirsty all the time. I can't think of much else except rationing out the water my husband and I have left. We have a water distillation unit, but it clogs with blood if we try to purify tap water."

"I haven't taken a shower in three days. I don't know how much longer I can hold out."

"Me neither. I must stink by now. I'd take a dip in the river if it weren't frozen or filled with blood."

"I wish my husband was still here. Or rather, I wish I had gone with him. He went in the second Disappearance. He resisted getting his mark. I did manage to cash in his stock portfolio, but I don't know how long I will last before having to go out and get a job."

"How much longer do you think the earth will last? How much more of this can we take?"

"I have no idea. I hope I live long enough to find out."

Forty-Nine

The Fourth Bowl – A Burning Plague

The Apostle John saw the fourth angel's bowl. Yellow smoke and sparks rose out of it. It bubbled and contained a fluid with blobs of red, purple, and yellow.

The fourth angel flew out with his bowl. He headed past the earth at a high rate of speed. He passed the SOHO satellite and caused it to spin. He stopped halfway between the Earth and the Sun and hurled the contents of his bowl at the sun.

The fluid penetrated the "skin" of the sun and disappeared. The deep rumble of the sun's violence increased. The sun's output multiplied.

***

The University of Arizona hired a new research staff at the Kitt Peak solar observatory and appointed Dr. Ronald Krim to head the new team. He knew Brad Huron well and kept familiar with his findings. Brad and his entire staff vanished after the second disappearance.

The first week on the job, he hired two solar physicists, Anders Sorenson and Stan Garrett. Other positions at the lab remained open, waiting on qualified personnel.

Dr. Krim inherited Brad Huron's instruction manual, which saved him weeks of tedious discovery. He knew what every computer in the lab monitored and how to work the video connections.

Anders Sorenson and Dr. Krim monitored the sun's brightness. Anders shook his right hand to ease the pain of his mark. His bandage showed blood oozing through.

Dr. Krim said, "You'd better change your bandage."

Anders accessed the SOHO satellite and noticed the sun brightening. He took a quick look at the clock on the wall. It was 3:54 p.m.

Anders said, "Dr. Krim, come here. The SOHO satellite shows the sun's radiation increasing. That could be a good thing."

"Put those images on the big screen."

When the images appeared, Dr. Krim and Anders studied them.

"Anders, what is the actual level of radiation? The sun looks like it is several times normal output."

The images on the big screen went blank. Several of the monitors in the lab went blank at the same time.

Anders said, "What happened? Let me check the telemetry stream."

He checked the telemetry stream coming from the satellite. "The SOHO satellite isn't broadcasting anymore. Something has gone wrong."

"Let us check the visual telescope using the McMath telescope. It isn't electronic."

Dr. Krim and Anders went down the elevator to the focal plane where the image of the sun appeared.

After checking, Dr. Krim said, "Uh oh. It looks like the sun is at several times normal intensity. SOHO may have been fried with this blast. This is *not* good news."

The pair of scientists returned to the lab. They searched for Stan.

Dr. Krim approached Stan and said, "Something has happened to the sun. From what we can see via the McMath telescope, the sun is outputting at several times normal radiation. We think the SOHO satellite is fried. We aren't receiving any telemetry from it."

Stan said, "Let me access another satellite."

He typed in commands on his computer. After a couple of minutes, he said, "The satellite I accessed shows this solar blast has enough power to fry power grids all over the world, and could kill people. I say we call our families before this blast hits cell phone transmissions and tell them to stay indoors. Or should we call the media first?"

Anders said, "There may not be enough time for either. I'm calling my family first."

Dr. Krim called his wife on his cell phone. When she answered, he said, "Hi there, honey. I'll be quick and to the point. You need to stay indoors, and get all the kids inside. *Now.* There's going to be a real hot blast from the sun and it will hit within minutes. Do it now."

His connection went silent.

He used a land line and called the local news agency and informed them of the impending crisis. Then he called scientists in Washington to get advice.

Dr. Krim told Anders and Stan, "You two better call your parents before you do anything else."

After making a few phone calls, Anders said, "Stan, turn on the news while I call the power companies. They will need the warning. This blast will hit the Earth in a few minutes. We'll watch TV until this event hits the news networks. Let's enjoy the air conditioning while we can."

Stan Garrett looked out the window. The sunlight intensified. In spite of being in the middle of March, the vegetation outside the lab wilted. Then he turned on the news.

Anders joined Dr. Krim and Stan in the employee's lounge after calling the power companies. They sat and waited for the news. They didn't wait long.

"This is Eric Boulder with Action8 News, Tucson. This is an emergency warning. The intensity of the sun's energy has increased to several times normal. Please stay indoors. If you are outside, please seek shelter now. People outdoors are in serious danger of severe burns, heat stroke, and other heat-related problems. Hospitals have been put on the alert and all media outlets are warning people to come indoors or seek shelter until the sun goes down. Again, you are advised to stay indoors and go outside only in an emergency until dark. The sun did not turn black at 4:00 p.m. today as it has for the last four years and ten months. Sunset should be around 6:54 p.m. The power companies have been notified of the impending disaster. Fortunately, it is March and not June or July."

***

Jorge and Juan Castaldo and their families picked strawberries in Southern California. Short-day strawberries ripened in March and burst with flavor. The cooler weather for the last few years made Jorge and Juan feel cold. They loved Mexico's hot sun. At 2:54 p.m. California time, the sun brightened several times normal. The heat felt good at first.

Juan said, "I feel like I'm back in Mexico. The sun is hot again."

They worked another hour picking strawberries.

Carlos, Juan's son collapsed in the field. Juan ran to help Carlos. His son had burns on his face. He called his wife, Carmelita to help take him into the barn.

Carmelita called to her daughters. "Get into the car. It is time to get out of the sun."

The girls got into the car and waited. Carlos' mother gave him some cold water, but he seemed delirious. She said, "I think we need to take him to the hospital. He is not doing well. Our daughters look scorched, too."

Juan agreed. "They are not used to this hot sun. Let's take them to the hospital."

The whole family got in the car and drove toward the hospital.

Halfway there, Carmelita said, "Turn the air conditioner on. It is hot in the car."

"It is on but doesn't seem to be working. Maybe it is too hot outside."

They arrived at the emergency room. Medics treated Carlos for burns and heat exhaustion.

Dozens of people came into the emergency room with severe burns. The victims included people working in backyard gardens, fishing in boats offshore, picnickers, landscapers, migrant workers, construction workers and policemen on their beat. People who tried to shield themselves from the sun arrived at the hospital with burned arms.

Carmelita and Juan watched the news in the emergency room waiting area.

"Candy Bushnell with SouthCal News. Eighteen people are dead because of heat-related issues in the last hour. Emergency rooms are filled with burn victims from the scorching sun. Most of them were migrant workers and people fishing on boats in area lakes. People in the open are in danger of severe burns and heat exhaustion. If you are outdoors, please seek shelter now. If you are indoors, please remain there until the sun goes down. The current temperature in the city is 114 degrees."

"The unseasonal heat has put a demand on the power grid for air conditioning. Power companies are advising they may not be able to keep up with the demand because of the intensity of solar radiation. Many Southwest Power customers are already without electricity."

"Many communication satellites are not working and cell phone networks are intermittent. Scientists report auroras as far south as Mexico City…"

A doctor at the hospital returned Carlos to his parents in the waiting room. He said, "Carlos has a few burns, but they aren't serious. He will be okay in a couple of days. Keep him hydrated and check the dressing on his burns. Bring him back here if anything goes wrong. Stay here in the waiting room until the sun goes down. We have free snacks available in the break room over there."

Juan and Carmelita thanked the doctor. When he left, the happy parents hugged Carlos.

Fifty

The Fifth Bowl – Darkness on the Beast's Throne

The Fifth angel left the Throne Room and went to Nist's headquarters in Jerusalem and poured out his bowl full of judgment. It looked like India ink.

Stile adjusted to the hot sun by working at night. While updating Nist's appointments, she heard the sound of breaking glass coming from his office.

Stile went into his office. Broken glass covered the floor. Nist broke eight TV monitors with bookends, paperweights, books, decorations and anything else he could get his hands on. Only one monitor remained intact. Sweat covered Nist's face and he had a wild look.

"What's going on? Why are you throwing things around your office?"

"I'm so angry."

"So I noticed. What has made you this way?"

"I am trying to rule the world. All of these disasters are causing panic and more rebellion."

"Why don't you get Eftas to make up a reason for these disasters and have a press conference or something?"

"Eftas is making me mad, too. Everyone is making fun of his statements. Nobody believes him anymore. I look stupid because I can't explain what is going on."

"Well, why don't you complete your temper tantrum by taking a bite out of the rug?"

Stile's last comment startled Nist.

Nist laughed at himself. "Maybe I will. I did make a fool of myself." He looked at the broken monitors and the glass on the floor. He buried his face in his hands for a minute. After regaining his composure, he asked, "What should I do?"

"Face these problems. Take them on, the same way you take on any other challenge. I don't think you need Eftas as much as you think you do. He's alright and I like him, but I don't think you need him."

"No, I still need him. For a while longer, perhaps. What I'm really mad about is that think tank I hired. They never told me what to do about these types of disasters. I don't think any other ruler had to solve these kinds of problems."

Stile said, "I think if you put your mind to it, you can find a way to use them to your advantage. Take on these challenges. You aren't a coward."

A knock on the door interrupted their conversation.

Nist asked, "Who is it?"

"Mallon Karth."

"Come in."

Stile said, "Its time I left. Let me know if you need a drink or something." Then she left.

***

Mallon entered Nist's office. Nist scowled at him and said, "What do you want?"

Mallon did his best to ignore the broken glass and damaged monitors. He did not know how Nist might act in this state of mind and thought about leaving. He decided to tell Nist the bad news. "There are several things I need to talk with you about."

"Like what?"

"Well, first of all, many of the religious leaders in Babylon are telling people in the world not to take your mark, but to take theirs instead."

Nist' face turned red. He slammed his fist on the desk. "What? After all I've done for that lazy, good for nothing crowd? Who is responsible in particular?"

"If you are asking my opinion, all of them. I came back from Babylon yesterday and none of them are working on your new one-world religion."

"What *are* they doing then?"

"They have brought out all kind of idols for people to worship other than your image and are sponsoring Black Arts classes."

Nist's face twisted. "Eftas isn't teaching those classes, is he?"

"No, he is not. I found out something else. The western religious leaders are critical of the former European nations for deserting them. They threaten them with hell if they don't attend their churches again. Most of them claim the sun's heat is judgment from God and that *you* are to blame for it. The Far East religious leaders are outright seditious and tell their people to stay with the old gods and to oppose you. They are all interfering with you in one way or another."

Nist screamed, "How dare they do this. They will have hell to pay."

He drummed his fingers on his desk and stared out of his window. Mallon waited for Nist's anger to cool.

Nist finally said, "Is there anything else you need to tell me?"

"Yes, there is. A lot of interns are quitting. They are simply not showing up for work. Some haven't adjusted to working during the night and the sun's behavior is scaring others. The sores around their marks are driving them crazy, too. The disasters we've seen are out of proportion with 'normal' ones and they don't think they will live another year. Not only that, the public executions you ordered are making them hate you."

Nist picked up a bookend and threw it at the remaining computer monitor and shattered it. Veins poked out of his forehead. He shook his fist at Mallon. "I didn't pay them to THINK. That's my job. I pay them to file things, run errands, and plug things in the wall. Now get out of here. I can do what I want."

Karth left. As he exited, Karl Willut, Nist's Latin American advisor, entered.

Nist scowled. "What do you want?

"Most of South America is in rebellion."

"Tell me something I don't know. Did you do what I told you to do?"

Karl said, "Yes. We turned them off like we turned off Germany, Belarus, Kazakhstan, the Republic of Georgia, and Afghanistan, but it isn't working. They have cut their network connections and destroyed the transmitters and receivers. We can't cut their electricity now. And their financial transactions are not coming through. They resent someone having as much authority over them as you do and have killed the majority of your troops there. It's the South American *machismo*. And their former religious leaders in Babylon encourage them."

Nist's face grew redder.

"How is this happening? How can they do this? How can they not worship me? I will need about an hour. Come back and I'll tell you what I will do."

"Okay." He looked at the clock on the wall. It was 4:54 p.m. Then he left Nist's office.

***

Gene Gregory, at last, found a good coffee shop in Brooklyn. He found out about it on the internet and decided to visit the store on the way home. The Bagel Castle had a huge selection of bagels and coffees. It did not take long for Gene to make it his favorite breakfast stop.

The owner, Murray Roth, loved his patrons. When Gene entered, he said, "You are new here. What do you like?"

Gene responded, "A pumpernickel bagel lightly toasted with peanut butter on the side and vanilla hazelnut coffee."

Murray responded, "I'll get them for you. Sit at this table."

When Murray returned with his order, Gene paid by passing his hand under the scanner. The steaming coffee tasted good. In spite of the heat and tough times, he remained optimistic. He felt the end of the plagues was near and that life could resume. The afternoon news showed on the TV.

"Good afternoon. I'm Dr. Kees Vorhees, with Channel 6 Medical News. Seven months have passed since people's identity marks became infected. President Callaghan assigned this problem to Dr. Andrew Reiner of the CDC in Atlanta, Georgia. We sent our associate reporter, Myron Kelly, to interview him. Myron, are you there?"

"Yes I am, Dr. Vorhees." Myron held his microphone to Dr. Reiner and asked, "Do you know the reason for these sores around our marks?"

Dr. Reiner said, "We don't at this point. We started our research six months ago. We think there are three possibilities. First of all, the transfer method of the tattoo may have allowed bacteria under the skin. Second, the inks used may be more reactive than other tattoo inks. And third, there is a possibility the lithium battery in the implanted GPS chips may have leaked. Any of these possibilities could cause this reaction."

"How long will it take you to find a solution, and how fast will it be made available to the public?"

"No real way of telling. We will keep you informed, though. It doesn't look like it will take a long time to figure out."

"You heard it from me, Myron Kelley, Channel 6 associate reporting LIVE from the CDC in Atlanta, Georgia. Now, back to Tina Levy with Special Edition News."

The camera changed to show Tina Levy in the Channel 6 studio. "President Callaghan has met with business leaders all over the country. In order to allow for safer working conditions, he has asked businesses to reverse working hours. That is, day hours to night hours."

A graphic appeared behind Tina showing a night sky outside an office window.

"People will report to work at 8:00 p.m. instead of 8:00 a.m., and get off work around 4:00 a.m. or 5:00 a.m. This will allow business to continue to operate and workers will be safer while commuting. Businesses are not required to do this, but are asked to. Any business which depends on daylight can opt out of this plan. This shift in hours will be effective tomorrow."

The good news encouraged Gene. He liked drinking coffee at night. The news of an imminent cure encouraged him.

**

About an hour later, Nist called Karl on the intercom. "Come to my office. I have something to tell you."

When Karl Willut entered Nist's office, he found the floor swept and the broken monitors replaced. Nist grinned and had his feet propped up on his desk. He looked calm.

Nist said, "Please sit."

Karl sat and asked, "Well, what have you decided to do?"

"I'm going to test the power of a neutron bomb on them."

Karl's jaw dropped and he turned pale. "On all of South America?"

Nist picked up his phone and dialed a number.

Nist spoke, "The General, please. ... How soon can you launch a neutron bomb attack on the South American rebels? ... How many do we need to cover the whole continent? ... Will that wipe out of all of South America? ... Okay. ... Send them all on their way. ... Yes, *now.*"

Nist hung up. Nist seemed rather calm. Karl's mouth hung open.

"Don't be a codfish and close your mouth. The South Americans have a half an hour before they meet their doom. Most will die in twenty-four hours. At most, forty-eight, and they will all be dead. *That's how you deal with rebellion.* The good news is there won't be any significant radioactive fallout. We still have over 100 neutron bombs in inventory and three new ones are made each month. Isn't that nice? You may go now."

Karl stood to leave.

Nist stopped him and said, "Oh, one more question."

"Yes?"

"About what percentage of the remaining population has my mark?"

"It has jumped up to 83 percent."

Nist pretended to be surprised, "Only 83 percent? Do I have to get tough with you to get the job done? Do I have to send out more beheading teams?"

Nist could see the look of fear on Karl's face.

Karl said, "We are doing the best we can. But we have been getting no cooperation with the Far East countries. The survivalists have fled into the wilderness with supplies, tents, hiding in caves, digging underground hideouts. Your death patrols are beheading many people in front of TV cameras to intensify the fear. They are doing their best to keep pace with their job."

"Who is resisting the most?"

"The Jewish people. They say their religion forbids them to have tattoos and refuse to take your mark. Other people are getting survival tips and being paid by the religious leaders in Babylon. They are using funds you gave them to help those people hide from you."

Nist screamed, "How are they eating? Oh, never mind. Get out of here and quit bothering me with details. I've had it with those religious people in Babylon."

Karl ran out of Nist's office.

***

Workers walked at Times Square near midnight. The new lunch hour started at 11:00 p.m., and ended at 2:00 a.m. Channel 6 news flashed on the Jumbotron. Jan Metz, the Channel 6 International News anchor had red eyes.

"Good evening. I'm Jan Metz with Channel 6 International News. One hour ago, Nist ordered the destruction of the entire population of South America. Over 100 neutron bombs wiped out all life on the continent. According to Nist, the rebellion of South America earned this punishment. They cut computer connections, destroyed the satellite linkups on the ground, and killed his troops.

"There will be no relief efforts. From Columbia in the north to Argentina in the south, the entire population is dead or dying. They are not expected to live longer than 48 hours at most. An insignificant amount of radioactive fallout will be produced according to Nist's spokesman."

"Our thoughts and prayers are with the people of South America."

Silence fell over the crowd at Times Square.

***

Three days later, a couple in their late 60s, Edward and Anna watched the TV news on their backyard patio. They enjoyed the cool night air. The bandages on their right hands showed traces of blood.

Edward said, "Thank God it is Saturday. I don't have to go to work tonight or tomorrow night. I'm still not used to working at night and trying to sleep during the day. It is May and the days are getting longer now. Let's turn on the news."

His wife Anna said, "I hate watching the news. It gets worse each day. It seems when things couldn't get worse, they do."

Edward turned on the TV to the Channel 6 News.

"Jan Metz reporting for Channel 6, breaking news. The sudden rebellion of Egypt and Russia and their allies have been defeated by the World Army. In a bold move, Nist's enemies moved a massive number of troops toward the World Peace Organization headquarters in Jerusalem."

"Nist responded by wiping the oncoming Egyptian and Russian military machines with tactical neutron bombs. The entire Egyptian army in the Sinai Peninsula is dead or dying, and there are few survivors of the Russian alliance to the north. Both Moscow and Cairo received a series of neutron bombs as a final blow to the invaders."

Edward turned off the TV.

"That's enough news for tonight."

Fifty-One

Time Off

The next day, Nist noticed Stile had her head on her desk as he came into the building.

"What's the matter, Stile?"

"I'm about to drop. I haven't had any time off in three years. I need a break."

"Yes, you do. I'll tell you what. I'll put ×500,000 ICU's in your account. I want you to take a vacation. Go someplace you've never been before. Get drunk. Party. Spend money. Buy clothes. Misbehave. And don't tell me where you are going. I want you to have some wonderful stories to tell me when I get back. Please stay out of the trouble spots of the world."

"I think I'll take you up on that."

"Is your Gold card still working?"

"Yes, it is. Thanks for not requiring me to get your mark. That makes just me and Eftas the only ones who are exempt."

"How could I do that to you, Stile?"

Stile pointed at him and said, "And you can't do it to Eftas because he conferred 'powers' on you."

"Let's not talk about Eftas. Take my private jet and go anywhere you want. Go home and pack your bags." He gave her a gentle hug.

Nist picked up his phone and requested his private jet be made ready for Stile. "Thanks. I'll see you when I get back."

Stile picked up her purse and left.

Fifty-Two

Far East Solution

Nist demanded Eftas to come to Jerusalem. He wanted some answers about the religious leaders in Babylon and he wanted an answer face to face.

When he arrived, Nist's temper exploded. Veins stood out on his forehead and his eyes glared. He screamed, "Why are those religious leaders getting away with the undermining my objectives?"

Eftas stood and kept his cool. He raised an eyebrow and said, "You have kept me too busy with other projects to manage them myself. It takes time to get such a diverse group to work together. I have allowed them this freedom for only a little while. You forget that Muslims, Catholics, Protestants, and all the smaller religions have never worked together. The new religion is in the works."

Nist face reddened. He waved his finger at Eftas and yelled, "But they helping people bypass my system. I want that stopped *today* as well as encouraging people not to worship me or my image."

Eftas replied, "If you wish I will do so. Did you call me here just for that?"

The veins in Nist's forehead disappeared. He said, "No. I've got to do something about the Far Eastern alliances. My military advisors tell me China, Japan, India and Korea are thinking of using massive force to oppose me. I've still got plenty of neutron and nuclear bombs. If they make their move, I can wipe them out. I am thinking of bombing that highway coming westward from China."

Eftas thought for a minute before he responded. "Maybe we should devise a plan to prevent that from happening. Let us meditate for a while. We get good ideas while meditating. And I know you like the drugs."

"You are right. I need to relax a bit. Let's get on with it."

They went to Eftas' recreation area. Nist took his coat and tie off and sat on several cushions. Eftas lit a few sticks of incense.

They inhaled the powerful drugs in the hookah. Nist went into a trance. His eyes rolled into his head. He breathed out a smoky cloud in the air above him. The smoke formed into an ugly, froglike demon. Helpphor also breathed out a smoke cloud which became another frog-like demon. A dragon demon writhing above their heads belched out a cloud of smoke which formed into a larger frog-like demon. These three demons rose into the air and headed toward the Far East countries.

***

The demons moved faster as they traveled. These spirits hovered over the Far East nations before descending and possessed the national leaders.

***

When the drug session ended Nist said, "I feel much better. Did you get any ideas?"

"No. Not yet. But I am relaxed. What about you?"

"The only thing I can think of is to find a common enemy and get them to join the fight. That will put off ideas of non-cooperation until we can think of something more lasting. I'm sure a plan will form soon. Good night. I mean 'Good morning.'"

Nist returned to the apartment below his building and went to sleep.

***

The next day, an object appeared approaching the earth from behind Moon. Nist wondered if he could turn it into an "alien invasion", so he called his science advisor, Darrin Denton, to get information on it.

When Darrin answered his phone, he said, "Darrin, you have a degree in astrophysics. Tell me what you know about the object approaching the Earth."

"I've been observing it via the space telescope. I have an appointment to call Dr. Albright at the university observatory in an hour to find out more. He is in seven time zones behind us in New York, so I'll have to wait until 4:00 p.m. or so."

"Well, do that and get back with me before you leave today." Nist ended the call.

***

Darrin called the Cornell University observatory at Ithaca, New York.

When Dr. Albright answered, Darrin said, "Do you have any more information on the object in space I e-mailed you about?"

"Yes, I do. I know it is not a comet, meteor or an asteroid. It is making independent movements. I also found some type of an electromagnetic shield around the object. Also, it radiates heat at 37 degrees, Celsius."

"That's body temperature, isn't it? Is it energy being reflected from the sun?"

"No. It is coming from the object itself."

"Is it alive?"

"It could be."

Darrin took notes while he talked.

Dr. Albright asked, "Anything else?"

"How big is it?"

"It is hard to tell. It seems a bit fluid. It is solid, but it flows."

"Is it a spaceship?"

"No. I'm sure it isn't. It is bigger than a spaceship."

Darrin heard a beeping noise.

Dr. Albright said, "Hold on for a second. My computer has some new information."

He checked his computer and said, "It looks like it stopped moving for the moment."

Darrin tapped his pen on his desk and thought. He asked, "What does radar reveal?"

"I find bits of metal reflection on radar. I can't figure out the surface of the object. The electromagnetic shield that covers it interferes with analysis. It does seem to have density above water, but barely. It doesn't make sense. If it is a transport of extra-terrestrial beings, it is beyond our technology."

Darrin leaned back in his chair. "How powerful is the electromagnetic shield? What is it made of?"

Dr. Albright thought for a minute and said, "I think it is made of pure electricity."

"Pure electricity? How could that be?"

"I don't know how, but that's my analysis."

"Is it intelligent?"

Dr. Albright considered his answer. "I'm going to catch some flak from my colleagues for saying this, but I think so. It can move, stop, and make lateral movements."

"Is it hostile?"

"I don't have enough information to determine that."

Darrin heard a beeping noise over the phone.

Dr. Albright said, "My alarm went off. The object is moving again. It is approaching Earth again."

"At its present speed, how long will it take to get here?"

"Wait a minute while I calculate."

Dr. Albright worked his calculator. "At its current rate of speed, to get to the upper regions of our atmosphere, it will take about twenty-one days. It is on a projected path to northern Israel."

"Northern Israel? Can you call me if you make any further discoveries? Like where it is going and if it changes its current course?"

"Yes, I can. I'll keep you posted of any changes. I'll let you know by e-mail of its projected arrival area about twice a day. Call me if you have any more questions."

"Thanks, Dr. Albright. I'll keep in touch. Bye for now."

***

Darrin went to Nist's office. After being seated, he said, "I've got some interesting things to tell you."

Nist said, "Go on."

Darrin opened his tablet and read from his notes. "The object in space is covered with an electromagnetic shield which limits analysis, but radar shows bits of metal. It is radiating heat, but only ninety-eight degrees, Fahrenheit. That's body temperature. It is very long and moving at forty-seven miles per hour. It will take three weeks at its present speed to get here."

Nist looked bored from the science lesson. His chin rested in his left hand and he played with his pen with his right hand. After Darrin finished he asked, "Is its speed constant?"

"Yes and no. When it is moving, it is constant, but it has stopped a few times. Its project arrival point is in northern Israel."

Nist asked, "Is it intelligent?"

"Dr. Albright at the university observatory seems to think it may be alive."

Darrin saw Nist smile when he heard that.

Nist put down his pen and said, "So it is alive, huh? Maybe I should gather the entire World Army to fight this invader and invite the Far East armies to fight with us."

"Why? It has shown no signs of hostility yet."

"But it pays to be prepared."

"Don't you have enough firepower without inviting the Far East armies?"

"That is not the issue. Fighting this thing from outer space could unite the world. I've been looking for a way to get more influence over the Far East and this could work. Don't you agree?"

Darrin leaned forward. "No I don't, and I'll tell you why. It is dangerous for too many forces to be too close together and the Far Eastern countries still don't like us. They need to be won over before I would be willing to fight beside them."

"You may be right. But there are more important issues here. I need them to participate in this fight against the invader from space. It will make them feel closer to the world community. You may go now."

Darrin rose and left the office.

***

Nist called Mallon Karth on his cell phone. "Come here. I need you right now."

In a couple of minutes Mallon Karth entered Nist's office.

Nist asked, "Is there a place in Israel big enough to hold an enormous number of troops?

Mallon put his tablet on Nist's desk and accessed a geographical map of Israel. He pointed to a particular location. "Yes. It is a bit north of here. It's called the Megiddo Valley. I've been there. Napoleon described it as the perfect battlefield. It is wide open. The Christian Bible calls it 'Armageddon', which is 'Valley of Megiddo' in Greek."

"Interesting. I will tell the commanding general to assemble the armies there. I'll meet them when they get there and decide what to do then."

"There is one major roadblock for the Eastern armies. The Euphrates River."

"Not my concern. You may go now. Keep your cell phone handy."

Mallon Karth left Nist's office.

***

Nist picked up his phone and called his commanding general, Sommy Hassad. After greeting him, Nist said, "Call the leaders of China, Japan and India. Request they join forces with us to fight these invaders from space. Request that they meet us in two weeks."

General Hassad objected. "But they don't like us. That is dangerous move."

"Are you disobeying me?"

"I'm giving you proper advisement."

Nist raised his voice. "This is a political decision. Do whatever it takes to make it work. Is that clear?"

"Yes it is. I don't know how wise it is, but the order is clear. Where should the armies meet?"

"In the Megiddo Valley."

General Hassad said, "I know the place. It is a good choice. Many battles have been fought there. I'll call them now."

Fifty-Three

The Sixth Bowl – Drying Up the Euphrates

John saw the sixth angel take off with his bowl of judgment. He headed for Iraq and poured out his bowl into the Euphrates River. The river receded and left a red stain in its path.

The Far East armies approached the Euphrates River with hundreds of mobile bridges to provide a path for their troop carriers, tanks, and missile launchers. When the troops tossed the first ten bridges in the water, the river subsided. The mobile bridges lay on the wet sand. In a mere ten minutes, the mighty Euphrates River stopped flowing. The military equipment ran full speed on the riverbed toward Israel.

In the War Room, Nist, Mallon Karth, and several advisors monitored troop movements.

Mallon Karth got a call on his cell phone. After a short conversation, he ended the call. "I have good news about the Far East armies."

Nist said, "If it's good news, tell us."

"My aide has been in contact with the leaders of India, China, and Japan. For some reason, they seem unusually cooperative. They, too, have seen the object in space and are worried about what to do. It seems their attitude has come around overnight."

"How nice. I wonder how that happened."

Nist called Eftas Helpphor on his phone. When he answered, Nist said, "I'm sending a helicopter to Babylon to pick you up. I need you now. Drop whatever you are doing."

Eftas said, "I'm in the middle of dinner now."

"I don't care. I need you now."

"As you wish. I will be at the heliport near my building in ten minutes."

Nist hung up.

Mallon's cell phone rang. He answered it and listened. After the call Mallon said, "I have more good news. We've received notice that the Euphrates is drying up."

Nist asked, "Did someone turn the switch at Atatürk dam in Turkey?"

"No. The river level is lowering. It seems nature is cooperating with you."

Nist called General Hassad in the field. "Tell the Far East Armies the Euphrates is drying up. ... Oh, they are aware of it? ... Well, good."

***

Nist's phone rang. The caller ID showed 'Darrin Denton'. He answered his phone and asked, "Do you have an update on the approaching object?"

"Yes. For now it has stopped its approach. It is halfway between the Earth and the Moon."

"Let me know when it moves again." Nist ended the call.

Fifty-Four

The Seventh Bowl – Armageddon

George Royal and Wayne Brown met at the Bagel Castle at sunset since Vasily's shop closed. George said, "This coffee is almost as good as Vasily's. I'm glad your friend Gene told us about this coffee shop."

Wayne said, "It was a year ago that Vasily and those other people disappeared. Time flies, doesn't it?"

"A year already? Wow. Time does fly."

"Let's get our bagels and coffee and watch the news. Let's hear what they are saying about the alien invaders."

"I'm Ronnie Einstein with Channel 6 News. Observatories and scientists around the globe report that the mysterious object approaching the Earth has stopped."

Ronnie's right hand had a small blood stain showing through his bandage.

"The invading object from space stopped mid-way between the Moon and the Earth. On the display behind me is the best photo we can obtain. Even with our best technology, we still can't determine its exact nature. The surrounding electromagnetic shield prevents further analysis. You are advised not to panic. Please stay tuned to this station for further developments. And now, Jan Metz, our International News anchor, with her story from Israel."

"The World Army has gathered in the Megiddo Valley in northern Israel. General Sommy Hassad arrived there today, prepared to meet the oncoming invaders from space. Massive sun shades are set up for the troops and they are wearing heavy goggles to protect their eyes from the sun's heightened output. The Far Eastern armies crossed the Euphrates River two hours ago and will join the World Army in a few hours."

George and Wayne shook their heads. George said, "Invaders from space, can you believe it? What next? An invasion of rabid Easter bunnies?"

***

George and Wayne talked for several hours. A news flash interrupted their conversation.

"Jan Metz with Channel 6 News with a breaking story. The meeting of the Far East armies and the World Army has erupted in heavy fighting. Thousands of casualties have been suffered by both sides. The eastern armies opened fire on the World Army within two miles of the Megiddo Valley."

On the display behind Jan, live scenes of the intense battle raged.

"General Hassad has launched a full attack on the Far East armies, but hasn't used his most powerful weapons because they are too close to his own troops. Bombs meant to kill troops from the Far East armies could kill his own troops. We will transfer to our reporter in Israel, David Lowe, at the edge of the battle area. Are you there, David?"

"Yes, Jan, I'm here. The battle is raging seventeen miles from here. The Far East armies used the opportunity to attack the World Army. Nist is watching the battle in a bunker at an undisclosed location."

George and Wayne stayed at the Bagel Castle all night watching the progress of the battle.

***

Eleven hours later, the battle ended. Both armies lost 90 percent of their soldiers. Thousands of bodies filled the Megiddo Valley.

General Hassad survived. He walked around the valley with his sunshade seeing nothing but dead bodies. He saw Charti Nist emerge from a helicopter and walked to the landing area.

Nist saw him and said, "Well, congratulations, General. That takes care of the Far East armies. It will take them a while to get over the loss of their entire army. I don't think that there is much fight left in them now. We kicked butt today, didn't we?"

General Hassad glared at Nist and said nothing.

Nist said, "I know the soldiers are tired, but they have to stay here. The object in space started moving again. That's why we came here in the first place. I'm going back to Jerusalem, but I'll be back when it arrives."

The general didn't complain and watched Nist's helicopter leave. Battle fatigue filled the surviving soldiers. Most of them suffered the loss of many of their friends. They grieved and watched the blood, already ankle deep, rise.

Nist returned to the War Room.

***

Back in the Throne Room of Heaven, John looked at the contents of the seventh angel's bowl. It contained large hailstones, pieces of metal shaped like lightning bolts, and clay balls that contained thunder.

The seventh angel emptied his bowl above the Earth's atmosphere. John heard a loud voice come from the throne: "IT IS DONE."

When the contents of the bowl reached the ground, a violent lightning storm erupted. Thick clouds covered the whole planet. Deep voices came from the sky.

A fierce lightning, hail, and wind storm ensued.

An *hour-long* earthquake shook the Earth.

Fifty-Five

The Brick Makers

On their land near Coffeyville, Kansas, brick makers Rita and Danny Platka surveyed the wreckage of their old farm house. Last night's earthquake leveled it. The sky was clear and at 8:00 a.m., the thermometer showed seventy degrees. The high for the day was going to be 128 degrees, so they worked while they could. They did not work at night like everybody else.

Danny wore overalls, steel-toe shoes and no shirt. His wore a Kansas City Royals baseball cap. His red beard nearly matched the color of Rita's hair. Rita wore a new pair of jeans and a University of Missouri t-shirt. She put on her St. Louis Cardinals baseball cap.

Rita said, "The house is gone and our barn is almost destroyed. But we still have our supplies intact and our underground shelter is strong."

Danny said, "I'll check on our forklift and backhoe."

He spent a half hour clearing debris from his equipment. Danny pressed the start button and they both fired up. Neither machine suffered any damage.

"Now, I'll check on my inventory of bricks."

Rita said, "I've already checked them. They are okay. No broken bricks. We'll have to stack them again."

"That's okay. I probably need to start a few more batches of bricks. With the damage the earthquake did, I'll be getting orders tomorrow. Help me turn the sunshield back on its feet."

Rita said, "I hope none of our friends were hurt."

The couple stood the sunshield in its proper position over Danny's workbench.

"Plug the lights back into that socket, and help me put my workbench right-side up."

The couple re-organized their workspace.

A truck drove up to their property. The driver parked and approached.

Danny said, "Well, I'll be. It is our neighbor Cameron Floyd. How are you doing?"

Cameron said, "You appear to be in a happy mood today. Other than cleaning up after last night's massive earthquake, what is going on?"

Danny laughed. "I'm just picking up the pieces."

Rita said, "And not a lot of pieces to pick up."

Danny asked, "What's the city look like? Are a lot of people hurt?"

Cameron said, "The whole town is on the streets. They are going house to house taking survivors out of the wreckage. So far, no deaths. Strange, isn't it? It seems after an earthquake that long that somebody should have been killed."

Danny said, "I'm glad. So, what are you doing here?"

"I've come to get my order of bricks."

"Got my groceries?"

"Yes, I do."

Cameron uncovered the bed of his truck. Rita came over with her list to check the items off.

Rita said, "Okay. Let's see. Two boxes of .38 ammo, one hundred pounds of ninety-two percent ground beef, ten boxes of baking soda, twenty gallons of diesel fuel, three cartons of AA batteries, three cases of soda, five jars of peanut butter, five boxes of teabags, five loaves of pumpernickel bread, five loaves of sourdough bread, five loaves of whole wheat bread, and a bottle of moisturizer."

Danny said, "I'll get my forklift and unload these supplies and load up your order of bricks."

Danny adjusted the forklift's sunshade and unloaded his food supplies and left them under his workshop's sunshade. Then he collected Cameron's order and loaded the bricks on his truck.

Cameron said, "What is this network of three-inch, black PVC pipes I brought you last time? You've got them connected all over your yard."

"That's my passive source of hot water. I pump water in it and the sun heats it. My well water goes into the acid-water treatment apparatus, then into these pipes for heating. I've got all the hot water I need."

"I can't believe a redneck like you could think of something like this. Everyone else is grumbling about the sun's heat. Especially since it is August."

Danny saw a cockroach on the ground and spit at it. "Got him."

Cameron said, "Wow. And he was eight feet away. Your aim has improved."

"Thanks. Not only that, but since bricks cure in half the time, it will be a real money-maker for me."

"Except that you don't make money. You barter for food and supplies. Why don't you take your mark like the rest of us?"

"I don't want somebody on the other side of the world telling me what to do."

"But it could be so much easier for me if you if you got into the system."

"I didn't take that mark because of the angel who shouted out his warning message not to take it. The angel was loud and clear."

"Are you one of those religious people?"

"Certainly not. My daddy was a preacher, and I rebelled against him. I didn't believe what he said until a short while ago. I've got my reasons."

"Okay. No problem. I'll see you two later after I repair my own house. This earthquake will make me rich since I'm a builder."

Danny said, "It won't hurt us either. Say hello to your wife Ginny for us."

Cameron handed Danny a piece of paper and said, "Here is my next order of bricks."

Rita and Danny waved bye and took their supplies into their shelter.

***

About 11:00 a.m., they quit work because of the sun's heat.

Rita said, "I've searched all the TV channels, but nothing is on yet. Even the satellite channels aren't working. I bet the earthquake has destroyed a lot of towers."

Danny said, "I'll see if there are any radio stations on the air. I'll get back to work at sunset unless something comes up."

After searching the local radio channels, he found nothing.

Rita said, "Try short-wave. Maybe there is something there."

Danny found a station still broadcasting. The broadcaster's clear British accent identified the station as the BBC.

"The sudden war between World Peace troops and the Far East troops is over. From what our foreign correspondent has found out, there was no real winner. Both sides lost 90 percent of their forces.

"The remaining troops at Megiddo have been ordered to remain where they are to fight the alien invaders.

"Our foreign correspondent in Jerusalem says the city has been split into three sections by the earthquake. There are over seven thousand casualties in the city and ten percent of the city is nothing but rubble.

"Last night's violent earthquake caused world-wide destruction. Scientists in the United Kingdom say it was a twelve on the Richter scale. Photos of Earth from the International Space Station reveal all small islands nations have disappeared. The main islands of the United Kingdom, Australia, New Zealand, and some of the Japanese islands have been spared. Hawaii has vanished as well as Indonesia, the Philippines, and the Caribbean islands. All round the globe, mountains have crumbled. The geography of the entire planet is different.

"Starting with the Great Disappearance almost seven years ago, and the subsequent disasters including yesterday's battle at the Megiddo Valley in Israel, it is the estimate of this station that the world's population has *decreased* by two-thirds.

"There is a little good news. Large, thick rainclouds are covering the entire earth. We have been in genuine need of rain worldwide. Let us hope this doesn't dampen (excuse the pun) the efforts of the World Army to stop the invaders from space. The thick cover of rainclouds has given the troops relief from the sun's intense heat."

Rita and Danny's radio ran down. Danny started to crank it up and Rita said, "Don't bother. It is all bad news. I'll check our supplies. At least we have food, water, and many cases of soda."

Danny said, "I'll check the radio tonight for the weather report. They said something about thick rain clouds gathering all over the planet. That may not be the good news it sounds like."

***

For their evening meal, they ate a simple meal of cold baked beans, potato chips and hot dogs. When the sun dipped below the horizon,

Danny lit a gas lantern and sat on his workbench. He faced the southern horizon for the best look at the night sky. Rita sat with him.

Rita asked, "When do you want to go into the shelter? It is nearly dark."

"I'm looking for those thick clouds. Besides it is cool tonight. The stars are still visible."

"When did your parents build this shelter? It looks like it is made of steel and concrete."

"It is. They built this bomb shelter in the 1950s. It has a re-enforced roof made of concrete and iron rebar. The foundation sits on heavy springs, and can withstand severe earthquakes and a nuclear hit five miles away."

"Why five miles?"

"There were missile silos at the Air Force base five miles from here during the Cold War."

Danny pointed to a shooting star. "Look over there. Did you see it?"

"Yes, I did. That was a bright one."

They watched the stars for a few minutes. Rita's train of thought finally got back on track.

Rita asked, "Was our shelter always as big as it is now? Some sections look newer than others."

"Yes, I expanded it six months before we got married. I also built three magneto generators for our electricity."

"I remember you building them. How do they work?"

"They generate electricity from the Earth's magnetic field and have no moving parts. The back room of the shelter has the generator, battery bank, and the voltage inverter."

Rita smiled and said, "I guess you made good use of your electrical engineering degree from Georgia Tech. Why do you dress like you are brainless?"

"It keeps nosy people out of my business. Besides that, I like to dress this way. It beats a shirt and tie every day."

Twenty minutes later Danny pointed to the horizon. "Those storm clouds are what I've been looking for. We better get in our shelter."

"Okay. I'll bring in your short-wave radio."

They descended the two flights of steps and entered their shelter. Danny turned on the lights, shut the solid, four-inch thick steel door and locked it.

Rita asked, "How long ago did we move into our shelter? Six years ago?"

"Four and a half years ago. In June I think. Yep. And next week will be the seventh anniversary of the Great Disappearance."

"How much longer are we going to live in this shelter?"

"Not much longer."

His dad's Bible lay on Danny's desk, open to the Book of Revelation. He taped his father's prophetic chart to the wall over his desk. It showed the events of the Book of Revelation in a timeline format.

Danny said, "Well, I'll check off this earthquake from Daddy's chart. That leaves one more disaster before Jesus returns. The next disaster will be a dangerous one."

Rita said, "Show me again."

Danny turned the light on his desk toward the chart on the wall. "Almost seven years ago the Great Disappearance happened. Six years ago, the first major earthquake hit. After the storm of fireballs and blood, I remembered Daddy preaching on this. I didn't look at this chart until the oceans turned to blood and the sun dimmed. I checked off these events as they happened and recorded the dates. We are nearly at the end of them."

Rita shook her head. "And to think that I never bothered to read that book."

Danny turned off the desk lamp. "After the sun dimmed we moved into this shelter and stopped living in Mom and Dad's house. At least until this whole mess of disasters is over. I kept the lights on in the old house to make people think we still lived there. I didn't want them getting into our supplies or knowing I have electric generators. That's why I lit a gas lantern outside.

"When the second rapture happened, I knew we had tough times ahead of us. I figured if we could survive until Jesus comes, there might be a chance for us."

"You mean you knew about all of this stuff? It seems like we ought to pray and get saved like your daddy asked us to. I think it is about time we did."

"I guess you are right. Here is the tract Daddy left me. Let's read it and do what it says."

***

Two weather scientists in Tuelon, Manitoba, fifteen miles north of Winnipeg entered their lab to study satellite images of the developing storm. The road conditions delayed them by several hours and they arrived at one o'clock in the morning. Their power consisted of two solar cell panels connected to batteries and a voltage inverter.

Torin McConnell said, "I'm glad I set up those solar panels. Electricity these days is so undependable. We are lucky they are still standing after the last earthquake."

Ian Travis, his partner said, "Right you are. I'll turn on the emergency power. Then we can straighten up our lab and see how big this storm is above us. The clouds look thick."

"What time is it anyway?"

"It is 1:08 a.m."

The two scientists put the tables upright, straightened up the shelves and checked their computer connections. They activated their satellite receivers and collected data.

"Ian, check the connection. I'm not receiving any data."

"Is the satellite still working? Check the frequency setting again."

"Okay. It was a little off. I suppose falling off the shelf didn't do our receiver any good. Let me try again."

Torin started his download from the weather satellite.

"Ian, it is working now, but it is slower than usual."

"Better hurry, the lightning is getting fierce. We might have to disconnect our antenna so we won't get hit by lightning."

"I've got the data. Now I have to process it. It will take about five or six minutes and we will have our answer. Fix us something cold to drink."

Ian looked through the lab refrigerator. "How about a root beer?"

"Why a root beer?"

"There's nothing else."

"That's good enough for me."

Torin imported the data into his weather modeling program. When he saw the resulting screen, his mouth fell open. He said, "Ian, come over here. I can't believe what I'm seeing."

Ian rushed over to take a look. "Wow. The whole world is full of convective cells. I've never seen so many. What about the moisture content? Do you have the data?"

"I will in a minute."

Torin accessed the satellite. "The data is coming. I'll feed it into the display."

Three minutes later, Torin said, "It is ready. Look at this. What do you make of it?"

Ian said, "I'd say this is quite dangerous. The large amount of moisture in those clouds will generate massive amounts of hail. I've never seen so many strong updrafts. This isn't local. It is worldwide. We'd better alert somebody."

"Who are we going to call?"

"I don't know. I'll see who I can raise on the short-wave."

Before Ian could turn on his transmitter, a hailstone hit the roof. Plaster fell from the ceiling and fell on Torin's keyboard. They both looked up and saw a crack in the ceiling.

Torin said, "Oh, no. It sounds like the hailstorm has already started. I hope it isn't as violent as it looks. I hope our solar panel survives it."

A second hailstone hit, penetrated the roof, and smashed the radio transmitter. The noise scared both men.

Torin's eyes grew big. "Look at the size of that hailstone. If there are more of those coming, we are in big trouble. Get the tape measure."

Ian said, "It is about a meter in diameter. I don't like the look of this."

A third hailstone smashed the roof and hit their refrigerator. The two weather scientists could see open sky above them. They also saw hundreds of hailstones falling.

Ian ran for a supply closet and opened the door. "Come with me. This is the sturdiest part of the lab."

Torin ran for the closet but a hailstone struck him in the head. He convulsed for a second or two and expired. Blood oozed out of his mouth onto the floor.

Ian wept for his friend since nothing could be done for him now. He surrounded himself with blankets and anything else that might take the shock of one of those hailstones.

A hailstone crashed through the closet ceiling and killed him.

***

Pounding noises roused Rita and Danny Platka out of a deep sleep.

Danny said, "What is going on?"

"Are we under attack?"

"No, we are not. It is probably a hailstorm. Don't open the door until the noise stops."

Rita asked, "What time is it?"

"It is 1:16 a.m."

"The shelter is holding up. That's good news."

***

The storm and the pounding stopped after three hours. Danny and Rita waited until daybreak to open the steel door.

Danny opened the door to find the boulder-sized hailstones blocking the steps to the surface.

"Wow. Look at the size of these hailstones. It will take us a while to get out of here. I hope Cameron and Ginny and their kids survived."

Rita said, "Turn on your short-wave radio."

Danny charged up his radio and listened for the BBC but couldn't find the station. He finally found Radio Netherlands broadcasting in English.

The Dutch radio announcer spoke English with a British accent. "This is Radio Netherlands in Hilversum. The English service resumed today because of the magnitude of this disaster. Today's hailstorm killed millions around the planet. We have learned this from our correspondents around the world. Survivors are scavenging for food and supplies."

"The only reliable communications around the world seems to be short-wave radio. A few television stations are operating. The recent earthquake and this morning's hailstorm destroyed most radio and TV towers. We are broadcasting from one of our mobile transmitters."

"In other news, the plague of hail killed about half of the remaining World Army soldiers gathered at Megiddo Valley in Israel. They had orders to stay there until the object from space arrived. The object in space is currently motionless. Please stay tuned for further developments."

Danny put fresh batteries in the radio and left it on. He said, "According to Dad's chart, this hailstorm was the last disaster. That is, the last world-wide disaster."

Rita said, "We need to eat. We have a big job ahead of us."

"How about coffee?"

"Of course. Both of us need breakfast. How long will it take us to get out of here?"

"We should be out of here later today. In a couple of hours, the heat of the sun will speed melting of those hailstones. I'll get my hammer and tools ready while you fix breakfast."

They switched their radio to music when they became tired of listening to the news.

Fifty-Six

The Destruction of Babylon

The angel who sounded the seventh trumpet said to the Apostle John, "Come here. I'll show you the judgment of the Great Whore that sits on many waters with whom the kings of the earth have committed adultery, and the inhabitants of the earth have been made drunk with the wine of her fornication."

The angel picked up John and took him into the wilderness surrounding Babylon. From the hilltop he stood on, he saw a woman sitting on a bright red beast. The beast had names like "Nimrod", "Ashtoreth", "Baal", "Mother religion", "Idolatry", "Universal Religion" written all over it. It had seven heads and ten horns. Three of the heads had two horns.

The woman wore the finest clothes in scarlet and purple. She wore expensive, gold rings, pearls, jewelry, bracelets, and necklaces. Each of her fingers had ornate rings from different parts of the world. Even her toes had rings. The gold cup in her hands had crusts of dried blood on the outside. A band around her forehead said, "MYSTERY, BABYLON THE GREAT, THE MOTHER OF HARLOTS AND ABOMINATIONS OF THE EARTH". She looked drunk and red fluid dripped out of her mouth.

John asked, "What *is* this woman?"

"She is Religion and seduces people using her wealth and luxury. Her delight is doing wrong and thinks nothing will happen to her."

"What is coming out of her mouth?"

"The blood of the saints she has murdered."

"What about the horrible beast she is riding? Can you tell me more?"

"I will tell you the mystery of the woman, and of the beast that carries her, which has the seven heads and ten horns.

"The beast that you see was, and is not; and shall ascend out of the bottomless pit, and go into perdition: and they that dwell on the earth shall wonder, whose names were not written in the book of life from the foundation of the world, when they behold the beast that was, and is not, and yet is. And here is the mind which hath wisdom. The seven heads are seven mountains, on which the woman sits. And there are seven kings: five are fallen, and one is, and the other is not yet come; and when he comes, he must continue a short space.

John wrote as fast as he could to record the angel's words. "You are speaking of the kingdoms of this world, aren't you?"

The angel nodded. "And the beast that was, and is not, even he is the eighth, and is of the seven, and goes into perdition. And the ten horns which you saw are ten kings, which have received no kingdom as yet; but receive power as kings one hour with the beast. These have one mind, and shall give their power and strength unto the beast. These shall make war with the Lamb, and the Lamb shall overcome them: for he is Lord of lords, and King of kings: and they that are with him are called, and chosen, and faithful."

John asked, "Isn't this what I saw – the man who took over the world and the nations that worked with him?"

"Yes."

John recorded the angel's words.

"The waters which you saw, where the whore sits, are peoples, and multitudes, and nations, and tongues. And the ten horns which you saw upon the beast, these shall hate the whore, and shall make her desolate and naked, and shall eat her flesh, and burn her with fire. For God hath put in their hearts to fulfill His will, and to agree, and give their kingdom unto the beast, until the words of God shall be fulfilled. And the woman which you saw is that great city, which reigns over the kings of the earth."

John finished writing and stood. He stretched and to gave his hands a rest.

***

<u>Another Angel's Prophesy of Babylon</u>

Another angel came out of Heaven toward the earth. He lit the Earth with his brightness.

He shouted his message to the whole Earth. "Babylon the great is fallen, is fallen, and is become the habitation of devils, and the hold of every foul spirit, and a cage of every unclean and hateful bird. Because all nations have drunk of the wine of the wrath of her fornication, and the kings of the earth have committed fornication with her, and the merchants of the earth are waxed rich through the abundance of her delicacies."

John wrote the angel's message.

When the angel finished his words, a voice came out of Heaven and said, "Come out of her, my people, that ye be not partakers of her sins, and that ye receive not of her plagues. For her sins have reached up to heaven, and God has remembered her iniquities. Reward her even as she rewarded you, and double unto her double according to her works: in the cup which she hath filled fill to her double. How much she hath glorified herself, and lived deliciously, so much torment and sorrow give her: for she says in her heart, I sit a queen, and am no widow, and shall see no sorrow. Therefore shall her plagues come in one day, death, and mourning, and famine; and she shall be utterly burned with fire: for strong is the Lord God who judges her."

As John wrote these words, he asked, "Is that God's voice?"

"Yes. The great whore has substituted religion in the place of the Gospel. She will persecute the Church through the ages until this time of judgment."

The voice from Heaven continued. "And the kings of the earth, who have committed fornication and lived deliciously with her, shall bewail her, and lament for her, when they shall see the smoke of her burning, standing afar off for the fear of her torment, saying, 'Alas, alas, that great city Babylon, that mighty city because in one hour is thy judgment come.' And the merchants of the earth shall weep and mourn over her; for no man buys their merchandise any more: The merchandise of gold, and silver, and precious stones, and of pearls, and fine linen, and purple, and silk, and scarlet, and all thy fine wood, and all manner vessels of ivory, and all manner vessels of most precious wood, and of brass, and iron, and marble, and cinnamon, and aromas, and ointments, and frankincense, and wine, and oil, and fine flour, and wheat, and beasts, and sheep, and horses, and chariots, and slaves, and souls of men."

John said, "What a terrible and fitting judgment for trading in men's souls." He wrote as fast as he could.

The voice from Heaven said, "And the fruits that thy soul lusted after are departed from thee, and all things which were dainty and goodly are departed from thee, and thou shalt find them no more at all. The merchants of these things, which were made rich by her, shall stand afar off for the fear of her torment, weeping and wailing, And saying, Alas, alas, that great city, that was clothed in fine linen, and purple, and scarlet, and decked with gold, and precious stones, and pearls. For in one hour so great riches is come to nothing. And every shipmaster, and all the company in ships, and sailors, and as many as trade by sea, stood afar off, And cried when they saw the smoke of her burning, saying, What city is like unto this great city And they cast dust on their heads, and cried, weeping and wailing, saying, Alas, alas, that great city, wherein were made rich all that had ships in the sea by reason of her costliness. For in one hour is she made desolate. Rejoice over her, thou heaven, and ye holy apostles and prophets; for God hath avenged you on her."

John asked the angel, "How can a city that big be destroyed in one hour?"

The angel responded, "Such power exists. God will take His vengeance for destroying His messengers." He flew over John's head, picked up a huge millstone from the Earth, and threw it into the sea.

He shouted, "Thus with violence shall that great city Babylon be thrown down, and shall be found no more at all. And the voice of harpers, and musicians, and of pipers, and trumpeters, shall be heard no more at all in thee; and no craftsman, of whatsoever craft he be, shall be found any more in thee; and the sound of a millstone shall be heard no more at all in thee; And the light of a candle shall shine no more at all in thee; and the voice of the bridegroom and of the bride shall be heard no more at all in thee: for thy merchants were the great men of the earth; for by thy sorceries were all nations deceived. And in her was found the blood of prophets, and of saints, and of all that were slain upon the earth."

John nodded and wrote all of the words he heard. He uttered a hearty "Amen" when he finished writing.

***

The Actual Destruction of Babylon

Rita and Danny Platka had plenty of bricks to build their new house. They spent a week clearing the foundation of the old farm house.

Danny said, "Let's build a large sunshade for our patio until the Sun starts behavin'."

Rita said, "Do you want to break for a snack? Let's pretend today is the Fourth of July and have an old-fashioned, American holiday. There's nobody around to tell us we can't."

"You're right. I think there is a flagpole in the barn somewhere. I'll put it up now."

"Turn on the radio and we'll catch the news and listen to music if we can find some."

Danny turned it on. "I'll find the news first."

He tuned his radio to the BBC. A news broadcast was in progress. "It is official. Babylon has been obliterated. Nist ordered the nuclear destruction of Babylon. A World Army plane from Turkey carried out the mission. The world leader gave permission to test the most advanced nuclear weapon on the city.

"The nuclear explosion ignited huge oil reserves under the city. Burning, high-sulfur content oil mixed with tar rained on the whole city. This sealed the destruction of the Far East army.

"The highways around Babylon are impassible because of the blast. No relief efforts will be made because of the high radioactivity and fallout. It will be another Chernobyl and many years will pass before the area will be useable.

"This is truly a tragedy. Babylon's commerce benefited the world. The merchants of the Earth have much to lose. Because of what has happened in the last three and a half years, we will never see another time when we've had such great entertainers. So much money has gone into rebuilding that great cultural center and now it is gone.

"Most of the countries of the world have complained to Nist about the various religious groups living in Babylon. According to our sources, they undermined the security of the nations. This was the primary reason given for the destruction of the city.

"In other news, some observatories report the object in space has resumed movement toward the Earth."

Danny said, "I wonder what else is getting ready to happen?"

Fifty-Seven

The Alien Object Arrives

John found himself back in the Throne Room. Cheering broke out in Heaven. Many people said, "Alleluia, Salvation and glory, and honor and power, unto the Lord our God: For true and righteous are his judgments: for he hath judged the great whore, which did corrupt the earth with her fornication, and hath avenged the blood of his servants at her hand. And again they said, Alleluia. And her smoke rose up forever and ever."

A voice came out of the Throne saying, "Praise our God, all ye his servants, and ye that fear him, both small and great."

All inhabitants of Heaven shouted out, "Alleluia: for the Lord God omnipotent reigns. Let us be glad and rejoice, and give honor to Him: for the marriage of the Lamb is come, and his wife hath made herself ready. And to her was granted that she should be arrayed in fine linen, clean and white: for the fine linen is the righteousness of saints."

The Elder tapped John on the shoulder and said, "Write, Blessed are they which are called unto the marriage supper of the Lamb. These are the true sayings of God."

John had such a sense of awe he fell on the floor and tried to worship the Elder. The Elder picked him up and commanded him, "See thou do it not: I am thy fellow servant, and of thy brethren that have the testimony of Jesus: worship God: for the testimony of Jesus is the spirit of prophecy."

The Elder pointed at Jesus, who prepared Himself for the battle. Jesus wore multiple crowns on His head, and had a name inscribed on it. John couldn't read what it said.

Jesus put a blood-red cape on his shoulders. On the back of it said, "The Word of God," and on His pant leg "KING OF KINGS, AND LORD OF LORDS" was written.

He mounted His white horse and took off, and His saints followed Him. They made a long trail behind Him.

***

Nist paced around the War Room waiting for the object in space to reach the Earth. He reached for his phone, but it rang before he touched it. He saw the caller ID and knew it was Darrin. He picked up the phone and said, "Is that object moving yet?"

"Yes. It started moving three minutes ago, and it has picked up speed. Its destination is still the Megiddo Valley. It should be there in an hour at most."

"Call me if anything changes."

***

Nist took the half hour ride in a helicopter to Megiddo Valley. He wanted to be at the scene of this battle. Eftas Helpphor, whom he summoned from Babylon, exited from a helicopter that landed nearby.

Nist saw anger in his face.

Helpphor said, "What did you do to Babylon?"

"I blew it to hell after I knew you were out of the danger area."

"Why did you do that?"

"I got tired of those religious people you mismanaged. They undermined my authority in the world and angered the European nations. I didn't want to have them around in the first place, so I got rid of them."

Eftas said, "You also blew away half of my staff that lived there."

"Well, easy come, easy go. You can always replace people."

"How are you going to replace Stile?"

"What do you mean by that?"

"I was eating dinner with her at her hotel in Babylon when you summoned me. Easy come, easy go?"

Nist was grief-stricken. He realized he murdered his secretary with an H-bomb. He turned his face away from Eftas and wept for a minute. He said, "I didn't like the idea of creating a new religion anyway. Mallon Karth told me what those religious people were doing. That made me mad. I wasn't willing to give them another chance."

Eftas saw something in the sky and pointed. "Look."

Next to the image of God in the sky, a gigantic CROSS formed.

Nist said, "What the hell is that?"

Near the cross in the sky, the object from space became visible.

He commanded General Hassad, "Sommy, attack it."

"What is it?"

"I don't care. Just attack it with all you have."

General Hassad ordered an all-out attack of the approaching object. He ordered firing of hundreds of short-range missiles. Nist couldn't even see the object in the sky because of the smoke created by the missiles.

But none of them exploded.

Nist said to the missile tech, "Why am I not hearing explosions?"

"I don't know. According to the radar, the missiles are vanishing."

"Vanishing? How can that happen?"

Nist saw the object from space approaching. It appeared to be about a half mile away. He took a gun from a nearby soldier's holster and fired at the object. He ran out of bullets, so he took a gun from another soldier and fired all rounds at it.

The shield melted away, and Jesus appeared in His red robe with millions of His saints. Jesus came into view about 300 yards above Nist.

Jesus opened His mouth. Inside His mouth a sharp, double-edged sword protruded. Lightning came out from the blade and killed all of the remaining soldiers in a split second. Only Nist and Helpphor survived.

The pair scrambled for a place to hide but found none. Jesus' and His horse moved in front of them. They recognized Jesus. Nist still had the smoking gun in his hand and dropped it in embarrassment. He said the first thing that came to his mind.

"Oh, crap."

Without saying a word, Jesus nodded to a nearby angel, who picked up Charti Nist and Eftas Helpphor. The angel took them a great distance from the battle scene and dropped them into the Lake of Fire. They screamed in pain when they fell in.

At Megiddo Valley, another angel called out to the birds of the air, "Come and gather yourselves together unto the supper of the great God; That ye may eat the flesh of kings, and the flesh of captains, and the flesh of mighty men, and the flesh of horses, and of them that sit on them, and the flesh of all men, both free and bond, both small and great."

Thousands of birds descended on the valley and ate the dead bodies.

***

Jesus headed for Jerusalem on His horse and dismounted on the Mount of Olives. The earthquake had split it in half. Part of it went north and the other part went south.

Jesus' footsteps made the only sounds. All survivors watched Him walk by and bowed in worship.

The sun returned to normal brightness and the image of God in the sky disappeared. The hailstones melted.

Jesus looked straight ahead and walked into Jerusalem toward the Temple.

The millions of saints following Jesus also landed and dismounted on the Mount of Olives.

When Jesus reached the Temple, He saw the idol of the Beast by the Altar. He snapped His fingers and the statue vanished. A cloud of glory cleansed the Temple. The locks and chains fell off of the front door and dissolved. Survivors of the Great Tribulation cheered. For the first time, Jesus smiled.

***

David Lowe, a news reporter with Channel 6, had survived. Since he and his camera team were Jewish, they had refused to take the mark of Nist. They followed Jesus to the Temple Mount.

The Orthodox Jews surrounded Him and bowed down in worship. When they stood, David could see Jesus speaking with them but couldn't get close enough to hear the conversation.

When the meeting ended, David approached one of the Orthodox Jews, and held up a microphone. He asked, "What are Jesus' plans? What is He talking to you about?"

"He intends to establish His personal rule of the planet."

"How soon will that happen?"

"Now."

David turned to his camera crew and said, "You heard it. Jesus Christ has returned to the Earth, and will rule the planet. The battles and plagues are over. Please stay tuned for further developments."

Celebrations broke out all over the planet.

Jesus had a little unfinished business with the devil.

Fifty-Eight

The Millennium

John saw an angel leave Heaven. He had a great key in one hand and a strong chain in the other. The angel used the key to open the *bottomless pit*, or the *abyss*.

The Dragon didn't go quietly. He snarled at the angel who brought the great chain. In a battle that lasted two hours, the angel cornered the Dragon in a canyon. He bound him with the great chain he brought and threw the dragon in the abyss, shut its door and locked it. He placed the Seal of God on it the door and said, "You won't be bothering us for 1,000 years. Then you will be released for a short period."

Jesus ruled the Earth from His capital in Jerusalem. He gave the martyrs first priority in ruling the planet. They ruled the area where they preached the Gospel.

John wrote what he saw. "And I saw thrones, and they sat upon them, and judgment was given unto them: and I saw the souls of them that were beheaded for the witness of Jesus, and for the word of God, and which had not worshipped the beast, neither his image, neither had received his mark upon their foreheads, or in their hands; and they lived and reigned with Christ a thousand years.

"But the rest of the dead lived not again until the thousand years were finished. This is the first resurrection. Blessed and holy is he that hath part in the first resurrection: on such the second death hath no power, but they shall be priests of God and of Christ, and shall reign with him a thousand years."

***

One by one, the TV stations re-appeared. The TV station crews broke out the emergency transmitters and connected with the existing news agencies. Television became a medium of the Gospel.

Jesus ordered many changes for the good of the planet. He ruled with righteousness.

Jesus commanded His saints to see justice done, corruption removed, bad laws repealed, porn eradicated, clubs and liquor stores closed, breweries closed, colleges curriculums cleansed, and churches opened.

Green grass re-appeared on Earth over the next few months. The blood disappeared from the world's oceans, rivers and streams. The acid poisoning of the water went away and fish became plentiful again.

Farms grew an enormous amount of food. Famines disappeared. Disease left the planet, and the people prospered.

Israel became the number one travel destination. People from all nations came to honor Christ.

Politics vanished. Only the commands of Jesus and His saints meant anything. And what they ordered happened.

The Earth became safe. Real peace and safety prevailed.

John saw these changes and wrote. "Blessed and holy is he that hath part in the first resurrection: on such the second death hath no power, but they shall be priests of God and of Christ, and shall reign with him a thousand years."

One more battle loomed.

Fifty-Nine

The Final Battle

At the end of the 1,000 years, a powerful angel released the devil. Satan searched the earth and found large numbers of people to rebel against goodness. They formed a large army and surrounded Jerusalem. The armies filled Saudi Arabia, Jordan, Lebanon and the Sinai Peninsula.

The armies sent bombs and missiles toward the Holy City, but they exploded harmlessly in the air. Jesus emerged from the City and stared at His enemies. When they saw Him, their feet stuck to the ground. While looking at him, their eyeballs melted from their sockets, their tongues fell out, and their flesh rotted. Fireballs rained down from Heaven and burned their bodies. The Final Battle was over.

John saw this event and recorded it. He looked at the Elder and said, "Zechariah prophesied that."

Several angels snatched up the Devil and cast him into the Lake of Fire. He joined Nist and Helpphor, who had been there for a thousand years.

John added these words to his scroll: "And the Devil shall be tormented day and night forever and ever."

He thought this would be an event worth celebrating but noticed that Jesus did not look happy. The moment Jesus dreaded for all eternity approached.

Sixty

The Great White Throne Judgment

John and the Elder found themselves on a large plain. A huge, terrible white throne was in the center of it. Seated on this throne was Jesus with tears on His face. Hell had been emptied and the people assembled in front of Him stood for their final judgment.

The Elder stood next to him. John asked, "Why is Jesus getting so sad here?"

"This is the moment of all Eternity that He dreads. He has to direct people He died for into the Lake of Fire. These are the people who rejected His gift of eternal life. His Father has commanded Him to do this. He is obeying, but it isn't easy for Him."

A trumpet sounded and an angel shouted, "Behold, the Book of Life and the Book of Deeds have been opened. Give honor to the Judge, the Son of God."

The Lake of Fire opened up beside them. It roared like a volcano and the foul smell of burning sulfur filled the air. Boiling waves of lava crashed together. The screams of Charti Nist, Eftas Helpphor, and the Devil could be heard above the roar of this place of eternal punishment.

Jesus beheld the first lost soul to be heard.

Jesus asked, "What is your name?"

"Andre Gaspé."

"Where are you from?"

"Argonne, France."

"You lived your whole life in the shadow of the village church. Yet you never went there. Why?"

"I didn't have the time. I took care of my farm."

"How long did you live?"

"Seventy-one years."

"Did you ever consider listening to me?"

"I thought someday I might get around to it, but never did."

Jesus looked at the angel with the Book of Life and asked, "Is his name written in the Book of Life?"

The angel said, "No, it is not."

At those words, tears came to Jesus' eyes, and He ordered Andre to be cast into the Lake of Fire. The angels shoved him in. His deep screams of pain faded the farther he fell. It affected the remaining sinners, knowing their fate will be the same.

***

"Who is next?"

"I am. My name is Ewen Cumberland. I lived in America."

"Why didn't you consider my Gospel?"

"I never cared much for religion. Besides the religious people I knew were the biggest hypocrites."

"Did any hypocrites work with you?"

"Well, yes. What of it?"

"Did you quit your job because of them?"

"Of course not."

"So, why didn't you venture out and visit a church?"

"Like I said, I didn't care much for religion."

"How long did you live?"

"Eighty-three years."

"Did you ever consider how to get into Heaven?"

"I didn't know if it existed."

"Did you ever think of finding a way to miss going to Hell?"

"Well, like Heaven, I didn't know for sure if it existed."

"During your eighty-three years on the Earth, did you ever think of how long Eternity is?"

"No."

"So you risked your *eternal* soul on the assumption Heaven and Hell may not exist and that churches are full of hypocrites? What did that get you?"

"Nothing, sir."

Jesus wiped tears from His eyes. He asked, "Is Ewen's name in the Book of Life?"

The angel replied, "No, it is not."

Jesus ordered him thrown in the Lake of Fire.

***

"Who is next?"

An angel brought a woman forward and announced, "Her name is Adrianna Rastovich."

"Where are you from?"

"A small village in Poland."

"Did you ever consider my Gospel to obtain everlasting life?"

"I didn't think I had to. After all, I did more good than evil, and my mother told me I deserved Heaven. I was a sweet girl. I did many good deeds. I don't know why I ended up in Hell."

"Did you have a Bible?"

"Yes."

"Did you ever read it?"

"I read some of it. My mother told me to read the Psalms and I did."

"Did you read the New Testament?"

"No, I never thought about it."

"Did you ever want to get saved?"

"Why should I? My mother told me I would make it to Heaven by my good deeds."

Jesus asked the angel, "Is her name written in the Book of Life?"

"No, it is not."

Tears came to Jesus' eyes as He ordered Adrianna thrown into the Lake of Fire.

John looked at the people burning in the Lake of Fire. The screams etched their way into his memory.

This judgment took years. John wept for the lost souls at their final judgment and had no tears left when it ended.

John recorded the event with these words: "And I saw the dead, small and great, stand before God; and the books were opened: and another book was opened, which is the book of life: and the dead were judged out of those things which were written in the books, according to their works. And the sea gave up the dead who were in it; and death and hell delivered up the dead who were in them: and they were judged every man according to their works. And death and hell were cast into the lake of fire. This is the second death. And whosoever was not found written in the book of life was cast into the lake of fire."

He wanted to write about something better.

Sixty-One

The New Heaven and the New Earth

John found himself back in the Throne Room with the Elder. A marvelous sight caught his attention. He saw another planet created next to the Earth and saw the people transported from the old Earth to the new one.

When all people were on the new planet, the old Earth exploded.

John asked, "What happened?"

The Elder laughed and said, "What does it look like? God created a new Earth without the presence of sin and destroyed the old Earth. All reminders of sin are gone except for the nail prints in Jesus' hands and the spear mark in His side."

A booming voice out of Heaven said, "Behold, the tabernacle of God is with men, and he will dwell with them, and they shall be his people, and God himself shall be with them, and be their God. And God shall wipe away all tears from their eyes; and there shall be no more death, neither sorrow, nor crying, neither shall there be any more pain: for the former things are passed away."

Jesus said, "Behold, I make all things new. Write: for these words are true and faithful."

John sat at his table to record His words.

***

Jesus approached John and spoke to him face-to-face. "It is done. I am Alpha and Omega, the beginning and the end. I will give unto him that is athirst of the fountain of the water of life freely. He that overcometh shall inherit all things; and I will be his God, and he shall be my son. But the fearful, and unbelieving, and the abominable, and murderers, and whoremongers, and sorcerers, and idolaters, and all liars, shall have their part in the lake which burneth with fire and brimstone: which is the second death."

Jesus pointed to the scroll and John wrote His words on it.

An angel who poured out one of the bowl judgments approached John. The angel said, "Come hither, I will show you the bride, the Lamb's wife." Jesus smiled at John and nodded.

John was almost used to his new method of traveling. Either angels took him somewhere or he found himself somewhere with no sense of traveling.

The angel took off with him and landed on a high mountain which overlooked the new earth. Bright stars illuminated the clear night sky. A beautiful city on a cloud descended to the large plain in front of him. The city sparkled like a gem. Light came from within and John sensed the holiness of it.

John later wrote these words. "And I John saw the holy city, new Jerusalem, coming down from God out of heaven, prepared as a bride adorned for her husband. It has the glory of God: and her light was like unto a stone most precious, even like a jasper stone, clear as crystal; And it has a wall great and high, and has twelve gates, and at each gate twelve angels, and names written thereon, which were the names of the twelve tribes of the children of Israel."

The angel motioned for John to follow him. He entered the city and walked at a slow pace. John didn't mind. He enjoyed the view. The people, gates, buildings and foundations fascinated John with their beauty.

John saw each side of Holy Jerusalem as he walked around the city. On each of the four sides, there were three gates. The wall had twelve foundations, and each foundation had written on it the name of an apostle. He noticed Paul's name written on one of the foundations. Judas' name was missing.

The angel handed John a golden reed and told him to measure the City, the gates, and the wall surrounding it.

He measured it and wrote, "And the city lieth foursquare, and the length is as large as the breadth: and he measured the city with the reed, twelve thousand furlongs. The length and the breadth and the height of it are equal.

"And he measured the wall thereof, an hundred and forty and four cubits, according to the measure of a man, that is, of the angel. And the building of the wall of it was made of jasper: and the city was pure gold, like unto clear glass. And the foundations of the wall of the city were garnished with all manner of precious stones. The first foundation was jasper; the second, sapphire; the third, chalcedony; the fourth, emerald; The fifth, sardonyx; the sixth, sardius; the seventh, chrysolite; the eighth, beryl; the ninth, topaz; the tenth, a chrysoprase; the eleventh, a jacinth; the twelfth, amethyst."

He thought, "Every color in the rainbow is in these stones."

John wrote more details of this City. "And the twelve gates were twelve pearls; every several gate was of one pearl: and the street of the city was pure gold, as it were transparent glass. And I saw no temple therein: for the Lord God Almighty and the Lamb are the temple of it. And the city had no need of the sun, neither of the Moon, to shine in it: for the glory of God did lighten it, and the Lamb is the light thereof. And the nations of them which are saved shall walk in the light of it: and the kings of the earth do bring their glory and honor into it. And the gates of it shall not be shut at all by day: for there shall be no night there. And they shall bring the glory and honor of the nations into it. And there shall in no wise enter into it anything that defiles, neither whatsoever works abomination, or makes a lie: but they which are written in the Lamb's book of life."

The angel pointed and said, "Look at the River of Life. It is clear as crystal, and comes out of the throne of God. In the middle of the street, and on either side of the river, is the Tree of Life, which produces twelve kinds of fruits, and yields fruit every month."

John said, "I wondered what happened to the Tree of Life."

"And the leaves of the tree are for the healing of the nations. And there shall be no more curse: but the throne of God and of the Lamb shall be in it; and his servants shall serve him."

John noticed the people in the city wearing the Name of God on a band around their foreheads. He wrote, "And they shall see his face; and his name shall be in their foreheads. And there shall be no night there; and they need no candle, neither light of the sun; for the Lord God giveth them light: and they shall reign forever and ever."

The angel said, "These sayings are faithful and true: and the Lord God of the holy prophets sent his angel to show unto his servants the things which must shortly be done."

Jesus approached John and said, "Behold, I come quickly: blessed is he that keeps the sayings of the prophecy of this book." Jesus pointed to John's scroll.

The sights overwhelmed John. He admired the angel who showed him these awesome sights. He bowed on his hands and knees and in order to worship him. The angel stood him to his feet and said, "See thou do it not: for I am thy fellow servant, and of thy brethren the prophets, and of them which keep the sayings of this book: worship God.

Jesus spoke again. "Seal not the sayings of the prophecy of this book: for the time is at hand. He that is unjust, let him be unjust still: and he which is filthy, let him be filthy still: and he that is righteous, let him be righteous still: and he that is holy, let him be holy still.

"And, behold, I come quickly; and my reward is with me, to give every man according as his work shall be. I am Alpha and Omega, the beginning and the end, the first and the last."

John wrote, "Blessed are they that do his commandments, that they may have right to the tree of life, and may enter in through the gates into the city. For without are dogs, and sorcerers, and whoremongers, and murderers, and idolaters, and whosoever loveth and maketh a lie."

When John finished writing, Jesus said, "I, Jesus, have sent mine angel to testify unto you these things in the churches. I am the root and the offspring of David, and the bright and morning star."

He found it difficult to write because he felt weak. After he wrote, he saw white and felt faint. Jesus and the City of Heaven vanished.

Sixty-Two

The Return

John felt a stinging sensation on his face. He heard a voice saying, "Hey, wake up. John, are you okay?"

He awoke and discovered Demos had smacked him on his face.

Melek, whose bed was across the aisle said, "Your eyes have been wide open and you've been motionless. Is something wrong?"

John gasped for breath. He didn't know what to say.

Petros asked, "Tell us something. Did the cat get your tongue?"

John came to. He realized where he was and looked at his surroundings. His fellow prisoners looked at him from their beds. The stench of sweat and fetid beds hit his nostrils. He was back on Patmos.

A look of concern was on Demos' face. "Did you have a seizure? You were almost stiff. We've been trying to rouse you. What has happened to you? Your skin is … glowing."

John saw the look of concern on Demos' face turn to astonishment. John remained speechless.

Demos noticed the beautiful scroll in John's right hand. He asked, "Hey, where did you get this scroll?"

John saw the scroll in his right hand.

He finally caught his breath and said, "I don't think you'd believe me if I told you."

Melek said, "Well, wherever you have been, we're glad to have you back. You worried us."

John asked, "How long have I been this way?"

Demos said, "Oh, about an hour or so. When we woke up, you stood there with your hands lifted up. What were you doing?"

John said, "I will need time to think about what happened. Maybe I will tell all of you later."

Melek said, "We are glad you are okay. We were worried that you had a seizure."

***

The next day, John noticed his scroll didn't look fresh. He held it so Demos could see it and said, "Look what is happening. My scroll is decaying fast. What am I going to do? I need to preserve what I've written on it."

Demos said, "Hand it to me."

John handed Demos the scroll. He felt the parchment, "I don't know what is happening, but it is rotting fast. Hey, this is all in your handwriting. How did you write this, anyway? And where did you get the ink?

John didn't say anything. He stared at the floor.

Demos said, "Yes, I know. You will tell me later."

John wondered how to preserve his message. He decided to pray and ask the Lord to provide for this need. "Demos, Let us agree in prayer like I taught you. We will see God do a miracle so I can make a copy of this scroll before it rots."

Demos agreed with John. He said, "I'd like to see a miracle happen because of our prayers. Let us pray together."

They both lifted up their hands and eyes toward Heaven. John prayed, "Father, in Jesus' Name I ask for a quill, ink, and parchment to copy this scroll before it decays. Thank You for answering our prayer of agreement. Amen."

Demos smiled at John and looked at the door.

John asked, "What are you looking at the door?"

"Someone could be bringing your parchment, quill and ink at any moment now. You better get ready to write."

John thought, "Demos is a real believer now. That took me off guard."

John's prayers had a remarkable tendency to get answered, so his fellow prisoners wondered how soon it might happen.

Dragon said, "Hey, why didn't you ask God to release us." John's friends nodded.

John said, "Well, you have faith in the same God I believe in. You pray."

His fellow prisoners still had lots of curiosity about what John went through. They didn't have to wonder long.

Sixty-Three

Where were you?

In the weeks following this vision, John considered what he might share with his fellow prisoners. He read and re-read his scroll. He thought, "This is my handwriting, and I remember it even without this scroll. I know God wants me to publish this. And it *will* be published throughout the Empire one way or another. God will find a way to get it done."

Two weeks after his return, he slipped in a conversation with Melek and said he had been to Heaven. Melek told the other prisoners. They wanted to know about the contents of the scroll and what he remembered about his visit.

Bit by bit, John shared bits and pieces of his heavenly experience. Each night he would share more.

Several nights later, after the guards left for the night, John pretended to fall asleep.

Melek broke this silence by saying, "Aren't you going to tell us anything tonight?"

John let out a sigh. He was tired from the day's work, but he propped himself on his elbows and said, "Of course. Who has a question?"

Melek said, "I do. Are people in Heaven ghosts or real people?"

"They are real people. I could touch them."

Nikos asked, "What was the strangest sight you saw?"

John thought for a minute. He thought about the Four Living Creatures and said, "The four creatures that stand guard around the Throne of Heaven have eyes all over them. Each of them had six wings. One of them had the face of a lion, another had the face of a calf, another had the face of a man, and the last one had the face of an eagle."

Melek had a sheepish look on his face. "You know, I saw something like that before I came here. But I had been drunk over a week. Even what I saw then wasn't as weird as what you saw."

John rolled his eyes and shook his head. "Melek, believe it or not, our prophet Daniel saw similar beasts. They are described in his prophetic writings and he never drank. The Medes and the Persians preserved his writings since he served as a high government official. Their wise men came to worship Jesus at His birth because they remembered the prophetic writings of Daniel. They came to Jerusalem during the time of Jesus' crucifixion and resurrection because of those same writings."

Petros asked, "How do you know that?"

John replied, "On the Day of Pentecost when the Holy Spirit filled us, we spoke in tongues. People in the crowd told us they understood us, even though we didn't even know their language or even what we were saying. Many of them came from the former Medo-Persian Empire. They knew Daniel's prophesies. Long ago, they calculated the time of fulfillment and came to Jerusalem to see Jesus ride into the city on the colt of a donkey."

Dragon asked, "Did Jesus remember you?"

John answered, "Oh yes. He remembered me well. He knew of the cities where I started churches, and what their current situations are. God gave me a specific message for each of them."

Nikos asked, "Do you have any idea how soon these things will happen?"

"No, but I know they will happen."

Jared, who had been quiet until now, asked, "Did God show you your future home in Heaven?"

"No, He didn't. But I am sure it will be perfect for me."

John closed out the question and answer session. "It is getting late and I'm tired. We have to work tomorrow. Let's get a good night's sleep. I'll answer more questions tomorrow night."

A hearty Amen resounded in the barracks, and they all went to sleep.

Sixty-Four

Answered Prayers

The next day, a guard opened the door and entered with several armed soldiers. He selected John and his friends and ordered their leg irons removed. The guard assembled them outside of the barracks. The camp commander of Patmos came to address the prisoners.

Lightning and thunder indicated an approaching storm.

The commander took a quick look at the storm clouds and said, "The Emperor Domitian died a week ago. We received the news this morning. The cases against you who are assembled here were personal cases. That is, cases the Emperor wanted to try on his own. By the terms of Roman law, we realize there is now no case against you. You will be released."

The assembled prisoners started to cheer, but the camp commander held his hand up and said, "But...." The prisoners got quiet.

The camp commander smiled and continued. "But the next supply ship on which you will return to civilian life isn't due here for another two weeks. You will no longer be on the work detail and you will not be chained in your beds anymore. We'll see if we can get a better quality of food for you. We have not had a lot of trouble out of you since John arrived here."

The commander looked directly at Melek, who had a sheepish grin.

The commander said, "We want your remaining stay to be comfortable. All of you will be transferred to a more comfortable barracks until the time of your departure."

He turned to John. He asked, "Is there anything you need that could make your remaining time more comfortable?

"I'd like a quill, some ink, and some parchments."

"Oh, you want to write memoirs of your stay here?"

All assembled prisoners and Roman guards laughed.

The camp commander smiled, "Yes, for whatever reason, I think we can find those items for you. You are all dismissed. You can retrieve any of your personal belongings at your old barracks before you go."

John hurried back to the old barracks to get his decaying scroll. John said goodbye to the remaining prisoners. He picked up his scroll, brushed off a cockroach, and went outside.

The commander escorted the former prisoners to the new barracks. "This isn't like any of the inns in the City of Rome, but they are better than where you were. I hope you will be comfortable."

A soldier brought John parchments, candles, ink, an inkwell, and several quills. John lit a candle and began to write.

***

John knew he had to write an introduction to his message. He dipped his quill into the ink and wrote, "The Revelation of Jesus Christ, which

God gave unto him, to show unto his servants things which must shortly come to pass...."

He realized how this heavenly vision strengthened his faith and wrote, "Blessed is he that reads, and they that hear the words of this prophecy, and keep those things which are written therein: for the time is at hand..."

John's testimony about Jesus is what brought him to Patmos, so he wrote, "I John, who also am your brother, and companion in tribulation, and in the kingdom and patience of Jesus Christ, was in the isle that is called Patmos, for the Word of God, and for the testimony of Jesus Christ. I was in the Spirit on the Lord's Day, and heard behind me a great voice, as of a trumpet, Saying, I am Alpha and Omega..."

John completed copying the scroll, but the Holy Spirit prompted him to write more. "And the Spirit and the bride say, Come. And let him that hears say, Come. And let him that is athirst come. And whosoever will, let him take the water of life freely. For I testify unto every man that hears the words of the prophecy of this book, If any man shall add unto these things, God shall add unto him the plagues that are written in this book: And if any man shall take away from the words of the book of this prophecy, God shall take away his part out of the book of life, and out of the holy city, and from the things which are written in this book. He which testifies these things says, Surely I come quickly."

John added, "Amen. Even so, come, Lord Jesus. The grace of our Lord Jesus Christ be with you all. Amen."

He laid down his pen and gently blew on the ink to speed the drying. He rolled it up. The afternoon sun set on the horizon, and John stared out of the window of his barracks. He felt he could rest now. He noticed the sea had calmed and his departure from Patmos was certain.

THE END

Appendix

For those who don't know...

<u>The Rapture</u>

In the Bible, 1 Thessalonians 4:15-18 says, "For this we say unto you by the word of the Lord, that we which are alive and remain unto the coming of the Lord shall not prevent them which are asleep. For the Lord himself shall descend from heaven with a shout, with the voice of the archangel, and with the trump of God: and the dead in Christ shall rise first: Then we which are alive and remain shall be caught up together with them in the clouds, to meet the Lord in the air: and so shall we ever be with the Lord. Wherefore comfort one another with these words."

The Rapture of the Church, which seems to take place in Revelation, chapter four, and is the rapture we are most familiar with. There is a second rapture in Revelation, Chapter fourteen of the people saved during the tribulation. This is not a new idea.

Please check out this link:

http://www.biblestudytools.com/commentaries/jamieson-fausset-brown/revelation/revelation-14.html?p=5

The Great Disappearance

News broadcasters don't like to use words that give credibility to what Christians believe. They didn't want to use the word, "rapture", so they coined the phrase, "The Great Disappearance" to replace it.

Mark of the Beast and "666"

This comes from Revelation 13:16-18. Damnation is promised to all that receive this mark. (See Revelation 14:9-11). Avoid this mark at all cost. This could be the number of a system and perhaps not the numerical value of a name. It might not even be a tattoo, as portrayed in this novel.

The Gideons

This is a Christian society dedicated to making copies of God's Word available to every person. You have only to request a Bible from them and you will get one. The plan of salvation is printed in the back of their pocket New Testaments.

Salvation

It will be easier to get saved *before* the events of this book take place. Take time to read the following section if you're not sure you'd go to Heaven if the Rapture (Great Disappearance) took place today.

Know that the events of the Book of Revelation *will* take place. Perhaps not *exactly* as I have described, but they will take place. Prepare yourself by getting saved now and take part in the "Great Disappearance".

I hope to see you in Heaven.

The Two Witnesses – Are they Moses and Elijah or Elijah and Enoch?

In my novel, I have chosen Moses and Elijah as the two witnesses in Revelation 11:3-12. These two seem to be experienced with floods, fire and plagues. They also appeared with Christ on the Mount of Transfiguration (Matthew 17:3-4). However, many people believe that the Two Witnesses will be Enoch and Elijah on the basis of Hebrews 9:27 that all men die once. Since the Bible does not record the death of these two individuals, many assume that these two will be asked to die here. We can't be dogmatic about their identities since the Bible does not reveal them.

Hebrews 9:24-28
24 For Christ is not entered into the holy places made with hands, which are the figures of the true; but into heaven itself, now to appear in the presence of God for us: 25 Nor yet that he should offer himself often, as the high priest entereth into the holy place every year with blood of others; 26 For then must he often have suffered since the foundation of the world: but now once in the end of the world hath he appeared to put away sin by the sacrifice of himself. 27 And as it is appointed unto men once to die, but after this the judgment: 28 So Christ was once offered to bear the sins of many; and unto them that look for him shall he appear the second time without sin unto salvation.

This scripture says that just as certain as men die once, and after that judgment, so Christ was offered once and salvation will follow.

Will the millions of Christians taken in the Rapture be required to die before they enter Heaven?

How to become a Born-Again Christian

Admit that you have sinned. Romans 3:23 says "For all have sinned and fallen short of the glory of God."

Believe that Jesus died on a cross for your sins and that he rose again on the third day. Romans 5:8 says "But God demonstrated His love for us, in that, while we were still sinners, Christ died for us."

The Resurrection of Jesus Christ from the dead is the most historically proven event in all of history.

Confess Jesus as the Lord of your life.

Romans 10:9-10 says "That if thou shalt confess with thy mouth the Lord Jesus, and shalt believe in thine heart that God hath raised him from the dead, thou shalt be saved. For with the heart man believeth unto righteousness; and with the mouth confession is made unto salvation."

Please make a decision to join us as we follow Christ, and share with the world the greatest gift of all ... The Gospel of Jesus Christ. It is God's ticket out of Hell and into Heaven.

A Model Prayer

"Dear Lord Jesus, I know I am a sinner. I believe you died for my sins. Right now, I turn from my sins and open the door of my heart and life to You. I receive You as my personal Lord and Savior. I believe in my heart that God raised You from the dead. Thank you for saving me. Amen."

If you prayed that prayer and meant it, Jesus Christ has now taken residence in your heart, and has forgiven you of all your sins.

The Bible tells us "If we confess our sins, he is faithful and just to forgive us our sins and cleanse us from all unrighteousness." (1 John 1:9)

If you sin after becoming a Christian, confess your sins to God and ask forgiveness every day.

God also promises, "As far as the east is from the west, so far has He removed our transgressions from us." (Psalms 103:12)

If you made a decision for Christ, please send me a message on my website www.booksbywillcarson.com on the Contact Us page.

Timetable

This is the timetable I used for my story. I did not get this from Scripture and created it from my imagination.

	Year 1	Year 2	Year 3
September	The Great Disappearance	First trumpet - Hail, fire, blood	Fifth Trumpet (stings)
October	Seals Opened		Fifth Trumpet (stings)
November	Wars, food shortages begin		Fifth Trumpet (stings)
December	Earthquake		Fifth Trumpet (stings)
January	The 144,000 sealed	Second trumpet - burning meteor, 1/3 of oceans become blood	Fifth Trumpet (stings)
February			Fifth Trumpet (stings)
March	Arab / Israeli Settlement. The two witnesses start		
April		Third Trumpet (star - bitter waters)	
May			Sixth Trumpet (200 Million demons kill 1/3 of mankind
June		Fourth Trumpet (1/3 sun darkened)	Plague lasts 1 year, 1 month, 1 day and 1 hour
July			
August	Chapter 8 - The 7th Seal - 2nd earthquake (3 minutes)		The Little Book and the Two Witnesses start; the 7th Seal; God meets Israel in the wilderness

REVELATION, THE NOVEL

	Year 4	Year 5	Year 6	Year 7
September	The antichrist assumes world power / Kevin and Dodi, Eftas, Brad Huron	Buckingham Park		Bowl 1 – Sores appear on marks
October	Eftas arrives in NY			
November				Bowl 2 – The Seas become blood
December	Move to Israel / ad campaign			
January				Bowl 3 – Springs become blood
February				
March	Moses flames a student	Marking starts / Dorian Janus	Marking required	Bowl 4 – Sun becomes hot
April	Jerusalem Event at the Temple. Nist declares himself to be god	Germany's rebellion		
May				Bowl 5 – Darkness on the Throne
June	End of the Sixth Trumpet plague			Bowl 6 – Euphrates dries up
July	The last of the 144,000 martyred and the Two Witnesses killed		The Seventh Trumpet	
August			The Second Disappearance	Bowl 7 – Armageddon. Earthquake. 100# Hailstones. Babylon destroyed

About the Author

William C. Carson has dedicated his career to studying and teaching the Bible and helping others achieve a greater understanding of its messages and meaning. He holds a degree in theology from Oral Roberts University in Tulsa, Oklahoma, where he wrote his senior paper on early church history.

Carson taught classes in Old Testament and New Testament survey and Bible study methods, and carried the word of God abroad on a short-term mission trip to Russia. He continues to support several missionaries and other humanitarian efforts.

Carson has been married to his wife, Jeanne, for more than forty years and is a proud patriarch to their three children and two grandchildren. Revelation, the Novel is his second book but his first novel.

***

Please visit his website to find out more and to browse other books he's written. Use the contact form to send a message.

Subscribe to his monthly newsletter. Exciting discoveries and Christian adventures will come your way.

Has this book created excitement about the Return of Jesus Christ? Any comments about the book would be appreciated.

www.booksbywillcarson.com